T0300598

MOST ARDENTLY

A PRIDE & PREJUDICE REMIX

THE
REMIXED CLASSICS
SERIES

MOST ARDENTLY

A Pride & Prejudice Remix

GABE COLE NOVOA

FEIWEL AND FRIENDS

New York

To my trans siblings:
We deserve romances that will sweep us off our feet too.
That's why this book is for you.

A Feiwel and Friends Book
An imprint of Macmillan Publishing Group, LLC
120 Broadway, New York, NY 10271 • fiercereads.com

Our books may be purchased in bulk for promotional, educational,
or business use. Please contact your local bookseller or the Macmillan
Corporate and Premium Sales Department at (800) 221-7945 ext. 5442 or
by email at MacmillanSpecialMarkets@macmillan.com.

Library of Congress Cataloging-in-Publication Data is available.

First edition, 2024
Book design by Samira Iravani
Feiwel and Friends logo designed by Filomena Tuosto
Printed in the United States of America

ISBN 978-1-250-86980-7
7   9   10   8

AUTHOR'S NOTE

MOST ARDENTLY IS OLIVER'S STORY, AND IN SOME WAYS IT WAS MINE as well. You'll find in these pages a trans boy who has not yet come out to his family navigating a rigidly cis-heteronormative society. The nature of this story means that Oliver's deadname is used repeatedly, he frequently experiences dysphoria, and he is misgendered by characters in the book (though never by the narrative). For many of us, these are wounds that can be painful to revisit, so while I did my best to broach these difficult moments with empathy, you know what you can handle best.

CHAPTER 1

İᴛ ɪs ᴀ ᴛʀᴜᴛʜ ᴜɴɪᴠᴇʀsᴀʟʟʏ ᴀᴄᴋɴᴏᴡʟᴇᴅɢᴇᴅ, ᴛʜᴀᴛ ᴀ sɪɴɢʟᴇ ʙᴏʏ ɪɴ possession of a good fortune must be in want of a future wife—unless that boy was Oliver Bennet. Not that Oliver was in possession of a good fortune, mind you, but it seemed impossible to him that having such a fortune would so completely transform his disinterest in one day having a wife.

Or, more importantly, being one.

So it was with no small amount of dismay that he listened to his mother share the exciting news about one Charles Bingley.

Mrs. Bennet yanked on the lacing of the stay pressed tight beneath his breasts as she said, "Have you girls heard that Netherfield has been let?"

Oliver gritted his teeth as the cinching fabric pushed his chest up and forward—accentuating a shape that made him utterly nauseous—and at the equally suffocating address of his sisters and him as *girls*. This could only be expected, however, as Mrs. Bennet, like most of the world, believed that Oliver was the second-eldest Bennet *daughter*, rather than the only Bennet *son*.

Oliver could count on one hand the number of people who knew the truth, and Mrs. Bennet was not one of them.

Stay tied, Mrs. Bennet pushed the wooden busk into the front opening, forcing him to stand up straight and further emphasizing the curves of his chest. There were few articles of clothing Oliver loathed more than the busked stay, if only because the pressure of the piece of wood pressed between his breasts was a constant reminder of a part of his body Oliver never wanted to see.

Satisfied and oblivious to his discomfort, Mrs. Bennet wrestled the emerald gown over Oliver's head and pulled it down, adjusting as necessary as it fell over the horrifying undergarments. Oliver shifted on the stool on which he stood, doing his best not to glower at his reflection in the mirror. He hated seeing himself in a dress, which was unfortunate given the amount of time he was forced to spend in one. Done up like this, his hair tied into two simple braids and a green ribbon to match the gown, he looked like a stranger.

"Netherfield has been let? To whom?" Jane asked, seated beside the window next to the mirror. She shot Oliver a sympathetic smile while he averted his gaze, studiously avoiding his own reflection.

"A young man by the name of Bingley, with an income of four or five thousand a year!" Mrs. Bennet responded. "How fortunate this turn of events is for you girls. I've already asked Mr. Bennet to introduce himself and invite him for tea."

Kitty and Lydia giggled on the other side of the room.

"Is he very handsome?" Lydia asked.

Mrs. Bennet frowned. "Well, I haven't yet met him, dear, but that should hardly be a priority."

"Do you know if he'll be at the Meryton Ball tonight?" Kitty asked.

"Why, I should hope so!" Mrs. Bennet beamed at Oliver's reflection as she finished smoothing out the gown. "Surely one of you girls will catch Mr. Bingley's eye tonight, if he does attend. I think it quite impossible that he won't notice such handsome company."

Oliver stepped off the stool. It wasn't so bad when he couldn't see himself. If he was careful not to look at his chest—or anything below the neck, really—

"Elizabeth," his mother admonished. "Could you at least *pretend* to be looking forward to the ball? Honestly, I don't know how you expect to ever be married when you plod about so morosely at every ball we attend."

Oliver's jaw clenched at the grating sensation of hearing the name he'd outgrown long ago. Still, the last thing he needed was attracting his mother's displeased attention. So, with practiced ease, he donned a small, apologetic smile.

"I'm sorry, Mama," he said. "You know how much I dislike wearing a busk—I'm simply adjusting still."

Seemingly satisfied, Mrs. Bennet nodded and clapped once, gesturing for the door. "Well, come along, girls! We mustn't be late."

Lydia, Mary, and Kitty all rushed out the door, with Mrs. Bennet right behind them. Oliver moved to follow with a sigh, until Jane lightly gripped his shoulder.

"Are you all right?" she asked softly. "I could tell Mama you aren't well if you'd prefer to stay home. You could even go out on your own . . ."

The suggestion blossomed inside him, filling him with hope, but Oliver crushed it before it grew large enough to hurt. He *would* go out on his own, in clothes that actually suited him, proudly bearing his true name . . . tomorrow.

"The Bartholomew Fair," he said softly. "I'll go out then. Do you think you could . . . ?"

Jane smiled. "I'll keep Mama busy. If the ball becomes too much tonight—"

"I'll let you know. Thank you, Jane."

She hugged him tightly and whispered, "Anything for my little brother."

Oliver closed his eyes, pressing his face into Jane's shoulder as her words filled him with warmth and pulled the corners of his lips up. *This* was what he would hold on to tonight. This feeling. This rightness of hearing Jane call him her brother.

One day, the rest of the world would know the truth too.

CHAPTER 2

THEY'D NO SOONER STEPPED INTO THE BALL AT MERYTON THAN Mrs. Bennet exclaimed, "Oh, isn't this just *lovely*?"

Kitty and Lydia cooed in agreement while Oliver took in the scene before him glumly. The ballroom was large, the painted walls casting an evergreen hue on the polished hardwood, which gleamed with a fresh coat of wax. Oliver estimated there were probably five dozen or so people in attendance, all dressed in not quite their *finest*, as this was a public affair, but dressed up all the same.

Mr. Bennet said something to Mrs. Bennet, then strode off confidently into the room, probably to mingle with the other husbands in a corner somewhere as he typically did at these affairs.

The dancing had already begun, pairs swooping together and apart in the center of the room while others mingled along the edges. It was there Oliver would prefer to stay—tucked away in a corner where fewer people might see him. But of course,

Mrs. Bennet would never allow that. As far as his mother was concerned, it was each of their responsibilities to attract an upper-class suitor with coquettish smiles and batted eyelashes. Oliver grimaced.

"There he is!" Mrs. Bennet whispered all too loudly. "In the north end of the room beside the large portrait of the master of the house! Yes, I'm quite sure of it—he fits the way Mrs. Long described perfectly. Why, he *is* handsome, isn't he?"

The young man in question was, Oliver had to admit, good-looking. His short hair was a golden-red, and his pale, freckled face seemed kind. But he wasn't alone; with him were two women—both of whom shared his coloring, so were likely his relatives—and a dark-haired young man, who looked to be between Oliver's and Jane's ages and seemed about as thrilled to be there as Oliver was. But at least Oliver had the decency to *pretend* he wasn't miserable; Bingley's companion appeared to have no such compulsion.

"Oh, he is handsome!" Lydia exclaimed. "And who is that with him?"

"Why, I believe Mrs. Long mentioned he was traveling with his companions," Mrs. Bennet answered. "That gentleman must be Fitzwilliam Darcy, and the women, Bingley's sisters."

Oliver stopped paying attention after that. Mrs. Bennet hovered over her children like a mother duck and her hatchlings, despite Oliver being seventeen and Jane even older, but eventually Jane and Oliver broke away from her. As they strayed out of earshot, Oliver's shoulders finally relaxed. The two of them wove between people, Jane smiling shyly at familiar faces and responding with quiet, polite conversation when respectability demanded. Oliver smiled and nodded at all the appropriate moments, though he hadn't the faintest idea what any of the conversations entailed.

It wasn't until they'd spoken to three or four people that Oliver realized they were nearing the end of the room where Bingley and his friends resided. His eyes narrowed at Jane, who had been leading the march. Was she approaching them on purpose? She hadn't looked at them once, but her path seemed clear.

She was, perhaps, approaching without *looking* like she was trying to approach, which suited her. Jane didn't particularly enjoy being the center of attention, and she would never presume to directly approach someone—even if that someone was a very handsome boy. In any case, if her motive was to attract Bingley's attention without appearing to, it was working. While Jane spoke to a young man who reminded Oliver of an overeager puppy (Oliver had already forgotten his name), Bingley's gaze settled on her. Jane laughed politely at something decidedly unamusing, then Bingley said something to his morose companion and began moving toward them.

Oliver's eyes widened, and he quickly turned back to the conversation Jane was having with the excitable boy. His pulse jumped as the sensation of someone nearing him from behind grew stronger. Should he alert Jane? Maybe it'd be best if she didn't know—then she could react more naturally. Yes, alerting Jane would likely only result in making her anxious.

"Don't you think?" It took Oliver a moment to realize Jane was looking at him.

"Oh." His face flushed. "I, uh, I beg your pardon, I was distracted. What was the question?"

Oliver was fated never to know, however, because at that moment a tall gentleman with golden-red hair approached the group and said, "Excuse me, miss." Bingley smiled at Jane. "I apologize for interrupting, but I couldn't help but notice you haven't a partner to dance with. Would you do me the honor of joining me on the floor?"

Jane's face pinked, a hint of a smile on her lips. "Oh, I would love to," she said softly. "That is, if Mr. Harrison doesn't mind?"

"Please!" The excitable boy—Mr. Harrison, apparently—gestured for Jane to go on. "Don't hold back on my account."

Jane's gaze met Oliver's, and he grinned and nodded encouragingly. "Enjoy."

So Jane took Bingley's outstretched hand, and the two of them stepped into the center of the room as a new set began. Oliver couldn't help but smile—Mrs. Bennet was going to be *thrilled*. And they *did* make a handsome pair. Jane certainly seemed happy enough about the development.

Of course, this now left Oliver in the awkward position of being alone with Mr. Harrison, who wanted to talk about embroidery, of all things.

"It's such a feminine art," he was saying, "so simple, but it can be truly beautiful with a skilled hand. I envy the ability of a woman to create such delicate work. Are you quite skilled in embroidery, Miss Bennet?"

Oliver pursed his lips at the address—and the implication that he would be skilled in a *feminine* art because Mr. Harrison mistook him for a woman—before forcing his shoulders to relax as he met Mr. Harrison's gaze. "I can't say I am. If you'll excuse me."

Oliver didn't wait for permission—or, more importantly, give him the opportunity to protest—before turning away and continuing along the perimeter of the room. He spotted Jane dancing with Bingley. She looked absolutely radiant, giggling shyly as they met in the center of the floor before separating again.

Jane looked happy, and for the moment, that was enough.

Oliver's gaze wandered across the room. He found Bingley's friend—Darcy, was it?—standing exactly where Bingley had left him when he went to ask Jane to dance. The two women had found dancing partners of their own, so there he stiffly stood, alone, his back to the green wall like it was his only protection.

It was a sentiment Oliver could relate to.

The boy's hair was longer than Bingley's and framed his face in loose waves that curled out like a crown. It looked very soft. What would it feel like to run his fingers through it?

A young, pretty woman with blond curls spilling over her shoulders approached Darcy. Oliver couldn't hear what was said from this distance, but he had a guess based on the way Darcy shook his head and waved his hand, and the woman frowned and walked away, looking slightly insulted.

Interesting.

Then Darcy was looking at him and Oliver froze. Everything in him demanded he look away before he was caught staring, but it was already too late, and Oliver found he couldn't pull his gaze from him. There was something magnetic about Darcy's dark eyes, about his slightly furrowed brow as the boy held eye contact with him. Oliver's face warmed, his heart pounding in his ears so loudly the music of the room fell away. Though he was trapped like a moth pinned to a board, from that distance Oliver couldn't quite make out the color of Darcy's eyes. Green? Brown? Somewhere in between? Whatever the color, the boy's eyes were pulling him in—until, all at once, they turned flinty. Darcy's lips thinned, his brow furrowed more deeply, and something like disgust flashed over his handsome features. He shook his head and looked away.

The spell broke, and Oliver's face flushed as he forced himself to turn away. He felt oddly like the entire room had caught him doing something illicit, though he couldn't fathom why. Still, the distaste in Darcy's face felt like a slap. It shouldn't have mattered—Darcy was a stranger, and they hadn't done anything but briefly *look* at each other. And yet, the apparent rejection stung more than it should have.

So what if Darcy wasn't interested in approaching him, or

even looking at him for that matter? Neither was Oliver. He needn't waste a second more of his time with a boy determined to be so miserable.

———

Sometime later, Jane found him again, her face flush with delight. "There you are!" She laughed breathlessly. "Have you not danced with anyone yet?"

"I haven't," Oliver answered with a small smile.

"Oh, but you should! It's so fun. Even Mama has begun dancing with Father!"

Oliver blinked—now *that* was a surprise. "Really? Well, that should lift Mama's spirits. You certainly seemed to have fun with Bingley." He grinned. "He seemed to be enjoying himself too."

Jane blushed. "Do you think? I was so focused on not making a fool of myself—he really *is* handsome."

"He seemed quite taken with you. He didn't look away from you once the entire time you were dancing."

Jane beamed, then took his hand. "Come, let's find you a dancing partner."

Oliver's stomach plummeted. "Oh. That's really not necessary—"

"Nonsense! I won't have you standing by miserably while the rest of us enjoy ourselves."

His face warmed. "Who said I was miserable? I've been

perfectly content watching you dance. I'll have you know, watching everyone is plenty entertaining. Did you not see the gentleman who tripped over his own two feet and fell on his arse?"

Jane shook her head with a laugh. "I know the perfect dancing partner for you. Bingley mentioned his friend, Darcy, hadn't found anyone to dance with thus far, so I told him about you and he agreed it'd be a great match!"

Oliver's eyes widened, dread dripping down his spine like ice water. "You did what?"

"Please, just give it a chance. At the very least it'll keep Mama from clucking about you all night."

That, Oliver had to admit, was true. Avoiding yet another lecture from Mrs. Bennet about Oliver's *vanishing prospects* might actually make the displeasure of dancing with a man who would ogle his chest and hips the entire time almost worth it.

But there was still a problem, namely that it was *Darcy* who Jane was trying to set him up with—the one boy Oliver had decided he absolutely *wouldn't* interact with any further.

"Jane," Oliver pleaded. "Does it have to be *him*? I don't think this is a good idea—he doesn't seem to like me very much."

Jane paused, interest sparking in her eyes. "What makes you say that? Did you speak to him?"

"Well, no . . ."

"Then?"

Oliver could feel the flush creeping up his neck and bleeding into his cheeks. He hadn't even said it yet, but he already knew how weak it was going to sound. Honestly, what was Jane going to think about *We looked at each other and he didn't seem interested*?

"He . . . glowered at me," Oliver said carefully. "I just didn't get the sense that he wants to be here, and he didn't seem particularly happy to catch my gaze—"

Jane didn't look impressed. "You think he doesn't like you because he *looked* at you?"

"I know that sounds ridiculous, but—"

"*Oliver.*" Jane said it softly, only loud enough for the two of them to hear, but it was enough. Hearing his name brought a flood of warmth, of rightness, and ridiculously, he found himself smiling at it, despite the dire situation.

Jane took his hands in hers and met his gaze. "Just give it a chance, for me. Please?"

Oliver was absolutely certain this was a terrible idea, but for his elder sister, there was little he wouldn't endure. And she knew it.

"Fine," he grumbled, and a grin spread across Jane's face.

Then, before he could think better of it, she was pulling him through the crowd toward Bingley and Darcy, who were in the middle of what appeared to be a heated discussion.

"You haven't danced with anyone yet!" Bingley was saying. "Surely there's *someone* here who has caught your eye by now?"

"There is not," Darcy said with finality.

Oliver pulled Jane to a stop. Even she seemed to notice the

tone of the conversation, because she nodded toward two unoc-cupied chairs nearby. Oliver and Jane sat, pretending not to be paying attention to Bingley and Darcy's conversation even though they were very much still within earshot.

"Darcy, I insist," Bingley said. "You must dance. You know how I dislike seeing you standing alone so miserably."

But Darcy didn't appear moved. "And *you* know how I detest dancing with strangers. There is not a girl here whom it wouldn't be an absolute punishment for me to dance with."

Oliver's face went hot. Darcy wasn't looking at him—his back was turned to Oliver, so it's unlikely he even saw Jane and him sitting nearby—but he *had* seen Oliver earlier. They'd locked eyes for far too long to be dismissed as a mere passing glance, and now Darcy had all but declared him a *punishment* to dance with.

"You are impossible to please!" Bingley exclaimed. "There are so many unusually pleasant girls here tonight who would be happy to dance with you."

"I have seen only one, and you are dancing with her."

"Oh, she is the most beautiful woman I've ever seen! But her sisters are very attractive too, and one of them is sitting just behind you."

Oliver's eyes widened. Bingley might as well have *told* him Oliver was eavesdropping on their conversation. Any moment now Darcy would turn around and see him. Oliver took a deep breath, trying to cool his face. He had to compose himself. Immediately.

Bingley went on, "Please, let me ask Jane to introduce you."

Jane squeezed Oliver's hand, but before either of them could react further, Darcy turned around.

And that is how Oliver found himself once again meeting Darcy's stormy gaze, his heart thudding in his ears so loudly he was all but convinced Jane could hear it. Oliver found himself unable to breathe as the obvious annoyance washed over Darcy's face. He knew at once that his instinct around Darcy's dislike had been correct, and he felt utterly foolish for thinking even for an instant that the other boy was handsome.

Darcy broke eye contact and, turning back to Bingley, said, "She's tolerable, but not handsome enough to interest me."

If in that moment the ground had opened up beneath Oliver's feet and swallowed him whole, it would have been a mercy. Instead, he was left feeling as though Darcy had dumped an entire tub of ice water on his head. Here he was, trying to be the good "daughter" everyone expected him to be, and for what? Insult upon insult.

Thankfully, Jane was also appalled by the other boy's lack of tact; this time, when Oliver turned to leave, she did not stop him.

CHAPTER 3

THE BARTHOLOMEW FAIR WAS THE PERFECT EVENT TO ATTEND IF you didn't want anyone to pay you any mind. The annual affair was one of Oliver's favorites—this year particularly so, because it was the very opportunity he needed to spend some time alone in the company of hundreds of strangers as himself.

But first, he needed to change.

It wasn't exactly advisable to waltz out of his and Jane's bedroom dressed as himself—as a boy—at least, not if he wanted to avoid incurring his mother's wrath. Given this reality, Oliver had developed two ways to go out as himself while the majority of his family was none the wiser.

When Oliver went out at night, he pulled his clothes from one of the many small trunks beneath his bed. There were six trunks total, each of them with innocuous labels like "books" (Oliver could only afford enough books to place in one small trunk), "trinkets," "embroidery" (in reality, Oliver despised embroidery with a deep and burning passion), "drawing" (he had actually enjoyed drawing once, but it had been over a year since that trunk had been opened), etcetera. The trunks were arranged in two rows of three, so that the most important trunk—the one in the center of the back row—was completely hidden from the front and sides. *This* was the trunk in which he hid a few boy outfits (gifted to him by his generous uncle about six months ago when Oliver had visited Gracechurch). The system had proved effective in keeping his secret safe from prying eyes, especially once he'd asked the staff to leave the trunks be. It was essential that no one found his clothes or saw him sneaking out—even a whisper of a rumor about a Bennet "daughter" going out on her own could ruin his family's reputation.

Society, unfortunately, wouldn't care that Oliver wasn't a daughter at all.

Once dressed, Oliver would replace the trunks as they were, then—after ensuring everyone had gone to bed or was otherwise occupied far on the other side of the house—climb out the window using the trellis running alongside the town house to lower himself to the ground. The first time he'd done this, Jane had nearly fainted in fright, but now that it had been several months without incident, it didn't make his sister so anxious anymore.

Of course, Oliver could hardly climb out their bedroom window unnoticed during the day, so a secondary strategy was required. When he went out during the day, he would tell his mother he was visiting his closest friend, Charlotte Lewis, who lived about a ten-minute walk from the Bennet family home, known as Longbourn. This was a half-truth, because he *did* go to Charlotte's, but he didn't stay there.

Charlotte was one of the five people who knew who Oliver was. Several months back, Oliver had stashed a couple boy outfits in her bedroom. The Lewises—comprised of just Charlotte and her father—couldn't afford staff, and Mr. Lewis worked so frequently he was rarely home. Charlotte kept Oliver's clothes folded neatly in her wardrobe beneath her underclothes, all but ensuring no one else would ever find them. This made Charlotte's room the perfect private abode, where Oliver could enter dressed as "Elizabeth" and leave as himself—and vice versa, when he stopped by Charlotte's to change back into his girl clothes before returning home.

As the Bartholomew Fair was a morning affair, this was the strategy Oliver employed that day. The early spring air was cool and crisp, and the grass and leaves shone with dew. When Oliver arrived at Charlotte's and knocked on the door, he was surprised to find not his friend opening the door, but Lu, Charlotte's close friend.

"Hello, Oliver!" Lu said cheerily, stepping aside to let him in. "Charlotte mentioned you'd be coming by this morning—to change, was it? I believe she's still in her room, if you'd like to say hello."

Oliver smiled and entered, thanking Lu as she closed the door behind him.

To all the world, Charlotte and Lu were friends, but in reality they were much more than that. It hadn't been long after Oliver entrusted Charlotte with the reality of who he was that Charlotte had shared a secret of her own with him—that she and Lu were lovers. Lu was a married woman, but being in the army, her husband was absent for months at a time, so Lu spent most of her days visiting with Charlotte. It had been the strangest relief to learn that Oliver's closest friend was breaking convention in her own way. While it wasn't the same as Oliver's experience, of course (Charlotte and Lu enjoyed presenting themselves femininely, for one, and Oliver was exclusively attracted to other boys), the honesty between them still made Oliver feel a little less alone.

Oliver was just about to knock on the door to Charlotte's bedroom when the door swung open. A smile lit up her face.

"I thought I heard you arrive! Please, come in—I've left your clothes out on the bed."

Oliver's clothes were freshly pressed—a courtesy he never asked for but always appreciated. He had enough boy clothes for four outfits total, half of which he kept at home under his bed, and the other half he stored at Charlotte's.

Here too he had a binding cloth to give him the appearance of a flat chest, a single pair of white trousers, an emerald-green double-breasted silk-and-linen vest with a high collar, a black double-breasted wool waistcoat, two white linen shirts (one frilled), a white linen cravat, and—his favorite piece—a black wool double-breasted tailcoat. He opted for the green vest in a nod to the oncoming spring weather and tied his cravat three times to get the knot just right. Satisfied with the clothing, he pulled his hair up and hid it beneath his top hat.

Once dressed, he looked in the mirror and beamed. Mrs. Bennet would surely faint if she saw him, but he felt *incredible*. The binding cloth he'd created with Jane's help—a flat corset-type material at the front with long fabric strips that wrapped around and pinned tight at the sides—worked perfectly beneath his shirt to flatten his chest. It had taken some finagling to get the measurements just right, but with some practice, Oliver had learned how to wrap it with the exact tension needed to keep the cloth snug against his flattened chest without hugging his ribs too tightly. Now fully dressed and styled, every glimpse of his reflection was absolutely thrilling.

It was such a contrast to his mood when he wore women's clothes, where even the silhouette of his shadow made him nauseous. He'd already thanked his uncle multiple times for providing him such a source of pure joy, but he made a mental note to send him another letter of gratitude.

It was a special thing, to have one's reflection in harmony with who they were.

Emerging from Charlotte's room and stepping into the foyer, Lu and Charlotte looked up from their conversation and broke out into twin smiles.

"Don't you look fetching!" Lu exclaimed. "Would you like some tea before you go?"

The Bartholomew Fair took place in Smithfield, a wide fairground divided into a variety of booths and stands. Somewhere in the center were animal pens that, oddly, were placed near the food stalls selling hot pies, sausages, oysters, and more. The cool mid-March air carried the scents of cooking meat, frying dough, and hay in a strange mélange. Outside the center were rows of booths, all turned to face inward. The booths sold a variety of wares, from unique glassware to clothing to brightly colored lamps.

Beyond the merchant stalls were show booths, which were elevated and large—about the size of an average parlor—to create pop-up stages for various performers. The one nearest Oliver held a London street band he'd seen sing and dance downtown before; it was composed of four men and a woman and featured drums, a violin, an organ, and pipes. The woman was the primary vocalist, and she sang while playing the violin— and occasionally shook her ankles, to which she'd tied bells.

People milled about around Oliver, but the day was still young, so the crowd would certainly grow over time. The first time he'd gone out in men's clothes, Oliver had been terrified that someone would recognize him. That someone would look at his face and see "Elizabeth" and react with horror. But he quickly learned that most didn't pay much attention to his face—once they saw the way he dressed, they made their own conclusions quickly. He suspected the notion that a "woman" would dress like a man was so preposterous to most of the populace that it never crossed anyone's mind that Oliver was anyone but who he said he was.

He was happy to use that assumption to his advantage.

The booth to the left of the London street band contained a sword-swallower. Oliver watched in grotesque fascination as a gangly boy, tall and thin as a reed, unsheathed a sword and tilted his head back. He positioned the sword above his open mouth and a shiver went through Oliver at the implication of what was about to come next.

"My God," said a familiar voice to Oliver's right. "He's really going to do it!"

Oliver turned to the source of the voice and very nearly blanched at seeing *Charles Bingley* of all people standing next to him. He appeared to be alone, at least for the moment, and he was pale as a sheet as he watched, wide-eyed, as the performer lowered the sword into his mouth.

Oliver's heart thrummed in his ears, the morning warmth gathering around his neck like a burning collar. It was one thing for strangers to see him, but quite another to run into some-one he'd met as Elizabeth—someone who had looked him in the face and called him pretty just the night before, no less. He needed to leave, *now*, before Bingley—

"Have you ever seen anything like this?" Bingley asked.

Oliver dared a glance over, half expecting to see Bingley's sisters or Darcy joining him, but none of his companions were there. There were other onlookers, of course, but Oliver was the only one standing directly next to him.

Which meant Bingley was talking to him.

Just act normal, Oliver reminded himself. *He's only being friendly. He hasn't really even looked at you yet.*

The performer had now swallowed the sword up to the hilt, drawing gasps from the sparse crowd around them. Bingley's eyes were fixated on the stage, which was advantageous. Oliver just had to respond banally so Bingley wouldn't remember the interaction, then politely excuse himself and walk away.

With a breath, Oliver kept the register of his voice low as he responded. "Well . . . I do think he was here last year, but it is impressive."

Responding, however, proved to be a mistake. The moment he spoke, Bingley looked at him. For a moment, Oliver was frozen, looking into Bingley's blue eyes and swallowing the panic rising in his chest. *Please*, he thought, *I'm Oliver. I'm not the girl you think you met last night. Please.*

But if Bingley was at all suspicious, he didn't show it. Instead, his face broke into a grin. "Oh! So you've been to the Bartholomew Fair before? How grand! My companions and I have wanted to visit for some time, but this is the first we've actually managed it."

"Oh," Oliver heard himself saying, even as his instinct to run made him feel as though he were floating away from his body. "I've been fortunate enough to attend since I was a child. I'm sure you'll enjoy yourself—there's something for everyone here."

"I should hope so!" Bingley exclaimed. "Are you expecting a companion yourself?"

Oliver hesitated, debating whether it'd be beneficial to lie about this. He chose to answer honestly. "No."

"Well, in that case, you should join my companion and me! It'd be wonderful to discover the fair with a knowledgeable guide. What do you say?"

Oliver blinked, uncertainty turning his tongue thick, like trying to speak through a mouthful of half-baked bread. If Bingley was inviting him to spend the day with them, then he really mustn't recognize him. Which meant he saw him as just another young man with whom he might like to become acquainted.

The possibility was dizzying. Oliver had been sneaking away from home to spend time in public as himself for months now, but he'd never had more than a fleeting, transient conversation with another boy as himself before. The opportunity to spend the day with boys who saw him as one of their own was more than tempting—it was a dream he never imagined he'd actually get to experience.

But to do that with Bingley seemed impossibly risky, and Oliver didn't even know who his companion was yet.

In the space of Oliver's hesitation, Bingley's eyes lit up as he looked at something—someone—over Oliver's shoulder. "Oh!" he said. "How perfect, that's my companion over there. Darcy!"

Oliver's eyes widened. Darcy? Bingley wanted him to spend the day with him and *Darcy*?

What were the odds, realistically, that Darcy wouldn't recognize him after glowering at him *twice* the night before? Bingley was one thing, but facing Darcy seemed far too much like tempting fate.

Unfortunately, Oliver didn't get much say in the matter because Darcy walked right up to Bingley, smiling softly at his friend before looking quizzically at Oliver.

Bingley swooped in with a grin. "Darcy, this is my new friend—ah, actually, I don't think I ever asked your name." He laughed. "How rude! Apologies, allow me to introduce myself. My name is Charles Bingley, and this is my friend, Fitzwilliam Darcy."

Oliver opened his mouth, ready to say Bennet before catching himself. The *B* had already formed on his lips so he spat out the first surname that came to mind. "Blake. Oliver Blake, but please, call me Oliver."

Darcy arched an eyebrow at his informality, and Oliver regretted it almost immediately, but he really couldn't count on remembering to respond to *Blake*, of all names. Still, if it bothered Darcy beyond mere curiosity, he didn't show it—he just nodded.

The grin that spread over Oliver's face was unstoppable. A lightness flooded his chest, and a giddying thought formed in his mind: *I can do this.* Neither Bingley nor Darcy had made the connection between him and the second-eldest Bennet they met last night.

"I was just asking Oliver if he'd be amenable to showing us around the fair," Bingley said to Darcy. "He's attended every year since he was a child, so he's quite familiar with the goings-on here."

He. Oliver couldn't stop smiling. It was such a simple thing, but the rightness of it was a balm. Being recognized for who he was brought him a euphoria like nothing else he had ever experienced. *You see me*, he thought, and it made him so happy he wanted to laugh out loud.

"That would be helpful," Darcy said, his gaze settling on Oliver. "I'm shocked there isn't a map readily available. This fair is much larger than I had anticipated."

"But only if it wouldn't be a bother," Bingley added quickly. "We'd completely understand if you weren't able to show us around." The redhead looked at Oliver pleadingly, a sheepish smile making him look even more boyish than usual. It was easy to see why Jane fancied him.

"I can do it." The words were out of his mouth before he could think better of it. "It might be nice to enjoy the fair with some new companions."

Bingley clapped and grinned widely. "Perfect! Where to now?"

After the incident last night, Oliver never would have imagined that spending the morning with Bingley and Darcy would be anywhere near enjoyable and yet, impossibly, it was. Once he realized neither Bingley nor Darcy had connected his face to any of the Bennets they'd encountered the night before, he'd been able to relax. And, once relaxed, he found himself laughing with genuine warmth.

Sometime later, the three realized it was well past noon and none of them had eaten since breakfast. Bingley volunteered to cross the fairgrounds to stand in what was sure to be a long line to get them all meat pies. With Bingley gone to get food, Oliver found himself, for the first time, alone with Darcy.

The reality made his stomach cramp with anxiety. Though he'd spent a couple hours with the two boys already, Bingley had largely led the conversation, and the few times Darcy spoke it was usually to his friend.

But now Bingley wasn't there, which meant they'd either have to speak to each other or ignore each other. Oliver wasn't sure which would be worse.

They stood in front of an elevated show booth, upon which stood a bear, two dogs, and a man. Absurdly, the bear was wearing red-and-yellow-trimmed pants, a matching open jacket, and a red fez. The dogs—both small white poodles—wore matching outfits, complete with their own tiny fezzes. The dogs hopped around the bear on their back legs while the bear stood in the center, balancing a ball on its nose.

The performance was driving the gathered crowd wild, but neither Oliver nor Darcy joined them in the applause and cheering. The display was deeply uncomfortable to him, but Oliver wasn't entirely sure why. Something about the juxtaposition of the bear in circus clothes, of all things, of the out-of-place-ness, the wrongness of it all, reverberated deeply.

It was a familiar discomfort, like the way he felt every time he had to wear a dress. Like it was all just a *performance*, and not one he was particularly adept at. Just the thought of it brought a bone-deep exhaustion.

"I've always found these performances a bit cruel," Darcy said, yanking Oliver out of his thoughts. He ripped his gaze away from the stage and looked at Darcy, who was frowning deeply at the act. "Animals aren't meant to perform for our entertainment. It's unnatural."

"We can watch something else," Oliver offered. "I'm sure Bingley will still find us as long as we don't stray far." He glanced around, quickly scanning the nearby show booths. "How about that one?" He nodded to a stage two booths over, where acrobats were stacking metal hoops and leaping over one another at incredible heights.

At that, Darcy's face softened. "That looks better."

They meandered over, neither of them in a hurry. Once there, Darcy watched the performance with an unreadable expression; he didn't turn to Oliver once. The air between them was full of tension so thick it was choking. Oliver wanted to fill the awkward silence, but standing next to Darcy, it was as though he'd forgotten every conversation starter he'd ever known. What did people even talk about? The weather? Oliver cringed internally at the thought of trying to talk to Darcy about the *weather*, of all things. And in any case, Darcy didn't seem to be much of a conversationalist.

After many excruciating minutes in which Oliver tried to enjoy the performance while hyperaware of the boy standing statue-still next to him, Bingley bounded up to them, arms full of meat pies wrapped in paper. "There you are! I was starting to think the bear had eaten you both. Am I interrupting?"

"Not at all." Darcy plucked a pie from Bingley's arms.

Oliver took a pie gratefully, smiling as the heat of it warmed his hands through the paper. He unwrapped it and the scent of flaky, buttery pastry made his mouth water. He broke off a bit of pastry with his fingers, creating a hole so the escaping steam would cool the inside faster, and popped it in his mouth.

"Darcy," Bingley said suddenly. "Didn't you say you wanted to purchase a couple more books for your library?"

Oliver's gaze snapped to Darcy before he could stop himself. He tried to disguise the surprise on his face—it was a testament to their wealth that they would casually discuss *purchasing* multiple books at once. Books were incredibly expensive—Oliver's family, who did perfectly well for themselves financially despite not being particularly wealthy, could only ever afford to purchase one on special occasions. Ordinarily, Oliver got books from the lending library. Having his own personal library was an unattainable dream.

"Well, we're in luck," Bingley continued. "Finsbury Square is but a quarter hour's walk from here."

Oliver's eyes widened. Finsbury Square was where the Temple of Muses, a rather popular bookstore, was located. Oliver had never gone himself, but he'd meant to take a look sometime, even if he couldn't afford to actually purchase anything.

Darcy's eyebrows rose. "Oh really? We should head over, then." He looked at Oliver. "Have you been to the Temple of Muses?"

"I haven't," Oliver replied almost breathlessly.

Darcy nodded. "You should join us. Their collection is quite impressive."

Oliver's mouth nearly fell open in shock. Was Darcy actually inviting him to spend *more* time with them? Darcy had been so quiet all morning Oliver had assumed he wasn't enjoying the company. But if he was inviting Oliver to join them, then maybe he'd misread the quiet boy.

"I would love to," Oliver said, and then the strangest thing happened.

Darcy smiled. Just a little.

———

Oliver had never given much thought to what the Temple of Muses might be like, if only to avoid tempting himself into visiting a place he would surely want to spend far too much time—and money—in. Now, stepping into the truly massive bookstore for the first time, he knew he'd made a grave mistake.

He was never going to want to leave.

The entry room was nearly as large as the entire bottom floor of Oliver's home, Longbourn. The far wall was comprised entirely of bookshelves, packed from floor to ceiling with books.

In the center of the room was an enormous round circulation desk, painted red and staffed by four men answering questions from a sizable crowd. Two iron columns extended from the desk to the ceiling, and directly above were even more bookshelves built into the walls of the upper floor—viewable through an enormous circle cut out of the ceiling. The air was heady with the scent of paper and glue—Oliver wished he could bottle the fragrance for his room.

"Impressive, isn't it?" Darcy asked, breaking Oliver from his stupor. He'd been so taken by the display—he'd never seen so many books in one place in his *life*, and they hadn't even gone to the upper floor yet!—that he'd forgotten about his companions entirely.

"This is incredible," Oliver breathed. "The books are . . . on display? Can we look at them?"

"That's the best part!" Bingley said cheerily. "In most book-shops, the books are all behind the counter, but here there are thousands of books, and you can look at however many you'd like. There's even a lounging area upstairs if you'd like to try reading a couple."

Oliver thought it a horrid crime that he'd never ventured here before.

He followed Darcy and Bingley up a staircase to the left, which opened onto a small landing with windows that over-looked the London streets below. They continued on up another set of stairs, which opened onto the second floor. Like the floor below, the walls were comprised of floor-to-ceiling bookshelves, but up here rows of shelves housed even more books on the right side of the room, and plush, large lounging chairs were set out as well. Oliver could see himself selecting a book, curling up in one of those chairs, and reading for hours. It was like something out of a fantasy.

"I'm afraid you've done me a disservice," Oliver said to Darcy. The other boy frowned, his brow furrowing in confusion before Oliver continued, "I'm never going to want to leave this place."

Darcy's face softened into a smile that filled Oliver with warmth. Bingley laughed and Darcy's gaze settled on Oliver, almost appraisingly, as he nodded. "It has that effect on me as well."

The three boys wandered down the aisles of shelves as Oliver marveled at the sheer number of books. When Bingley had said there were thousands of books here, Oliver had thought he'd been hyperbolizing, but now standing among the seemingly endless rows of books, he didn't doubt that was the case. The capital required to acquire such an inventory was so immense Oliver couldn't begin to put a number to it.

Darcy strode with purpose to one particular bookshelf and knelt, running his fingers over the books' spines as he searched. His fingers were long and elegant—perfect for playing an instrument, though Oliver doubted he did because, as ridiculous as it was, most men and boys left the music playing to the women and girls. Then all at once his fingers paused on a book, and with a twitch of his lips, he pulled it from the shelf and stood. In black lettering, the title read *The Farther Adventures of Robinson Crusoe: Being the Second and Last Part of His Life, and Strange Surprizing Accounts of His Travels Round Three Parts of the Globe.*

"Are you familiar with the title?" Darcy asked.

Oliver frowned and shook his head. "I can't say I am."

"It's a sequel. Perhaps you've heard of the first book, *The Life and Strange Surprizing Adventures of Robinson Crusoe, of York, Mariner: Who Lived Eight and Twenty Years, All Alone in an Un-inhabited Island on the Coast of America, Near the Mouth of the Great River of Oroonoque?*" He frowned. "There's more to the title but I can't remember it in its entirety. Something about being the only survivor of a shipwreck . . . and pirates."

Oliver arched an eyebrow. "I haven't read it, but it does sound interesting."

Darcy nodded. "I thoroughly enjoyed it. Some of the depictions were . . . questionable, to say the least, but from a purely for-entertainment standpoint, I found it enjoyable. Do you like to read?"

Just a few hours earlier, Oliver would have thought this conversation with Darcy—that they found a common point of interest between them—an impossibility. But it seemed the key to Darcy's heart was books.

Oliver could relate.

"I do!" he said. "I'll admit I haven't had quite as much

opportunity to read as I would like, but when I have a good book, there's little that will tear me away from it."

"I'm the same way," Darcy responded. "It's truly a singular experience, being captivated by an excellent story."

Together, the three of them wandered around exploring the shelves. As they conversed about the selection, it was the first time all day that Darcy seemed interested in including Oliver in the conversation. His aloofness from earlier in the day wasn't gone entirely, but as the day went on Darcy seemed less reticent to address Oliver directly. It was a small thing, but for reasons Oliver chose not to explore, it felt like a victory.

After Darcy painstakingly selected four books to add to his home library (with Oliver's help, much to his delight) they stepped back out into the cool spring air. Oliver had become so accustomed to the warm scent of the books inside that the outside air felt almost tart in comparison.

They'd barely been outside for ten seconds before Bingley said, "Just a minute, I think I saw a lavatory inside," then slipped back into the bookstore. As Darcy and Oliver turned to each other, it occurred to Oliver that this was probably the time he should excuse himself and go home, but before he could speak, Darcy beat him to it.

"Bingley and I go to Watier's every week—Tuesday nights, which are designated for boys and young men, specifically. Are you perchance a member?"

Oliver's face warmed. Watier's was a gentleman's club, where highbrow men gambled, drank, and socialized away from the eyes of women. Oliver had never been in one for obvious reasons, but even if he *had* been recognized as a boy at birth, he certainly wouldn't have had the wealth to afford the outrageous membership fees.

"I'm afraid not," Oliver responded evenly.

Darcy nodded. "I suspected as much."

If Oliver hadn't flushed before, he certainly did now. The gall! Was this Darcy's way of telling him he wasn't wealthy enough to associate with them? And here Oliver had actually thought maybe Darcy was beginning to warm up to him. But perhaps he was just putting on the niceties for Bingley's sake, and now that he was gone, so was the act.

And to think he'd almost fallen for it.

"I see," Oliver said stiffly.

Darcy frowned, looking at him quizzically. Then his eyes widened. "Oh! Apologies, I wasn't trying to imply—I only meant that I hadn't seen you there before."

Oh. Oliver's shoulders relaxed, feeling a bit foolish. Darcy pinched the bridge of his nose and closed his eyes and it almost looked like—was *he* blushing now?

He dropped his hand and opened his eyes. "I'm not . . . like Bingley. I'm not good at this." He gestured airily between them.

Oliver had to admit, this whole display was oddly endearing. He found himself smiling softly without meaning to. "This?"

"Socializing. Meeting new people. It's an art I've accepted I'll likely never master. Oftentimes I don't have to, as Bingley is skilled enough for the both of us, but when I'm left to interact with someone I don't know, alone . . . well. They either bore me and I lack the ability and desire to pretend otherwise, or I inevitably make a fool of myself. I apologize."

Oliver's smile grew. Bored Darcy might be an arse, but flustered Darcy was adorable. "Well, I suppose I'm happy to know I don't bore you."

"Absolutely not," Darcy said, so quickly that the simple reassurance filled Oliver's chest with warmth.

It was then that Bingley emerged from the Temple of Muses once more. "Apologies!" he said. "Did I miss anything?"

"I was just inviting Oliver to join us at Watier's," Darcy said.

Oliver's eyes widened. He was?

"Oh!" Bingley exclaimed. "Yes, of course! You must join us, Oliver. It'll be a grand old time. What do you say?"

Oliver's head was spinning. Darcy and Bingley wanted to spend more time with him? At *Watier's* of all places? The thought of going there felt terrifyingly illicit, but why should it be? He *was* a boy. The rest of the world may not see it most of the time, but Darcy and Bingley did, and they were the ones offering the invitation.

"Are you sure?" Oliver asked. "I didn't think I was allowed entrance without a membership."

"We're permitted to bring a guest," Darcy said. "We could

bring a guest every week if we wanted to. I'd be happy to make you mine."

Oliver arched an eyebrow.

Darcy's face flushed pink. "My . . . guest. That is."

Oliver grinned. How on earth was it possible that this was the same Darcy as last night? Or even this morning? "I'd be honored."

Darcy's smile was small and sweet—and Oliver found he couldn't look away.

For some reason, he didn't want to.

CHAPTER 4

THE NEXT MORNING OLIVER MOVED ABOUT IN A DAZE. THOUGH HE performed his morning routine flawlessly—dressing as expected and sitting at the table just in time for breakfast—his mind was caught up in the previous day's events.

He'd spent the entire *day* with Bingley and Darcy. He could hardly believe how smoothly it had gone—and how different Darcy was in the company of boys. And they'd invited him to Watier's of all places, and thoughtlessly, he'd accepted!

Now in the harsh reality of the morning, going to Watier's with Bingley and Darcy seemed like a terrible idea. He'd passed all day as a boy with just the two of them, but would he really be able to do so in a roomful of wealthy young gentlemen?

Why not? he asked himself. *No one has ever questioned you before. Why would this be any different?*

That was probably true, but it was still terrifying to contemplate. Oliver had never gone into such an exclusively gendered place before—at least, not one meant for boys.

Still, wasn't that what made it so exhilarating?

"After dancing with our dear Jane, he didn't look at another girl for the rest of the night!" Mrs. Bennet was saying. She'd been crooning about the Meryton Ball for nearly forty-eight hours straight now. Oliver wasn't tired of it yet, if only because the attention on Jane meant Mrs. Bennet wasn't focused on turning him into a "proper lady." And anyway, Jane seemed to be quietly enjoying the excitement, even if she was far too cautious to declare a victory herself.

"That's wonderful, dear," Mr. Bennet said, probably for the fourth or fifth time during this meal alone, as he wiped crumbs from his mouth with a cloth serviette.

It was then that Oliver realized most everyone else had nearly finished their breakfasts, while he had barely eaten anything at all. He dug in quickly, eating his toast in large bites and gulping his tea—which had now cooled to room temperature. This was a transgression that likely would not have gone unnoticed had Mrs. Bennet not been too busy already planning out Jane and Bingley's future together.

"You should have several children," she was saying. "At least three, I should think. Oh, you'll make me the most *beautiful* grandchildren, Jane."

Oliver grimaced and met Mr. Bennet's gaze, who raised his eyebrows and lifted a shoulder as if to say *Are you really surprised?* His grimace deepened and he stopped listening before his insides withered to dust. Across the table, Kitty and Lydia were whispering to each other. He tried to focus on their hushed voices, though it was difficult with Mrs. Bennet (who was now proposing names for the grandchildren she didn't yet have) right beside him.

"If we go downtown, I should think we'd be able to see them," Lydia was saying. "We could propose taking a walk once they've arrived."

Oliver frowned. Who were his sisters planning to visit?

Kitty's eyes gleamed with excitement. "I can't wait. There will be so *many*—"

"Elizabeth," Mrs. Bennet said, for possibly not the first time.

Oliver looked up, hiding his flinch with an embarrassed smile. "Yes?"

Across the table, Mary snickered at him. Oliver resisted the urge to stick his tongue out at her.

Mrs. Bennet sighed with unnecessary force. "I was just discussing with Jane how after she's married, *you* should be next."

A full-body shudder of revulsion rolled through him, spreading from his stomach to his toes and the tips of his fingers. It wasn't so much the thought of marriage itself that was so off-putting, just the role he was expected to play in one.

He couldn't be someone's wife. It would kill him.

"Well," Oliver said smoothly, somehow maintaining a smile, "I think perhaps we shouldn't rush ahead. After all, Jane isn't even engaged yet. She and Bingley have only met once."

Mrs. Bennet clutched her hand over her heart. "My dear, have you been completely lost in your head this morning? Did you not hear Jane discussing the letter she received today?"

Oliver had not, in fact, heard Jane discussing any such letter.

He looked at his elder sister with surprise, and she smiled apologetically at him.

"The Bingleys invited me to join them for tea later this week," she said softly. "I intend to accept."

"Of *course* you'll accept!" Mrs. Bennet exclaimed, aghast at any implication otherwise. "Don't you see, Elizabeth? Mr. Bingley was so taken with our Jane the other night that he wants to get to know her personally! And of course he'll be even more enamored with her after spending more time with her. It's only a matter of time before he proposes."

Oliver still thought it a leap to assume Jane's engagement was all but certain, but it was a happy turn of events nevertheless. He couldn't share it with Mrs. Bennet, of course, but he *had* spent the day with Bingley and found him to be perfectly amicable. It'd be a good match.

Still, Oliver didn't want to have any part of this conversation with his mother. Instead, he turned to Jane with a smile. "Should we decide what you're going to wear, then?"

"I know you don't actually care about what dress I choose for the occasion," Jane said the moment their bedroom door closed behind them. "Is everything all right?"

Oliver thought it probably said something unflattering about him that Jane's first assumption was that he'd pulled her away from a happy conversation to give her bad news, but she *was* right that he wasn't actually interested in her dress of choice.

"No!" he said quickly. "Nothing's wrong—quite the opposite actually." He sat on his bed, in the farthest corner of the room from the door, and beckoned for Jane to sit near him. The walls of their bedroom were painted a garish yellow-green, which reminded Oliver of one of his least favorite meals, split pea soup. A thin strip of wallpaper ran along the very topmost portion of the wall, depicting a yellow frieze, with deep-green drapes trimmed in gold.

As Jane sat, Oliver pressed his bare feet into the floral Wilton rug—also green—its fibers soft against his soles. Once Jane was settled, he lowered his voice. "I didn't get the chance to tell you this morning about my day yesterday."

Jane's eyes widened. "Oh yes! I'd wanted to ask, but Mama kept us both so busy last night . . ."

Oliver nodded. Neither Jane nor he had taken to the pianoforte like Mary, or painting like Kitty and Lydia, so every so often she insisted on giving them both sewing lessons. Jane didn't really need it—she was an excellent seamstress, as evidenced by her help in creating Oliver's binding cloth—but Oliver had never really developed the same level of skill as she had. This often frustrated Mrs. Bennet, which meant their lessons went on for far longer than he would have liked.

"The fair itself was fine," Oliver said, "but you'll never guess who I ran into while I was there."

Jane frowned. "Who?"

"Bingley and Darcy!"

Jane gasped, her hand flying to her mouth. "Oh no. Did they recognize you from the ball?"

"No!" Oliver laughed, his grin easy as yesterday's events filled him with a sense of buoyancy. "That's the best part! I spent *the entire day* with them both, introduced myself as Oliver, and neither of them questioned it. I was just . . . I was just another boy who they met at the fair. We even spent a couple hours at the Temple of Muses afterward!"

"Oh Oliver, that's wonderful!" Jane exclaimed. "And Darcy . . . ?"

"I think . . . he was starting to warm up to me, by the end." Oliver smiled softly. "He was a completely different person in the company of men. He seemed more at ease—and he even invited me to join Bingley and him at Watier's later this week!"

Jane's eyes widened. "He did?"

"Yes!" And this was where his excitement deflated to something like anxiety. His smile faltered and his gaze drifted to his lap. "I accepted, but . . . I'm not sure if it's wise for me to go."

Jane tsked. "And why not?"

Oliver looked at her with a frown. "You know why, Jane. If someone realizes who I am . . . Women aren't permitted there."

"Well, it's a good thing you aren't a woman, then," Jane said without missing a beat. "Oliver, *I* barely recognize you when you're dressed in your proper clothes, and I'm your sister. You said Darcy was a different person in the company of men— well, *you're* a different person when you're permitted to be yourself. You're so much more at ease, so much happier. It's not just that your clothes have changed, your entire demeanor is more authentic."

Oliver wasn't sure what to say to that. It was true that the person he saw in the mirror was totally different when he wore men's clothes, but there was always a part of his brain whispering that he was a fraud. That he would never be like Darcy, or Bingley, or any other person recognized as a boy at birth. There was always a fear that someone might notice the very slight bump of his chest beneath his binding cloth, or might think his hips too wide, or his voice too high, to truly be a man.

But of course, who was really looking at him that closely besides himself? If Jane was telling him he was a transformed person as Oliver, as himself, then he should trust her.

"You really think I'd be able to pass for a boy at Watier's?"

"It's not a question in my mind at all," she responded confidently. "Let me ask you something: If you weren't at all worried about someone recognizing you, do you think you'd enjoy yourself at Watier's with Bingley and Darcy?"

Oliver didn't even have to think about it. "Absolutely," he responded. "I know it seems impossible after the Meryton Ball, but Darcy was significantly more pleasant to be around, if a little awkward. And Bingley! I completely understand what you see in him. They really did make great company."

"Then you should go." Jane stood, dusting her hands off as if the matter was settled.

And maybe it was.

CHAPTER 5

TODAY WAS A RARITY, IN THAT WHEN OLIVER TOLD HIS MOTHER HE would be visiting with Charlotte, he actually meant it. Unfortunately, Kitty and Lydia wanted to join him for reasons he couldn't begin to fathom, which meant he had to pretend to be Elizabeth the entire time.

It was far from ideal, but at the very least it added credibility to his claim that he was spending so much time with Charlotte.

Upon arrival, he was happy to find Lu there too. It wasn't until Charlotte suggested they all take advantage of the unseasonably warm day to walk into London proper and Lydia and Kitty squealed with excitement, cooing about how they should all go immediately, that Oliver began to understand why they were so desperate to join him to begin with. Being the youngest Bennets, Kitty and Lydia weren't permitted to wander far from Longbourn themselves, but with a chaperone—like, say, Oliver, Charlotte, and Lu—it was perfectly permissible.

What he was less clear on was why they were so excited about going into the city, but he supposed that wasn't really his concern as long as they didn't do anything dangerous. Still, as they all set off down the walking path, the younger girls rushed on ahead, remaining in view, but abandoning all pretense of wanting to spend time with Charlotte, Lu, and Oliver.

This also suited Oliver perfectly, as it meant he could speak to Charlotte and Lu frankly without worrying about his sisters hearing something they shouldn't and parroting it back to Mrs. Bennet.

"They certainly seem excited about something," Charlotte observed, a note of amusement in her voice.

"I'd thought their insistence that they hadn't seen you in ages was suspicious," Oliver responded with a laugh. "Although, I'm not certain what's happening in London proper that they're so eager to see. Do either of you know of anything going on?"

Charlotte pursed her lips and shook her head. "The Bartholomew Fair ended over the weekend, though that was in Smithfield. Still, it's London. There's always something happening."

That was true, at least. Oliver cleared his throat. "Speaking of the Bartholomew Fair, I attended on my own two days ago. As myself."

"Oh, did you?" Lu arched an eyebrow and smiled widely. "And how did that go?"

"Surprisingly well, actually."

Lu grinned. "I hardly think *that* a surprise. You make quite the handsome young man, Oliver." She winked at him, and Oliver's face warmed as he bit back a smile. "Don't you agree, Charlotte?"

"Naturally," Charlotte said.

"Thank you," Oliver answered. "It's more than you think, though. Charlotte, did you show Lu my letter about what happened at the Meryton Ball?"

The morning after the ball, before Oliver had gone to the fair, he'd written Charlotte a letter detailing the events of the night before—down to Darcy's exact words. Charlotte had written back in appropriate horror.

Lu frowned. "She certainly *told* me about it. That Darcy's behavior was truly appalling."

Charlotte shook her head and tsked. "To think that such a respectable young man could be so abjectly disagreeable."

"It *was* terrible," Oliver agreed. "But something strange happened . . ." Oliver recounted the story of the weekend's adventure, from running into Bingley and Darcy, to spending the morning exploring the fair together, to the Temple of Muses and finally the invitation to Watier's.

When he was finished, Lu's eyes were wide as shillings. "Why didn't you mention it when you returned to change back into your dress?"

"I needed time to process before I spoke to anyone about it,"

Oliver said, shaking his hand like batting away a fly. "I didn't even mention it to Jane until yesterday morning."

Lu laughed, shaking her head. It was then that Oliver noticed Charlotte, who, contrary to expectations, didn't look pleased. Her mouth was thin and unsmiling. A crease furrowed her brow, and for an uncomfortable moment neither of them said anything. This was a very different reaction from Lu, or when Oliver had shared the news with Jane. He wasn't sure how to interpret her sudden change in mood. Lu seemed to notice it too, because as her gaze slid to Charlotte, her smile melted off her face like ice on a summer day.

They were entering the more populous part of London now. Though the sounds of horse hooves on the packed road, squeaky carriage wheels, and conversation as people walked past them were impossible to escape, Charlotte's silence felt like an absence of all sound. Like Oliver had fallen into a dream in which he couldn't hear.

Finally, Charlotte said carefully, "And . . . what did you say?"

Oliver was no longer sure he wanted to have this conversation with Charlotte, but it was far too late to change course now. "Well, it would have been rude to refuse," he said, trying to infuse his voice with more confidence than he had. "And anyway, Jane thinks I should go."

"I agree with Jane," Lu said. "It's an opportunity to get to know more boys your age. If you want to go, I think you should."

Charlotte's lips became a flat line. Oliver bit his lip, forcing himself not to look at the disapproval clear on her face. The following silence made him want to squirm. Why was she acting like he was doing something wrong? She'd always been supportive before.

"Can I ask you something?" she said after many uncomfortable moments.

Given the tone of the interaction so far, Oliver was tempted to say no. But Charlotte was his closest friend, and he had to trust that she wouldn't steer this conversation in a way that would hurt him.

"I suppose," he answered, his gaze focused on his sisters far ahead of them. Lydia paused and looked back, then waved at them, beckoning for them to hurry up. Oliver pretended he didn't notice.

"Where do you imagine this going?" Charlotte asked.

Oliver looked at her at last. "Going to Watier's?"

She shook her head. "Not just that. All of it. You know I support you being yourself, and I'm glad it brings you joy, but where do you see it leading? Five years from now, where do you see yourself?"

Oliver's brow furrowed. The truth of it was that he hadn't really thought that far ahead. He'd only started finding happiness a handful of months ago. There was still so much to explore, so much to try. How was he supposed to know what his adult life would look like?

"I have time to figure it out," he answered nonchalantly.

"That's what worries me."

Oliver's frown deepened. "What do you mean?"

Charlotte sighed, sounding uncomfortably like his mother every time she presented him with a new dress he would inevitably detest. "I'm only two years older than you, Oliver, but I must be thinking about how I'll shape my adult life. You know how much I wish Lu and I could marry, but that's not our reality. Lu needed to find a husband to support herself, and she was fortunate enough to find one who is absent for long periods of time so we can still see each other. I'll need to do the same because neither of us were born with the capital to survive on our own. I'll likely marry the first man who will take me, regardless of my feelings about him, because people in our position don't have the luxury of marrying for love. We must make sacrifices if we want to survive. I just worry you don't have as much time as you think you do."

Oliver barely contained the full-body shudder that rolled through him at the picture Charlotte was painting. The thought of marrying at all, of pretending to be someone's wife for the rest of his life, echoed bone-deep with wrongness. Even the simple notion of marrying someone he didn't like, who would look at him and see a woman, was nauseating.

"Surely you don't expect me to be someone's wife," he said tightly.

Charlotte sighed again. "I don't have any expectations,

Oliver, but I . . . I hope you'll give some thought to your long-term plans. You need to know how you'll survive when your father isn't able to provide for you anymore."

The three walked in silence for a while, as Oliver ignored the ache in the back of his throat. Finally, he took in a shuddering breath. "I would rather live alone for the rest of my life than become someone's wife. Maybe you can survive a life like that, but I can't."

"Oliver—"

Lu placed her hand on Charlotte's arm and shook her head. Charlotte bit her lip.

"*This* is pretending." Oliver gestured to his day dress, his long, tied-back hair. "*This* isn't me. Do you want to know where I see myself in five years? I see *myself*. I won't pretend like this forever. I would rather die."

Charlotte gasped quietly, but Oliver didn't care. Every word of what he said was true. He wiped his eyes, composing himself. And a good thing too, because Lydia and Kitty had stopped and were looking back at them, suspicious.

Oliver began walking again, and Charlotte and Lu hurried to keep up.

"I'm sorry," Charlotte said quickly. "I didn't mean to upset you. I'm just concerned about your future."

"Try being concerned about *me* instead," Oliver snapped. "I won't submit myself to a life that would make me absolutely miserable, and you shouldn't want me to."

Charlotte looked away, her face turning pink. She looked embarrassed.

Good.

"Perhaps," Lu said after a long pause, "you'll be able to find someone who you can be yourself with at home. Even if you have to pretend to be Elizabeth in certain public situations, perhaps you'll find someone you can be a husband with in the privacy of your home."

The suggestion was better than the future Charlotte had been alluding to, but the thought of having to pretend to be someone's wife, even in just "certain public situations," twisted and soured in his stomach. He supposed he could survive it. But why should he have to compromise and settle for a future that was only *half* of what he wanted?

Do you really think you'll ever meet someone who will take you as a husband at all? Oliver clenched his jaw, forcing the thought out of his mind. But even as he silenced the doubt, it left behind a cold emptiness that made him feel like a cored apple.

"Come *on!*" Lydia shouted, hands on her hips as she stomped toward them. "You three are so slow! We're going to miss the soldiers!"

Oliver frowned as he neared his sister. "Soldiers?"

"The Forty-Second regiment," Kitty responded dreamily. "They're in town. Lydia and I hoped we might spot them."

Ah. So *that* was why they were so eager to go out today. To gawk at handsome young men.

"But we *won't* if you three keep walking like you have anchors attached to your feet," Lydia huffed. "Now let's go!"

———

They'd been walking for about ten minutes when Lu suddenly perked up and turned to Oliver with a conspiratorial smile. "Do you see that building up ahead? The tavern?"

Oliver looked in the direction Lu had indicated, peering at the shops there. The storefronts were all built next to one another with virtually no space between them, creating the impression of strips of different buildings mashed together. A tailor's shop in a stucco building detailed with dark-brown wood was beside a redbrick cobbler's store with a deep-blue awning in need of a wash, which was beside a pale brick tavern that jutted out ahead of the other two. Beneath its own awning—this one striped blue and white—were two small tables and chairs set out for patrons who wanted to enjoy a bite outside. A sign hung well above the awning labeled it AVERY'S TAVERN.

"I see it," Oliver responded cautiously.

"Do you know what it is?"

Oliver frowned. "Do I know . . . what a tavern is?"

Lu laughed, then leaned toward Oliver, lowering her voice. "That's a Molly House. Specifically for younger people."

Oliver blinked, his gaze sliding back to Avery's with interest. Molly Houses were a hush-hush part of society—one that the Bennets certainly didn't speak of. They were places where men who were attracted to men, women who were attracted to women, people who weren't either gender, and others of the like frequented. He'd even heard others like him occasionally attended—boys mistaken as girls and vice versa. Just the knowledge that there *were* others like him had been a balm even though he'd yet to step foot in a Molly House. But Oliver hadn't realized there were any specifically meant for younger patrons.

"Really?" he asked. "How do you know?"

"It was William's favorite spot before he became too old," Lu responded with a smile. William was Lu's elder brother—and the very first boy he'd met who was attracted to other boys. It was William who'd taught Oliver the truth about Molly Houses—that they were safe places for people to be themselves, and not the scandalous sex dens that society at large painted them as. Last Oliver had heard, William had moved to Paris, where it was a little safer for men like him to be themselves.

"I've been myself a couple times," Lu went on. "It's a very welcoming environment—quite pleasant, isn't it, Charlotte?"

Oliver's mouth nearly fell open as his gaze snapped to Charlotte. "*You've* been as well?"

Charlotte blushed and covered a small smile with her hand. "It was Lu's idea."

"And you loved it," Lu said.

"It was . . . a surprisingly pleasant experience," Charlotte conceded.

Lu made a triumphant noise while Oliver laughed. "Maybe I should visit," he said.

"Oh Oliver, you must!" Lu exclaimed. "It really is such fun. Just ask for the coffeehouse at the bar and they'll show you where to go."

Oliver had never actually been to a Molly House, but he'd very much wanted to go for some time. It had all just seemed so intimidating—what if he arrived and people laughed at him? Or didn't accept him as a boy who liked boys? But if this Molly House was specifically intended for younger people and even *Charlotte* of all people had gone . . .

Maybe it wouldn't be as scary as Oliver thought.

"Who are Lydia and Kitty speaking to?" Charlotte suddenly asked.

Oliver's sisters had remained well ahead of them throughout their walk, which wasn't a surprise. What was a surprise was finding them standing outside of a gray-brick tailor shop with menswear displayed in the glass window shop front, speaking to a tall blond boy in a military uniform. He was handsome, with a strong jaw and broad shoulders.

As Oliver, Lu, and Charlotte approached, his sisters were giggling and blushing.

"Kitty, Lydia," Oliver said, balancing his tone between firm and polite. "You shouldn't wander off so far ahead. We almost lost track of you two."

The boy turned to Oliver, and up close, Oliver realized he

was more man than boy—probably twenty or so, in contrast to Lydia's fourteen years and Kitty's fifteen. Something in the man's gaze as he sized Oliver up made him shiver, and Oliver found himself wanting to look away from those piercing blue eyes, but he forced himself to meet them.

"Hello," the man said. "My name is Wickham."

When he was pretending to be a girl, Oliver *despised* introductions. It was difficult enough forcing himself to respond to a name that didn't remotely suit him, but there was something uniquely painful about forcing that name off his own tongue. About denying who he was out loud, in words. It was a self-betrayal that cut deep.

"Elizabeth Bennet," Oliver forced himself to say, after Charlotte and Lu introduced themselves. "Pleasure to meet you."

"The pleasure is mine." Wickham's smile was the kind that made many weak at the knees. Oliver returned it with a polite smile of his own before turning to his sisters.

"We really ought to return home," he said, fully prepared for his siblings to protest, but to his shock—and deep suspicion—Lydia lit up at the mention of home instead.

"Why, that's perfect!" Lydia exclaimed. "Wickham here just told us he was walking in the same direction and offered to escort us home. He could join us!"

"Oh, that won't be necessary," Oliver said quickly, but Wickham cut in.

"Nonsense! What caliber of gentleman would I be if I allowed five beautiful women to travel home without an escort? I simply cannot allow it. You must accept my offer."

Oliver's jaw clenched, despising every moment of this conversation more than the last. Charlotte must have sensed his distress, because she placed her hand on Oliver's arm and smiled genially at Wickham.

"Thank you, that is a most generous offer," she said.

Wickham smiled.

As they walked home, Lydia and Kitty engaged Wickham in conversation while Oliver bit back burning humiliation. There was a time when being referred to as a girl or a woman felt *off*, like trying to force two ill-matched puzzle pieces together, damaging both in the process. But the discomfort that was once easily ignored became exponentially more painful once Oliver experienced the euphoria of being seen as himself, as a boy, for the first time. It seemed the longer he spent in the bliss of being the boy he was always meant to be, the more miserable he was forcing himself to play the part of the girl he never was.

"Why, isn't that the same Mr. Bingley who danced with Jane at the Meryton Ball?" Lydia asked, yanking Oliver out of his thoughts like a fish caught on a line. Lydia was right, but it wasn't just Bingley strolling down the walkway on the opposite side of the road—beside him was, of course, Darcy.

Truthfully, Oliver wasn't sure what to feel as he watched the two boys walk, oblivious to Oliver's presence. But now that he'd spent several hours with the both of them as himself, part of him didn't want either of them to see him as Elizabeth ever again.

Of course, that was highly impractical and, given Jane's interest in Bingley, unlikely to be avoidable. Still, Oliver pulled his gaze away from the two boys, forcing his expression into non-chalance.

"Our elder sister Jane had a *wonderful* night dancing with Bingley at the Meryton Ball," Lydia was explaining to Wickham.

"He seemed to be a kind man," Kitty added.

Wickham's face tightened into something like a grimace before he smoothed his expression and looked away from the pair. "Bingley is a kind person," he said slowly, "but I'd advise all of you avoid associating with Darcy as much as possible."

Oliver frowned as Kitty's eyebrows raised in interest. "Really? What makes you say so?"

Wickham sighed and shook his head. "I . . . I won't gossip," he said, though he sounded reluctant. "All that I will say is he's been known to be unkind to women."

Oliver's frown deepened. Darcy *had* been rude to him at the Meryton Ball, when he'd been dressed as a woman. But he seemed different on the day of the fair . . .

Yes, but he knew you weren't a woman then, a small voice whispered in his mind.

He wanted to brush the thought away as easily as wiping dust off a polished table. But what if there was some merit to the accusation?

CHAPTER 6

Standing at the entrance of a room bursting at the seams with upper-crust boys and young men, Oliver could hardly believe he'd actually agreed to come here.

The room was truly enormous—and there were so many people he could barely see the far end of the room. The walls were papered in wine red, with a subtle but intricate design repeated in a sheen tone of the same color. Not one but two large chandeliers hung from the ceiling. On the left side of the room was a long dining room table, so large it may have actually been two dining tables pushed together, end to end. Place settings were already set up, and the chairs were lushly upholstered in red velvet cushions with golden trim.

The rest of the room seemed to be set up with more gambling tables than Oliver could count, save for the elaborate bar set against the right wall. From his vantage point at the door, it looked like probably seventy-five percent of the right wall from bar level to the ceiling were shelves of various alcohols. The bottles glinted with the chandelier light, like a rainbow of stars.

The room was a riot of noise—laughing and dozens upon dozens of conversations layered upon one another. The clink of glasses, the scuffle of shoes over rugs and hardwood, the squeak of moving chairs and explosions of laughter like fireworks—it was overwhelming. Oliver felt like he was floating on a sea of sound, blinking as he took in the room, slightly light-headed.

Was this a bad idea?

"It's a lot to take in at first," Darcy said beside him.

Oliver startled, forgetting for a moment that Darcy was, indeed, with him. As was Bingley, but he was already wandering off toward the dining table, greeting some of the others with a wide smile.

Darcy's voice was strangely gentle. Oliver hadn't heard this tenderness from him yet, and when he met Darcy's gaze, the other boy *smiled*—just at the corners, just for a second.

It was a nice smile.

Maybe this wasn't a bad idea. For reasons he didn't care to examine, meeting Darcy's gaze was calming. Like the gentle push and pull of the tide, he felt himself slowly drifting out to sea, but it didn't scare him as much as it should have.

He wasn't alone in this strange place. Bingley may have wandered off, but Darcy was here with him. With Darcy at his side, he could do this.

"Frankly," Oliver said, collecting his wits again, "I didn't peg you for the type to enjoy such a rowdy atmosphere."

Darcy looked bashful, running his hand through his locks, mussing his hair in a way that was truly adorable. He nodded toward the dining table, beckoning him forward so they weren't blocking the door. "You're right, I'm not at all. To be honest, the first time Bingley brought me here, I loathed it so much I swore to never return."

"And yet you sought to invite me here yourself," Oliver responded with a wry smile.

Darcy laughed, and Oliver was so shocked he couldn't hide the surprise from his face. Darcy's laugh was genuine; it rolled up Oliver's spine and filled him with warmth. He couldn't help but grin in return.

"Well, I don't *still* loathe it," Darcy said. "It grew on me. I hope it will do the same for you."

"Be careful what you wish for," Oliver said. "If I like it *too* much, I might want to come every week."

"Hopefully so," Darcy said without missing a beat.

Oliver's face warmed. Was Darcy saying he wanted to spend more time with him? He looked at the taller boy carefully, taking in his wavy dark hair and sharp jawline. In contrast with the near chaos around them, he seemed so relaxed.

Oliver didn't have the chance to prod this line of conversation any further, however, because they'd reached the dining table. Darcy pulled a chair aside for him, and Oliver met his gaze with an arched eyebrow. Darcy's face tinged pink, probably realizing that was more of an expected gesture for a woman, but he didn't release the back of the chair until Oliver sat down. Darcy sat next to him, his face still a little red, but he was smiling softly, and Oliver was finding he really enjoyed Darcy's smile.

"Careful," Oliver said softly, "if you're *too* gentlemanlike, I might think you're trying to court me."

The moment the words were out of his mouth, Oliver could have kicked himself. What was he doing being so forward with Darcy? But he'd kept his tone light so Darcy could plausibly interpret his statement as jesting . . .

Darcy's eyes widened just slightly, but his face morphed into a conspiratorial smile. "You're right," he said in a low voice, "that would be terrible."

Oliver couldn't contain his grin as relief flooded his chest. He forced himself to look away, suddenly warm, suddenly barely able to hear over the pounding of his heart. He couldn't believe this was happening. He'd just flirted with Darcy. And was Darcy flirting back?

When Bingley sat on Darcy's other side, Oliver was practically buzzing with excitement. It wasn't long before the table was full of diners, and men dressed in black and white streamed out of two doors in the back of the room, each carrying trays. They spaced themselves perfectly on both sides of the table, serving everyone a small bowl of steaming white soup.

Oliver's stomach growled. Once everyone was served, he

glanced at Darcy out of the corner of his eye. The other boy had picked up his spoon and was reaching toward his bowl. Oliver did the same, careful to let the steaming hot soup air out a little on the spoon before taking a bite. The soup was thick, warm, and full of rich flavor. This variety seemed to be chicken-based, but there was a tang to it that made Oliver want to lick the bowl clean—lemon, perhaps?

He'd barely finished his bowl before the wave of servers returned; a new plate was set out before him, and to his astonishment it wasn't yet the main meal. Instead, the plate held small prawns placed delicately in a pool of some kind of yellow sauce. The prawns were perfectly tender, and the lemony sauce complemented the flavor of the white soup lingering in his mouth.

This was followed by the actual main meal: turbot in a thick lobster sauce. Oliver was sure he hadn't eaten so much rich food in one sitting in some time. He'd known Watier's had a reputation for good food—unlike most of the gentleman's clubs—but this was far beyond his expectations.

"I'm starting to see why this place grew on you," he said to Darcy as the servers took his dish away and replaced it with a cup of lemon ice.

Darcy laughed. "The food isn't the *only* reason, but it certainly helped."

"It might be enough of a reason for me," Oliver said with a grin.

Once the food was gone, few people lingered at the table.

Most seemed eager to settle down at a gambling table—which, Oliver supposed, was probably the main reason anyone went to a club like Watier's.

Unfortunately, card games weren't part of the *becoming a lady* repertoire that his mother had taught him and his sisters. As Oliver dared a glance around the room from his seat at the dining table, his stomach twisted at the fluency with which everyone seemed to have with the cards.

Would he look like a fool if he didn't know how to play? He didn't even know *what* card game they were playing.

Bingley said something to Darcy that Oliver didn't catch, then made a beeline for a table in the back of the room. When Darcy turned to Oliver, he did his best to keep the twinge of panic from showing on his face.

"Do you play Macau?" Darcy asked.

Oliver smiled sheepishly. "I'm afraid not."

But to Oliver's surprise, Darcy said, "Oh good."

Oliver arched an eyebrow. "Is it?"

"I'm afraid no one here actually *wins* at Macau. It's an excellent game to play if you want to throw away your money, but it's certainly not a lucrative hobby."

Oliver nodded, looking around the room with renewed interest. "Is that what everyone here is playing? Dozens of separate Macau games?"

"Mostly, with some Loo and Whist undoubtedly thrown in there as well. Are you familiar with either of those?"

Oliver bit his lip and leaned toward Darcy, heart pounding as he kept his voice steady, cool. "Can I share a secret with you?" he asked conspiratorially.

Darcy's eyebrow twitched and he leaned in, his face only inches from Oliver's. "I can keep a secret."

"I don't know how to play any card games at all."

Darcy's brows rose into the soft fringe over his forehead, then his face split into a smile. "Can I share a secret with you as well?"

Oliver blinked. "Don't tell me you don't know how to play cards either."

Darcy laughed. "No, no, that's not it."

"Go on, then."

Darcy's grin slid into a sly smile. "I absolutely loathe card games."

Oliver laughed, a rush of relief washing over him like a cool rain in the dead of summer. "Why doesn't that surprise me?"

"Perhaps you've picked up that I'm a rather discerning individual."

"*Discerning*, yes. I suppose that's one way to look at it. Some might say choosy, perhaps."

"Is that so wrong?" Darcy leaned back in his seat, his smile softening into gentle amusement. "I like to think it means that the people and things I do enjoy are special. I appreciate them more than I would otherwise, I think."

Oliver tilted his head. "You think you would enjoy things less if you enjoyed a larger variety of activities?"

"It's logical, isn't it?"

"Only if you believe yourself to have a limited amount of amusement that can be exhausted."

"Don't you?"

Oliver shook his head, pulling his gaze away from Darcy's intense eyes. He spotted Bingley across the room—it wasn't difficult, what with his eye-catching red hair—who seemed very focused on whatever card game he was playing.

"I try to enjoy as much of the world as possible. Life is short— what better way to spend it than try to find amusement out of as much as possible?"

"And do you succeed?"

Oliver met Darcy's questioning stare. His face was so soft, so drawn in; Darcy hadn't looked away from him once. He seemed genuinely interested in Oliver's response. The realization made his stomach flutter and brought a lightness to his bones.

"Not always," he admitted after a pause. "But that doesn't stop me from trying."

"I think that's admirable," Darcy said.

Then, for the first time since this conversation had started, Darcy pulled his gaze away and glanced over the room. All at once his shoulders stiffened, the calm in his face dissolving into a stormy expression worryingly close to fury.

Frowning, Oliver followed his gaze to the eastern side of the room. Bingley was seated there playing Macau, but Oliver thought it unlikely that Bingley had caused Darcy's sudden change in temperament. Just as he began to turn back to Darcy to ask him what was the matter, his gaze caught on a boy who was scowling back in their direction. Oliver's breath caught in his chest—he *knew* that boy. His face was unmistakable—after all, it'd been just the day before that he'd met Wickham.

Darcy pursed his lips, then turned back to Oliver, his face barely concealing his rage. But then he inhaled deeply through his nose, and slowly his expression smoothed. "I know I invited you here to Watier's specifically," he said with surprising calm, "but would you like to take a walk?"

Oliver hesitated. "Oh. Well, I wouldn't want to ruin Bingley's fun . . ."

"He can stay here. I'll let him know we're leaving. I'm sure he won't mind—that is, if you want to. We can also stay if you'd like to learn how to play a card game or two."

Oliver smirked. "I thought you said you don't enjoy card games."

"I believe I said I loathe them, which is absolutely true. But I'd be willing to teach you nevertheless, if you wanted to learn."

That Darcy offered such a thing despite clearly no longer wanting to be here made Oliver feel like he was floating. He could hardly believe he was having this conversation—with Darcy, of all people! Even more incredible was that Darcy wanted to spend more time with him, *without* Bingley. It would be an unthinkable scandal if he were a woman.

Good thing he wasn't.

"I wouldn't mind a walk."

Darcy grinned. "I hoped you'd say that."

The March night was cold, the air fresh with the dewy scent of a recent rain. Oliver and Darcy strolled along the walking path into a public garden, so close their shoulders were almost touching. If Oliver swayed even a little to the left, he'd bump into Darcy's arm. It was a temptation that was difficult to ignore.

This is the same Darcy who treated you terribly at the Meryton Ball, he reminded himself. *Even if he didn't know it was you, it still doesn't speak well of his character.*

That was true, and it should matter. But the longer Oliver spent with Darcy, the harder it was to care.

"I enjoy walking here to think," Darcy said. "Especially this time of night. It's very soothing."

Oliver nodded, taking in the faint scent of greenery. It was hard to see in the dark, but he imagined there were likely not-yet-bloomed flower bushes mixed among the hedges. The cold night air stung his nose and cheeks, but he didn't mind.

"I enjoy going to Westminster Bridge for that purpose," Oliver said. "I'll lean against the rail and stare across the Thames. It helps clear my head, especially when I need some time alone."

Darcy nodded. "Is it difficult for you to find solitude at home?"

Oliver laughed lightly. "Well, I have four siblings who all live at home with our parents, so yes, you could say that."

Darcy arched an eyebrow. "Four siblings! I can only imagine."

"Do you have any siblings?"

"Just one, my younger sister, Georgiana." He paused, then added, "Our parents passed on two years ago."

Oliver frowned. "I'm sorry to hear that."

"Thank you. I was still too young to officially take on the role of head of household at the time, so until I turned eighteen the two of us lived with our aunt. Now Georgiana and I primarily reside at our family estate, Pemberly, though she sometimes opts to stay with our aunt while I'm away."

"So it's likely not necessary for you to leave home to find some quiet, then," Oliver said with a wry smile.

"No," Darcy agreed, smiling softly. After some quiet, he added, "I'm glad to have met you, Oliver."

Oliver blinked at him with a slight laugh. "That's a relief, given the circumstances. This would be an entirely different walk if you secretly disliked spending time with me."

Darcy laughed once, a quick, shocked sound. "Impossible."

Oliver was absolutely buoyant. He'd never expected this— not with any boy really, let alone someone like Darcy. But was Darcy being friendly, or was this something more?

And will he still feel that way once he learns about Elizabeth?

And with that single thought, a dark cloud loomed over his mood. Darcy may be amicable now, but it seemed improbable that he had ever met a boy like Oliver. The notion that this new friendship may be conditional on something Oliver couldn't control made him feel ill.

His own parents would never accept Oliver for who he really was. Why should Darcy be any different?

Ordinarily, by the time Oliver returned from his nightly outings, everyone had long gone to sleep. He'd yet to rouse any suspicion this way—after all, the last anyone had seen him he'd been going to bed along with most of the household, and Jane always covered for him the few times they'd been disturbed.

Mr. Bennet was always the last to go to sleep, but on most nights that didn't matter; by the time Oliver returned, even he was abed for the night.

But as Oliver crossed the front yard, he spotted candlelight from his father's office. The warm yellow of the flickering flames spilled out onto the grass, painting a spot of bright in the otherwise cool night.

A chill crept up Oliver's spine, his steps slowing. The trellis leading to Oliver and Jane's bedroom crossed directly over Mr. Bennet's office window. This had never been a problem before.

Still, tonight was proving to be the exception. The situation gave him pause. The only way up to their bedroom without going inside was to scale the trellis to his unlatched window. Theoretically, he could probably enter through the front door as well—he knew where the key was left in case someone accidentally locked themselves out—but there was no way he'd be able to unlock the door, open it, close it, and creep all the way up to their room without his father noticing. And that was assuming no one else woke at the noise.

No, the trellis was the only way. Oliver supposed he could try to wait his father out—it *was* late after all, and Mr. Bennet was bound to be going to bed soon—but what if he wasn't? The only thing Oliver could think of that would keep his father awake so late was work, and he had no way of knowing how much his father had left to do. Not to mention that he was exhausted himself. And it was cold out.

Maybe if he just moved quietly and quickly he could climb the side of the town house without his father noticing. Oliver bit his lip, approaching the trellis from the side, out of view from the window. There were about six inches of space where the trellis was against the brick rather than the window. It was certainly not enough space for Oliver to climb, but it at least allowed him to approach without worrying about being spotted. Yet.

With shaking fingers, Oliver grabbed the trellis with his left hand. The notion of potentially being caught was making his palms sweat—not ideal for climbing. He took a deep breath, wiping both of his palms against his trousers, trying to breathe as deeply as possible to calm his racing heart.

It'll be fine, he reassured himself. *You've done this dozens of times without a problem. You could climb this with your eyes closed. Just move quickly, and even if he hears you, he won't see you.*

With one last deep breath, Oliver gripped the trellis and hoisted himself up. He moved quickly, holding his breath as his hands and feet found familiar footholds, and he pulled himself higher. His torso was directly over his father's window for only a few seconds, then just his legs, then just his boots.

Once he had cleared the window entirely, Oliver paused, pressing his forehead against the cool wooden trellis, slowing his still-panicked heartbeat. He did it! With a small, nervous laugh, Oliver reached up to continue the climb.

His left foot slipped beneath him and he gasped as he slid down a couple inches with a bone-jarring scrape. Oliver jammed his right foot into the trellis hard, gripping the wood and scrambling back up before—

The scrape of an opening window stopped Oliver cold. Now that he had slipped, he was *just* over the office window. He didn't dare move. He barely breathed, pressing his cheek against the trellis, praying his father didn't look up.

Don't look at me, he pleaded. *It was probably just some animal. Go to bed. Please.*

For a long moment, there was only silence. Oliver's pulse roared in his ears, his arms and legs burning, shivering, as he held himself utterly still. His hot breath puffed against the brick behind the trellis and warmed his face. His muscles were really starting to hurt now—he wasn't sure how much longer he could hold on without giving out.

"Lizzy, is that you?"

Oliver groaned, pressing his forehead against the brick. "No," he responded, knowing full well just how ridiculous he sounded to his father, though it was actually the truth.

Oddly, his father actually chuckled. "While I admire your athleticism, you might find my office window easier to climb into."

There was no way around this. He was trembling so hard it was a miracle he hadn't slipped again. Slowly, he lowered himself to the open window, swung his legs inside, and landed softly on a large rug. His pulse was a roar in his ears. There he was, standing in his father's office, with Mr. Bennet himself, dressed from head to toe in menswear. He might just pass out from anxiety. Or vomit.

Behind him, Mr. Bennet closed the window with a *squeak-scrape*. Oliver stood absolutely frozen as his father stepped around him, looking him over with an appraising eye. Finally, his gaze met Oliver's and the most unexpected thing happened.

Mr. Bennet smiled.

"Well," he said. "This is quite the surprise."

Oliver opened his mouth, ready to say that he could explain, but . . . could he? There was no excuse that he could come up with fast enough to explain why Mr. Bennet's second-eldest child had snuck out in the middle of the night dressed as a boy. And in any case, he wasn't sure that he wanted to lie. At least, not to his father.

Which meant there was nothing left but the truth.

The reality of the situation made Oliver hot and cold all over. His underarms were instantly damp, his palms clammy. So then, this was it. Time to tell his father the truth. But even as Oliver tried to muster up the courage to speak, fear choked out his voice.

"I must say," Mr. Bennet said, his voice shockingly gentle, "you look *very* handsome."

And that was when Oliver saw it—the twinkle in his father's eye that looked almost like . . .

Pride?

"Thank you," he finally managed to say, though his voice was small and soft. But his father didn't look upset—in fact, he was still smiling, and the more Oliver looked at him, the more certain he became that Mr. Bennet was, in fact, inexplicably proud of him.

"Father," Oliver forced himself to say before his voice failed him again. "You should know . . ." God, he was trembling. His insides felt like a plucked string, reverberating with sound. "You should know my name is Oliver. And I'm . . . I'm your son."

Mr. Bennet's smile grew into a full grin, spreading across his face like a plant turning its leaves to the sun. "You most certainly are," he said, and then his arms were around Oliver.

Oliver melted into the embrace, squeezing his eyes closed as relief washed over him. He held his father tight, tears spilling down his cheeks despite his best efforts to keep them at bay.

"My son," Mr. Bennet said, and Oliver nearly imploded from happiness. *Son.* The word he'd been so desperate to hear, the word he thought he'd *never* hear, not directed at him. The word from Mr. Bennet rang true, echoing in his chest and filling him with warmth.

His father pulled away first and held Oliver's shoulders. A jolt struck Oliver as he spotted the tears slipping down his cheeks too. He frowned. "Papa—"

"I'm so happy, Oliver," Mr. Bennet said. "I'm so proud of you. And I'm so glad you've told me. Thank you for telling me."

Oliver felt if he smiled any wider his face might just break. "You don't seem surprised," he said with a slight laugh.

Mr. Bennet arched an eyebrow. "Should I be?"

Oliver hesitated. He would have thought yes, but maybe his father was right. Out of everyone in the family, Jane and Mr. Bennet had always known him best. Was it so far-fetched to think his father might have seen something in him even before Oliver was ready to admit it aloud?

And then he said, "Oliver, you didn't really believe I never saw you climbing up and down the trellis from your room before tonight, did you?" and Oliver's face burst with heat. Mr. Bennet laughed and clapped his shoulder. "Don't worry, son. I won't mention that bit to your mother." He winked.

Oliver smiled weakly, but the mention of his mother brought

a new wave of nausea through him. "About that . . . Jane and my aunt and uncle are aware of who I am, but I'm not ready to tell Mother anything."

His father's face sobered and he nodded. "I understand. Truthfully, I don't know how she'd react. I think it's sensible to hold off on telling her for the moment, but you *should* tell her eventually."

Oliver's gaze slid to his boots. "I know."

His father squeezed his shoulders. "When you're ready, son, I'll be right there with you."

Oliver hadn't realized how much he needed to hear those words. His whole body relaxed with an inaudible sigh, and though tears gathered in the corners of Oliver's eyes, he was smiling.

CHAPTER 7

In typical spring London fashion, it was raining. Not a drizzle, but the variety that soaked you to the bone the moment you stepped outside. The wind was strong too, carrying the rain directly into the windowpane with so much force it almost appeared to be raining sideways.

Oliver frowned out the window, arms crossed over his chest as the endless hum of rain against the house pattered like quiet thunder. He wouldn't be going anywhere, not if this didn't let up. He hadn't exactly had any specific plan in mind today—during the past few days at home, he'd been forced to carry out his usual chores but had spent most of his time mentally replaying the night he'd spent with Darcy. Still, if he was going to stay in, he wanted it to be of his own volition, not because the weather was trapping him inside.

With a sigh, Oliver descended the stairs, trying to ignore the way his skirts swished around his ankles. He was home, so at least he didn't have to wear a bust-accentuating bodice today. His day dress was simple, deep blue, and felt light on his body in contrast to the usual bodices and constricting clothes he ordinarily wore.

It made the clothing slightly less suffocating, slightly easier to ignore. But it also meant he felt the movement of his chest as he walked, which was excruciatingly difficult to overlook. *How much simpler and more comfortable it would be*, he thought, *if my chest had remained flat.* It was a reality that he could, unfortunately, do little about, but that didn't stop the yearning for his body to change.

As he pattered into the dining room, he found himself walking into the middle of a lively conversation.

"It's cold and *raining*," Jane was saying. "Surely we could spare the carriage today."

"My dear, it's precisely *because* it is raining that we most assuredly *cannot* spare the carriage," Mrs. Bennet responded. "You may take the horse. Surely that will be sufficient to get you to the Bingleys' quickly enough."

Oliver frowned. "Mama, Jane will get soaked if she takes the horse. It's not exactly warm out either—she'll be freezing."

Inexplicably, Mrs. Bennet's eyes sparkled with delight as she turned to Oliver. "I should hope so," she declared. "Then she just might catch a chill and she'll *have* to stay with the Bingleys longer to recover. It will allow her more time with a *certain* Bingley."

Jane and Oliver gaped at her. Even Mary, who had been quietly eating while politely ignoring the argument, looked up, wide-eyed.

"You can't be serious," Oliver said. "You *want* her to get ill?"

"Catching a cold is nothing to worry about," Mrs. Bennet said. "It's enough that polite company will demand she stay without it being life-endangering. Trust me, this is what's best for our Jane."

Jane looked down at her lap, and something like rage sparked inside of Oliver. Jane was going to accept this. She was going to go out there, in the pouring rain, and arrive at the Bingleys' looking like a wet dog.

This was his mother's master plan for Jane to attract Bingley? To arrive like a damsel in distress?

Oliver shook his head, anger seeping into his voice as he seethed. "I can't believe you're doing this to her."

Mrs. Bennet tsked. "You'll thank me when Mr. Bingley is worrying after Jane and taking care of her in his own home."

Oliver highly doubted that, but when he opened his mouth to argue, Jane looked at him and shook her head. "It's all right," she said. "The ride isn't terribly long. And it may be a little chilly, but I'll wear a coat and bring an umbrella."

"Much good an umbrella will do in this wind," Oliver muttered, but if Jane—or Mrs. Bennet, for that matter—heard him, neither of them showed it.

———

It came as a shock to absolutely no one when a messenger arrived hours later, carrying a letter from the Bingleys. Mrs. Bennet

accepted the note with much enthusiasm and turned to Oliver—
who was sitting in a reading chair nearby, book open in his lap—
with a victorious smile.

"You see?" she said. "It's from the Bingleys!"

Oliver didn't respond.

Mrs. Bennet slid her finger beneath the wax seal and hastily
opened the letter. After a moment she gave a triumphant shout
and exclaimed, "Jane is ill!"

Oliver slowly closed his book, meeting his mother's excitement with a dead-eyed stare. "Strange for a mother to celebrate
her child's misfortune, don't you think?"

"Oh, stop it," Mrs. Bennet chided, turning the letter to him.
"The Bingleys have written to say Jane will be staying with them
for a few *days* to recover. Days! Plural! What an incredible opportunity for our Jane, to better acquaint herself with the Bingleys."

"I'm not sure how much *acquainting* she'll be doing from her
sickbed." Oliver rose, barely holding in the furious heat simmer-
ing in his chest. "I should go check on her."

Mrs. Bennet's eyes widened, then her face broke into further
delight. "Yes! What an excellent idea, Elizabeth. To have the
Bingleys further acquaint themselves with our family—"

"I'm *not* going for the Bingleys," Oliver gritted out. "I'm
going for Jane."

"Of course you are, dear."

Oliver bit his lip. There was no sense in arguing this any further. "I don't suppose you'll allow *me* to take the carriage."

Mrs. Bennet looked at him, aghast. "And how would that look, if I sent Jane to attend on horseback in the middle of a rainstorm but lent the carriage to you after? Absolutely not."

Oliver pinched the bridge of his nose, then glanced out the nearest window. The rain had let up significantly, though it was still drizzling. Even so, it wasn't nearly as bad as when Jane had gone earlier that morning.

"Fine," he grumbled, "I'll take the other horse."

"I'm afraid Mr. Bennet has taken the second horse already," Mrs. Bennet responded. "The walk isn't terribly long, is it?"

As Oliver's laced half boot sank an inch into slick, cold mud for the umpteenth time, he swore at the heavens above and hells below. It was bad enough that he had to make this walk directly after a terrible storm—worse still that he couldn't even wear his own boots and trousers while he did.

Mrs. Bennet had forced him to change from his simple day dress before he left, of course, so now he was trapped in another suffocating bodice that made him feel nauseous every time he looked down at his curved chest. He hadn't worn his best day dress at least—Mrs. Bennet had seen sense when Oliver pointed out he'd be trudging through mud most of the way as soon as he was outside of the city proper. Not that he cared about getting mud on his dresses, but Mrs. Bennet certainly would have, despite the fact that it was she who insisted he walk after a rain-storm.

Oliver unstuck his foot with an unseemly squelch, taking care to step on the thicker-looking tufts of grass. It was slow going, forcing him to walk awkwardly on islands of thicker grass better able to hold his weight—and having to pause to unstick himself every fifteen feet or so anyway. It didn't help that he was carrying a bag full of his and Jane's clothes, which unbalanced him further. All the while he imagined how much easier this would be in trousers. Yes, it would still be muddy, but at least he wouldn't *feel* the cold mud splattered up his legs, and the lack of lacing on men's boots would have made them much easier to clean.

"This never would have happened with trousers," he whispered to no one at all.

CHAPTER 8

WHEN CHARLES BINGLEY'S SISTER CAROLINE GREETED OLIVER AT THE door, her gaze rolled slowly from his muddy boots, up to the muddy hem of his dress, to his mud-splattered skirts, and finally to his slightly sweaty face. Her eyes widened slowly as she took him in, her lips thinning until they became all but invisible against her pale skin.

"Did you . . . walk here?" she asked slowly.

"I did," Oliver responded promptly. "I apologize for my disheveled nature. I can clean my boots out here if you'd be so kind as to provide me a washcloth and some water?"

"Yes," Caroline responded tightly. "I think that would be for the best."

Ten minutes later, Oliver stepped inside in damp, stained (but significantly less muddy) boots, which were mostly covered by his mud-stained skirts. There was little he could do about that, and frankly, he didn't care. He ignored the open disgust on Caroline's face as she stood stiffly nearby.

"My sister?" he asked. "Where is she? Do you know how she is?"

"She's resting. I'll show you to the guest room."

Neither Oliver nor Caroline said a word to each other in the awkward short walk to the guest room. As soon as Caroline gestured to the door, Oliver thanked her and entered without looking back. Caroline didn't follow him in.

As the door closed behind him, Oliver blinked in the brightly lit—and expansive—guest room. The walls were papered in powder blue, the windows large and plentiful with swooping silk curtains. The floor was hardwood, but there were multiple rugs placed throughout the room, each a deep blue of Turkish design. A desk and chair were placed by the farthest window, near a small bookshelf completely filled with books.

"It's elaborate, isn't it?" Jane asked with a soft laugh.

Oliver spun toward her voice, finding his sister in a four-poster bed so large three people could fit comfortably. Half a dozen pillows were crammed beside her, and the sheets appeared to also be silk, judging by their luminescence.

"Wow," Oliver said. "Maybe Mama was onto something."

"Oliver!" Jane hissed, but she was laughing. She patted the bed next to her, clearing space for him.

"I don't know if that's a good idea." Oliver gestured to his muddy skirts. "I wouldn't want to dirty the bed."

Jane's eyes widened, as if noticing the state of him for the first time. "Don't tell me Mama had you *walk* here."

Oliver forced a smile. "She said it would have looked bad if she'd given me the carriage when she refused it to you."

Jane groaned and gestured to a large white wardrobe against

the left side of the room. "Caroline bid me use of any of the dresses in the dresser. Please, avail yourself."

Oliver recoiled at the suggestion. "Oh, I certainly won't be doing that."

Jane frowned. "I'm sure Caroline won't mind."

"I'm sure you're wrong. In any case, it's not necessary." He lifted the bag stuffed full of Jane's clothes. "I brought you some clothes to change into over the next couple days. And I included an extra dress for myself, just in case."

Once he had changed and wiped the dry mud from his legs with a damp cloth, he sat on the bed at Jane's feet. "So. What is there to do around here?"

———

To Oliver's pleasant surprise, the bookshelf in Jane's room had a variety of interesting titles. Oliver selected one, then when Jane mentioned wanting some time to rest, he left her room and ventured over to the drawing room.

Stepping inside, he found essentially what he expected, given the luxuriousness of the rest of the estate: an unnecessarily large room with enormous windows, a crystal chandelier, some small tables with pairs of chairs spaced out along the walls, and two sitting areas in the center of the room. He was not surprised to find Bingley's sisters, Caroline and Louisa, already in the sitting area, speaking in hushed voices.

What he did not expect to find was the tall, dark-haired boy sitting at a table near a large window, his long legs stretched out in front of him, crossed at the ankles. In hindsight, it probably shouldn't have been such a surprise to find Darcy at Netherfield—after all, he'd known the Bingleys and Darcys had let the place together. But Oliver had forgotten about that, and he hadn't prepared himself to see Darcy, let alone interact with him.

He froze in the doorway, book clenched in his hand at his side. It had been only a number of days since he'd gone to Watier's with Bingley and Darcy, and since he and Darcy had taken a night stroll together. But it'd been about a week since "Elizabeth" had interacted with Darcy, which had gone . . . well, poorly.

Oliver bit his lip and, before anyone noticed him standing in the doorway gawking at Darcy, walked over to the nearest table and pulled a chair aside. He'd attempted to move the chair as quietly as possible, but the wooden legs squeaked against the waxed wooden floor, making him wince. In the quiet of the room Oliver might as well have slammed a door. Darcy, Caroline, and Louisa all looked up at once.

Oliver cringed, his face warming as he pretended not to notice the room's stares. He sat quickly, promptly opening the book, staring at the text on the page as he waited for his face to cool. Eventually, the quiet of the room was restored, and only Caroline's and Louisa's whispers carried through the silence.

"I still can't believe she *walked* the three miles here through all that mud," Caroline said.

"It *is* shockingly improper behavior," Louisa responded.

Oliver turned the page of the book, though he had no idea what the last page had said. Caroline and Louisa had to know he could hear them, but they didn't seem to care.

"Mama never would have allowed us to behave in such a way," Caroline said.

"Oh, certainly not."

"I suspect we shouldn't expect anything more from someone of *their* status. It really is a shame; Jane is very beautiful, but can you imagine our brother marrying into such a family?"

Louisa and Caroline broke into a fit of giggles. Oliver could barely breathe. That they would be so blatantly rude—talking about his family *while he was in the room*—the audacity! His pulse rushed in his ears. All his interactions with Bingley made him conclude he was a perfectly genial individual, but Bingley's sisters made him want to throw his book at them.

Darcy snapped his own book shut with a clap, making Oliver jump. The two girls hushed as Darcy abruptly stood, pushed his chair back in, and marched out of the room.

The drawing room fell quiet, and this time, no poisonous whispers ruined the atmosphere.

Oliver had hoped that he might complete this unwanted visit without his mother's appearance, but he was quickly disappointed.

Not twenty-four hours had passed before Mrs. Bennet sent word of her arrival, and just two hours later she had arrived at Netherfield with Mary, Kitty, Lydia, and two trunks full of Jane's and Oliver's clothes in tow.

They had taken the carriage. Of course.

"Why, I'd heard Netherfield was beautiful, but I never imagined *this*!" Mrs. Bennet crooned. "The land is just beautiful—are there any gardens?"

Bingley smiled awkwardly. "There are, in the back. Would you like to see them?"

"Oh, we better not, I'm quite allergic to a number of flowers," Mrs. Bennet responded. "Still, it does add such a calming atmosphere."

It was all Oliver could do to avoid grimacing. Mrs. Bennet meant well, but she tended toward overenthusiasm in situations like these—a reality that could easily further degrade his family's reputation in the eyes of the Bingleys. Given the way the Bingley sisters had treated *him* thus far, he strongly suspected it wouldn't go unnoticed. At least Jane was still resting in the guest room, so she was spared this embarrassment.

"This really is something here," Mrs. Bennet said, for she was still talking. "Do you plan to stay long?"

Bingley hesitated, then lifted a shoulder. "We haven't really decided the full length of our stay yet."

Mrs. Bennet gasped. "Oh, but you *must* stay! This is such a lovely property, and so conveniently located! You really must consider staying full-time. I strongly believe it would be worth your while."

Bingley laughed slightly. "Well, we'll certainly take that into consideration. I do believe the decision will ultimately rest with Darcy's aunt, however. It was she who selected this location to begin with."

"You don't say!"

Oliver cleared his throat. "Jane still isn't well, I'm afraid."

Mrs. Bennet looked at him like she was noticing him for the first time. "Oh! My poor Jane, of course. Has she seen any improvement at all?"

"I'm not sure," Oliver admitted. "She's been sleeping most of the day. I hope that all this rest today might energize her tomorrow."

Mrs. Bennet nodded. "I should hope so. My poor, beautiful Jane! Seeing her ill like this really does upset my nerves."

"I assure you she's being well taken care of," Bingley said quickly. "We summoned our family physician, who assured us a few days of rest should help tremendously."

"That is a relief to hear," Mrs. Bennet said. "Thank you again for taking such good care of our Jane. It's truly such a wonderful gesture."

Bingley smiled. "I'm happy to."

"They say Jane is one of the most beautiful girls in all of London," Mrs. Bennet said confidently. "Did you know? She really is so unusually handsome. The pride of our family."

Oliver's eyes went wide as saucers. What on earth was she doing? Jane *was* beautiful, obviously, but this was so transparent.

Louisa and Caroline, who were standing several feet behind their brother, giggled quietly. Bingley, ever the gentleman, took this humiliating display in stride. "I must agree. She's the most attractive girl I've ever met. I feel quite fortunate to have been at the Meryton Ball the very same night she attended."

Though Bingley was just being polite, this declaration only encouraged Mrs. Bennet all the more.

"Oh indeed!" she exclaimed. "Why, that's wonderful to hear. The two of you really do make such a fortuitous match."

Bingley only smiled.

Oliver scrambled to think of a topic change to a less delicate matter, but in the end he didn't have to, because Lydia spoke up first.

"Mr. Bingley," she said, "you really do have such a wonderful estate here at Netherfield. Do you think you'll ever throw a ball?"

Bingley, presumably eager for a change of topic himself, leapt right into the new conversation. "A ball! Well, that's an idea."

"You really must consider it," Lydia insisted. "Netherfield is just *perfect* for it. Don't you think, Elizabeth?"

Oliver flinched. "Oh. Well, it would be nice, I imagine. If Mr. Bingley is so inclined, that is."

Bingley nodded slowly, considering. "We'd have to wait until

Jane has fully recovered, of course, but I *am* amenable to the idea. I'll give it some serious thought."

"Wonderful!" Lydia exclaimed.

"Oh, wonderful indeed," Mrs. Bennet agreed.

Oliver prayed Jane woke soon so she could dispatch the family before the Bingleys wrote them off forever.

CHAPTER 9

THE BENNETS DID LEAVE, EVENTUALLY.

It had been an exhausting day enduring his mother's indulgent enthusiasm and endless bragging. Oliver understood perfectly what she was attempting—she wanted to present Jane in the best light possible, to convince Bingley they would be an excellent match. But a part of Oliver feared she may have done Jane—and the rest of the family—a disservice in the process.

More exhausting still had been pointedly ignoring Caroline and Louisa whispering about his mother—and his family—right in front of them all. Oliver didn't think Mrs. Bennet had noticed, but their disrespect certainly didn't go unnoticed by *him*.

And yet, he couldn't do a thing about it. Confronting them during the visit would have resulted in nothing more than shining a spotlight on his family's embarrassment—and further disparaging himself in the eyes of Bingley's sisters. The latter might not have bothered him at all if it weren't for Jane's feelings for their brother, and how his behavior would reflect on the rest of the family.

Now in the drawing room, Oliver was reading—or trying to—while Darcy sat a few tables away writing a letter. Caroline was playing the pianoforte, and Bingley was sitting on the lounge, tapping his foot to Caroline's playing. She was an average enough player of the pianoforte—certainly not as good as Mary, but undoubtedly better than Oliver. Still, she leaned a little too heavily on the notes, creating a single, steady, loud volume and unintentional staccato effect. In truth, he might not have noticed except that her playing made it impossible to pretend she wasn't in the room, and his abuse at her hands made him less than charitable toward either of the Bingley sisters.

They would be terrible sisters-in-law, he thought with no small amount of chagrin. Caroline and Louisa would be, without a doubt, the worst part of Jane and Bingley's match—if they did end up a match.

"We should dance!" Louisa suddenly declared. "Brother, don't you think? Join me!"

Bingley laughed and stood. "A splendid idea. Darcy—"

"No," Darcy said at once.

"Oh, come now," Bingley responded. "I'm sure Elizabeth would like to dance with you."

Oliver froze, then slowly glanced up from the book. Bingley was grinning at him. Had he forgotten about what had happened at the Meryton Ball? Was he really going to put him through further humiliation at Darcy's hands?

Though Oliver had fully expected Darcy to immediately refuse, instead, he paused and looked at Oliver. Panic flared hot and fast in Oliver's chest as he met Darcy's gaze. He and Darcy had stared into each other's eyes just a few nights back. Would Darcy recognize him if he looked closely enough?

"I might not mind that," Darcy said, to Oliver's utter astonishment.

He couldn't dance with Darcy, not as Elizabeth. He couldn't risk Darcy getting that close to him, really looking at him. Bingley may not be looking at him closely, but Darcy *would*, and if he realized—

"Are you sure?" Oliver said dryly. "I seem to remember not being handsome enough for your tastes."

Darcy's eyes widened and Bingley laughed. Oliver looked back at his book, heart thrumming in his ears, praying that would be the end of this conversation. After a full minute of staring at the same page in his book without anyone interrupting him, Oliver dared a glance back up at Darcy.

He had resumed writing his letter. Oliver relaxed, taking a slow, calming breath. He could hardly believe how well he'd played that off.

Eventually, Bingley stood and said something about checking in on Jane before leaving the room. Not long after that, Caroline stopped playing, huffing as she stood, and closed the case over the pianoforte's keys.

"Oh no!" Louisa said, "We were having so much fun!"

"*You* were, certainly," Caroline responded briskly. "My fingers are tired. I think I shall read a book instead."

She wandered over to the far wall, where the built-in book-shelves were located. Dragging her finger across the spines, she hummed loudly as she considered the selection.

"Oh!" Caroline pulled a book from the shelf. "*An Unusual Year in Usual Times*. Isn't this the sequel to the book you were reading the other day, Darcy?"

Darcy did not look up from his letter. "It is."

"How marvelous! Then I'm sure to enjoy this." She walked across the room, heels clacking loudly on the hardwood between rugs, before depositing herself just one table over from where Darcy sat. She opened the book and began to read, all the while Darcy continued working on his letter.

It was then that it occurred to Oliver that Caroline wasn't being obnoxious just for the sake of being obnoxious. She sighed loudly as she stared at the page with odd ferocity. It seemed far too much of a coincidence that the book she selected was one Darcy would know so well. She'd even taken pains to point that out to him. *And* now she was sitting next to him, sighing every couple seconds, attempting to read in the most obtrusive way possible.

Evidently growing bored, Caroline closed the book and set it on the table beside her. "I must say, there is nothing like reading! Truly, every other form of entertainment pales in comparison. One day when I am married and manage a beautiful home, I shall be utterly dejected if I haven't an extensive library of my own."

Oliver began to wonder if Caroline had ever read a book at all.

If her aim was to get Darcy's attention, however, not even that declaration worked. He continued writing, not glancing up or even pausing once. Oliver almost wanted to laugh. Caroline was frowning at Darcy, and he was none the wiser.

Suddenly, she stood and began strolling around the room. "I do enjoy walking," she said loudly. "It's so wonderful to stretch one's legs and take in the brisk air."

Oliver wasn't sure what brisk air she was experiencing in this large room without a single open window, but he didn't comment.

"Elizabeth!" Caroline said at once.

Oliver jumped, the sound of *that* name so grating on Caroline's lips that she might as well have raked her nails down his back. He looked up warily from his book, regretting doing so the moment he met Caroline's gaze.

"You must walk with me! Come, join me."

Oliver cringed. "Oh, I think I better not. I—"

"Nonsense! Walking is really so important, we mustn't allow ourselves to *sit* all day. Join me."

It was more of a command than a request, but when no one else spoke up to save him, he reluctantly closed his book and stood. As he did, Darcy glanced up, something like curiosity in his gaze as he met Oliver's eyes.

Don't look too closely, he begged, and ripped his gaze away, forcing himself to smile at Caroline. It felt like trying to stretch a stiff, unused muscle. Caroline extended her arm, and seeing no way to refuse without being rude, he took her arm. Together, they walked around the room in slow circles, floorboards creaking beneath them.

"Isn't this so much the better?" Caroline asked. "It really is so refreshing to move around after a long day of sitting in place."

Oliver couldn't speak for Caroline, but between entertaining his mother and sisters and checking on Jane periodically throughout the day, he had *not* had a long day of *sitting in place*. But he didn't bother trying to correct her. He didn't think she was really paying attention to half of what she said anyway. She was clearly speaking to fill the air.

"It's nice," he allowed.

"What *are* you doing?" Darcy asked.

This seemed to delight Caroline. She giggled and shot him a buoyant smile. "Why, we're taking a walk, of course."

"Around the room?"

"Indeed."

"Why would you circle the room? It can't possibly be that entertaining to endlessly walk the perimeter of a room you've been in dozens of times."

Oliver couldn't help but agree. Still, he pretended he wasn't paying attention to the conversation awkwardly being had over him, allowing his gaze to wander around the room instead, catching the sheen stripes of the decorated walls.

"It's a simple pleasure for simple ladies," Caroline responded.

Oliver couldn't stop the look of revulsion that washed over his face. Even if he *was* a woman, he would never describe himself as a "simple lady." Was this really Caroline's best attempt at flirting?

Darcy leaned back in his seat, stretching his legs out in front of him. "Is that truly why you've started this? Or have you convinced Elizabeth to take a walk around the room with you to catch my attention?"

Caroline gasped in mock offense. "Mr. Darcy!"

"That wasn't a no."

Beside him, she giggled again. "I couldn't say. Is it working?"

This was truly the most painful walk Oliver had ever taken, and he'd once forgotten to break in a pair of new leather boots before walking two miles in them.

"To be clear," Oliver interrupted at last, "*I'm* only walking because Caroline insisted. I couldn't care less whether that was enough to pique your interest."

It was true, at least as long as he had to present as Elizabeth. The less he interacted with Darcy as a girl, the better—it was humiliating enough to have to be in the same room as him dressed like this after spending so much time with the other boy as himself.

Darcy smirked. "Of course. I would never assume as much from you."

Oliver frowned. "Are you trying to say something about my character?"

"If I were to make a statement about your character, Miss

Bennet, rest assured I would say it directly. I haven't any interest in wasting time playing verbal games."

Oliver snorted and before he could stop himself, said, "You haven't any interest in *wasting time* with anybody at all."

He regretted the words immediately. Not because they weren't true, but because "Elizabeth" wasn't supposed to be engaging Darcy in conversation. Darcy wasn't supposed to notice "Elizabeth" at all.

Unfortunately, it was exceedingly difficult for Oliver to turn down a battle of wit.

"I am discerning with my time, that's true," Darcy said. "But I like to think it means those I *do* spend my time with are especially deserving of my attention."

"You don't think it bold to assume others don't?"

"I know!" Caroline interrupted loudly. "We must play a game, Elizabeth. For the sake of amusement, we should determine what Darcy's worst qualities are."

Oliver couldn't believe he actually agreed with Caroline on something, but he had to admit that *did* sound fun. And the way Darcy's eyes narrowed at the suggestion only convinced him all the more that it was an excellent idea.

"You know what, Caroline? That sounds like a splendid idea. Would you like to go first?"

"And do I not have to consent to this game?" Darcy asked.

"No," Oliver and Caroline said at once. Oliver smiled, laughter already gathering in his chest.

"I can start," Caroline said. "Darcy thinks himself more

intelligent than everyone around him. He *is* very intelligent, so as a result he comes off as intimidating."

Oliver resisted the urge to side-eye Caroline. They were *supposed* to be poking fun at Darcy's character, but that "flaw" seemed more like Caroline's attempt to continue flirting with him.

"Hmm," Darcy said. "I suppose I can accept that."

Oliver rolled his eyes. "Of course you can; that was hardly a character flaw at all."

"I'm not sure I agree, though. I would say my worst characteristic is that my good opinion, once lost, is lost forever." Darcy crossed his arms over his chest and smiled wryly. "And what is *your* conclusion about my character?"

"I should think your inclination to abhor everybody would be your more accurate flaw," Oliver responded.

"And yours is your inclination to misunderstand everyone."

Oliver opened his mouth to argue, but Caroline dropped his arm and huffed. "I'm bored," she said. "I have a better idea. Who would like to play the pianoforte? I did so last, so it should be someone else this time. Elizabeth, won't you be a dear and play for us?"

Oliver clenched his jaw, quickly growing tired of hearing that name thrown at him repeatedly. It was obvious what Caroline was doing—next she would insist that Darcy dance with her, thereby securing the full force of his attention. Though Darcy didn't seem any more interested in her flirtations than he had at the beginning of this encounter, Caroline had succeeded in one thing: Oliver was exhausted from dealing with her.

"Actually, I think I'll go sit with Jane for a while. Thank you all for the entertainment."

And with that he walked out of the room, ignoring Caroline's triumphant smile and the prickle of Darcy's gaze on his back.

Oliver found Jane not in the guest room she'd been occupying as he'd expected, but sitting on a bench set out in the hallway with Bingley beside her. The two were laughing over something Oliver hadn't heard, and the tone of Jane's gentle laughter made Oliver stop in his tracks. He knew all too well the difference between Jane's polite, quiet laugh and her genuine amusement. This was the latter.

He hesitated, not wanting to disturb them. The two were leaning toward each other, perhaps a little closer than was proper, but not egregiously so. And though Oliver couldn't see Jane's face, he could hear the smile in her voice.

"I must thank you again for your hospitality," she said. "I was so disappointed when I began feeling poorly. I'd really been hoping for a pleasant, uneventful visit."

"Would it be absolutely horrid of me to say that I'm glad you had cause to stay longer than expected?" Bingley asked with a small smile of his own. "Of course I'm not happy that you're feeling poorly, but it has been nice to have the opportunity to offer you some extra care."

"I suppose I could forgive that," Jane said coyly, and Oliver's mouth nearly fell open in shock. Jane was *flirting*!

The two laughed, and the ease of their joy should have made him happy—and it did. But it also hit him in the stomach with an ugly pang. Because the truth was, he wanted that easy camaraderie. He wanted to be able to court someone without fearing how they might react if they knew the full truth about him. He wanted an openness with someone without fear, without worry. He wanted that ease, but it all seemed impossible. What were the odds, truly, that he would ever find someone who knew how to love someone like him?

The truth was he didn't know. And the not knowing hurt more than he wanted to admit.

CHAPTER 10

Mama,

Jane and I are ready to return home. While Jane isn't yet fully recovered, she has agreed she's well enough to travel and would prefer to complete her rest in the comfort of her bedroom. If you could arrange for the carriage to bring us home, it would be most appreciated.

Love,

Elizabeth

Elizabeth,

Your father has use of the carriage today, so I'm afraid that won't be possible. Maybe it would be best to stay for another day? I'm sure Jane won't mind spending more time with the handsome Mr. Bingley.

Love,
Your mother

Oliver very nearly ripped the letter into shreds upon receipt. While it was plausible that Mr. Bennet really was using the carriage today, the rest of the letter made him suspect otherwise. Did she really want them to overstay their welcome?

He supposed Mama didn't think it possible for anyone to tire of Jane, and maybe that was true, but *he* was there as well, and after two days he was certainly exhausted of being around two Bingleys in particular.

After finishing a breakfast of crumpets with strawberry jam and a cup of tea, Oliver wandered around Netherfield searching for Bingley. But the estate was sprawling, and he quickly realized despite spending two days here, he'd only been to a handful of rooms, none of which contained the redheaded boy.

When he checked the library, he wasn't surprised to find Darcy there, reading the book he'd pointed out to Oliver at the Temple of Muses. The cover brought back the memory of wandering the bookstore with Darcy at his side so strongly that he stopped in his tracks. He could almost smell the warm scent of the paper and glue, and Darcy's smile . . .

Oliver ripped his gaze away from the other boy. He wasn't here for Darcy. And Bingley wasn't here either. With a sigh, he turned on his heel. He'd just faced the door to leave when a voice stopped him.

"Can I help you, Miss Bennet?"

Oliver closed his eyes. That address coming from Darcy felt

like taking a boot to the stomach. It wasn't that he hadn't grown accustomed to being referred to as *Miss* Bennet, but it felt different now—worse somehow—coming from Darcy after hearing him use Oliver's true name.

Worse still that it had been *days* since he'd been able to be himself. With every passing moment performing as Elizabeth, it became more difficult to breathe.

When Oliver opened his eyes and turned around, Darcy was looking at him expectantly. He'd paused for too long.

"Apologies," he said quickly. "I was searching for Mr. Bingley. Do you happen to know where he is?"

"No."

Oliver waited, expecting more, but after a couple seconds it became apparent that was the entirety of Darcy's response. The other boy looked at Oliver with a flatness that conveyed pure disinterest with a note of something like irritation. As if Darcy couldn't believe he was being interrupted with such a banal exchange.

He hadn't wanted to believe Wickham's accusation that Darcy hated women, but it was becoming increasingly difficult to deny the possibility.

"Right, then," Oliver said. "I won't take up any more of your time."

"Do you intend to stay at Netherfield for much longer?" Darcy asked coolly.

Oliver's face warmed. He had known, of course, that he and

Jane had overstayed their welcome, which was the entire reason he was trying to find Bingley. But hearing it so obviously implied, from someone who was doing little to hide his disdain, was humiliating nevertheless.

Oliver fought to keep the embarrassment from showing on his face. He pulled his shoulders back and cleared his throat. "Actually, that's why I was looking for Mr. Bingley. I was hoping perhaps Jane and I could borrow his carriage to return to Longbourn. Jane has recovered enough to return home, but I received a letter from our mother this morning informing us our father is using the carriage, so they won't be able to send it today."

"Oh," said a soft voice behind him. "You're leaving."

Oliver turned with a start and found Bingley at last, looking at him with something like sadness in his eyes. It almost made him feel bad for insisting that they leave today. Almost.

"I'm afraid we must," Oliver said.

"You're welcome to stay another day if you'd like," Bingley said. "I hope you know you and Jane aren't imposing at all."

Oliver forced a small smile and made a point not to look at Darcy. Still, even if Bingley's friend *had* agreed they were welcome to stay, the notion of being trapped here pretending to be Elizabeth another day made him absolutely nauseous. "That's very generous of you, but I believe Jane would prefer to complete her recovery in the comfort of her own bed."

Bingley nodded. "That's understandable. Of course we'd be happy to lend you a carriage."

No sooner had Jane and Oliver stepped through the front door of their home than Mrs. Bennet greeted them with a pinched expression conveying her displeasure.

"How did you return home?" she asked. Then she turned on Oliver, her quickly souring mood twisting her features. "Surely you didn't force Jane to *walk* home in her condition?"

Jane opened her mouth to respond but coughed weakly instead, so Oliver stepped forward. "No, Mama. Mr. Bingley was kind enough to lend us his carriage."

Mrs. Bennet's eyes narrowed. "He asked you to leave?"

"Mr. Darcy did," Oliver responded, which was mostly true.

"I wanted to return home," Jane interrupted, before Mrs. Bennet could argue any further. "I'm still not well, Mama. I want to rest at home, in my own bedroom."

Mrs. Bennet's expression softened. "Of course you do, poor dear. Do you need any assistance?"

Jane shook her head. "No, thank you, Mama. But if someone could bring my trunk . . . ?"

"I'll bring it up along with my own," Oliver said.

Jane thanked him, then continued on up the stairs to their shared bedroom. Oliver moved to follow, but Mrs. Bennet stopped him.

"Just a moment, dear. I'd like to hear all about your visit. Was Jane able to spend some time with Mr. Bingley?"

Oliver bit his lip and lowered both trunks to the floor before his arms began to ache. "Some. She spent most of the visit resting, but Mr. Bingley did check on her frequently."

"Good! Oh, that is excellent news. And what about you? Did you learn anything from the Bingley sisters?"

Oliver blinked. "Pardon?"

"The Bingley sisters are two very beautiful, feminine women. I thought it might be educational for you to spend some time with two proper ladies, given your proclivities."

Oliver's heart pounded so hard his chest hurt, heat creeping up his neck. Mrs. Bennet didn't know that he went out dressed as a boy—there wasn't a snowflake's chance in summer that she wouldn't have blown up immediately the moment she learned the truth. So if she didn't know that he preferred to dress as a boy—that he *was* a boy—then what on earth was she referring to?

"I don't understand," Oliver said carefully. "What 'proclivities,' exactly?"

Mrs. Bennet let out an exasperated sigh. "Honestly, Elizabeth, did you really think your own mother wouldn't notice how much you detest your most beautiful dresses? Or how miserably you hold yourself when you're expected to dance with a gentleman? Not to mention the way you cringe at the merest mention of a suitor—"

"All right," Oliver interrupted. "I understand your meaning. But, Mama, none of that is novel. I've *always* disliked those things."

"Precisely. Which is why I believe it is in your best interests to spend more time with proper ladies. Perhaps being a lady doesn't come as naturally to you as it does your sisters, but that's nothing that can't be fixed. You just need the right education."

The heat in Oliver's neck spread to the rest of his body, broiling him alive as his stomach flopped in sickening waves. What Mrs. Bennet was suggesting made his blood roar in his ears and his lungs constrict. He needed out of this conversation and he needed out *now*.

"No thank you," Oliver said, fighting to keep his voice casually polite. His voice sounded distant, his movements disjointed as he reached toward the trunks. It was as though he were watching himself speak and move, but someone else was controlling his body. He was just an observer, buoyed in a roiling place with his pulse a storm in his ears.

"I'm quite all right," he said, his tone just a note away from breaking. "I'm going to check on Jane now."

With that he ascended the stairs to the second floor, his head light as he fought to stay grounded. Mrs. Bennet didn't stop him.

Jane was asleep, which suited Oliver perfectly well.

Oliver threw himself onto his bed, hitting the mattress with a thump that almost winded him. Lying on his bed, arms crossed behind his head, his mother's words swirled in his mind, making him dizzy with dread.

The fabric of his dress was, all at once, much too tight. Oliver leapt to his feet, cringing at the creaky floorboard beneath him, and ripped the dress up over his head and into a heap at his feet. Freed from his fabric prison, he grabbed a wooden chair from the small desk and propped it against the door to prevent anyone from entering unannounced. Satisfied, Oliver returned to his bed, dropped to his knees, and reached beneath the bed to push the decoy trunks aside and pull his hidden trunk free.

Though he would have liked to change into a full outfit—coat, cravat, boots, and all—that would be a lot harder to change out of quickly if need be, so he opted just for trousers, his chest flattener, and a shirt. Once dressed, he ran his hand over his now-flat chest and sighed, cool relief washing over him as a small smile tugged at his lips. His flattener ran tight around his ribs like a hug, and it was oddly comforting.

As his panic ebbed away, Oliver grabbed a quill pen, inkpot, and a sheet of paper. He'd used the chair to block the door, so he couldn't sit at the desk. Instead, he sat on the floor in front of his open trunk, closed the lid, and spread the paper on top of it. Dipping his pen into the inkpot, he wrote *Aspirations*, and below it, he began a list:

—*Visit a Molly House*
—*Spend several subsequent days dressed as myself
without pretending to be a girl*

—*Tell the rest of the family and the staff*
    who I am so I can be myself at home

Oliver hesitated. The last item he wanted to add felt impossible. But this was a list of aspirations, and if he couldn't allow himself to even dream for this, then what was the point of this list at all?

So, taking a deep breath, he wrote down the impossible with shaking fingers:

—*Kiss a boy as a boy*

CHAPTER 11

MUCH TO LYDIA'S DELIGHT, IT WASN'T LONG AFTER THEIR DEPARTURE from Netherfield that Jane recovered. And sooner still before they received an invitation to the Netherfield Ball. Lydia crooned about the handsome men sure to be there, while Jane tried to play down her excitement about spending more time with Bingley without being ill.

"It's only been a week since we've seen them last, but it will be nice to see him again," she said, her cheeks becoming powder pink. "Of course, I'm sure there will be many people there. I can't expect to be the sole object of his attention."

"Maybe you can't expect it," Oliver conceded. "But I suspect you will be."

Oliver, meanwhile, hadn't had the opportunity even once since returning from Netherfield to go out on his own. It left him feeling like an animal with a foot snagged in a trap, the teeth of his mother's expectations sinking deeper into him every time he struggled.

Mrs. Bennet had insisted on Oliver's help all week to *prepare the home* for their cousin, Mr. Collins, who had let them know he'd shortly be coming to visit for the first time. As the Bennets didn't have any legally recognized sons, Collins was due to inherit Longbourn in the event of Father's passing. Oliver had absolutely no interest in meeting the man, but Mrs. Bennet seemed to think he might take a liking to one of them to marry. It was a truly vile notion, and Oliver was determined to make himself as unlikable as possible.

But tonight Oliver didn't have to worry about Collins—tonight was the Netherfield Ball. Once they'd arrived at Netherfield and followed the crowd to the ballroom, Oliver was taken by the grandeur of the room. Though he'd stayed on the premises for a number of days, he'd never ventured over to the ballroom—after all, there hadn't really been much cause to. Now there, he found himself looking around the enormous room, wide-eyed.

The dark hardwood floors were freshly waxed and gleamed in the light—they were so well polished Oliver could see his reflection in the wood. Two large crystal chandeliers spilled light across the room like twinkling stars. The walls were a deep royal blue, the curtains gold-trimmed silk.

Though the Meryton Ball had been a public affair, this was a private ball, which meant everyone was in their finest. Oliver did his best not to look at his evening gown. He knew it was blue, not dissimilar from the color of the walls, and the busk dug into his skin just beneath his breasts every time he was tempted to slouch to de-emphasize the shape of his chest. He'd mostly dressed—and allowed Mrs. Bennet to assist him—while looking at his reflection as little as possible. His hair was up at least. He'd had to argue with Mrs. Bennet to keep it that way, but in the end she'd conceded.

At any rate, it wasn't his dress that he was interested in. Oliver had a unique opportunity tonight to take in the best of the best of menswear. It wasn't an opportunity he had often, and he wouldn't squander it.

They'd barely stepped into the room before Bingley approached them, absolutely beaming. He looked at Jane like she was the most beautiful woman he'd ever seen, his smile gleaming in the light.

"You look absolutely stunning," he said, offering Jane his hand. "May I have this dance?"

Jane flushed, smiling as she took his hand. "You may have as many dances as you'd like, Mr. Bingley."

And with that they were off.

Seeing Bingley reminded Oliver that Darcy must be here too—after all, he did live at Netherfield. For reasons Oliver didn't care to investigate, he found himself looking around the room, trying to pull him from the crowd. It didn't take long to spot him standing with his back to the wall, arms crossed. He looked vexed, which struck Oliver as odd. Of course, he already knew Darcy wasn't a huge fan of dances, but this was one that *he* had helped to arrange. Surely he wasn't as irritated by the affair as he had been by the Meryton Ball.

The longer Oliver looked at Darcy, the more it seemed like the other boy was glowering at someone in particular. Oliver followed his gaze across the room to Wickham, of all people, dressed in the ceremonial attire of a soldier. He seemed to be returning Darcy's glare with his own.

He understood, somewhat, why Wickham didn't like Darcy. But why did Darcy seem so furious to see Wickham?

Lydia, Kitty, and Mary all scurried off somewhere into the thick of the crowd. Oliver moved to walk in the opposite direction when a hand clasped his shoulder.

"Dear," Mrs. Bennet said, squeezing his shoulder tight. "I do want to encourage you to dance with someone tonight. With Jane all but engaged to Mr. Bingley—"

"That's a bit presumptuous, don't you think?" Oliver interrupted with a smile.

"Presumptuous!" Mrs. Bennet scoffed. "Mark my words, my dear, Mr. Bingley will not take his eyes off Jane once throughout the night! I am absolutely certain he will dance with no one else."

"I suppose we'll see, then," Oliver said, turning away, but Mrs. Bennet grabbed his arm again. He sighed and looked back at her. "Sorry, was there more?"

"I want you to promise me you'll dance with at least one gentleman tonight."

Oliver grimaced. "I'm sure Kitty and Lydia will dance with

more than enough gentlemen for the three of us." Mrs. Bennet's eyes narrowed, and Oliver bit his lip and finally conceded. "*If* a gentleman asks me to dance, I'll accept. But I won't go parade myself about in front of them like a peacock looking for a mate."

"Fine." Mrs. Bennet sounded far more triumphant than Oliver was comfortable with. It was then he realized she wasn't looking at him, rather something over his shoulder. "Oh, Mr. Collins! What a lovely surprise."

Oliver's stomach dropped to his toes. Mr. Collins? As in his cousin, Mr. Collins? *Here?* He wasn't supposed to arrive until tomorrow evening—

"Good evening, Mrs. Bennet. Miss Bennet." A man approached them, removing his hat as he nodded at them both. "What a pleasant surprise! And here I hadn't expected to have the pleasure of your company for another twenty-four hours."

Oliver forced himself to smile even though everything inside him demanded he find an excuse to leave immediately. Mrs. Bennet couldn't have set this up better if she tried—which perhaps she had.

"Why, Miss Bennet, you look absolutely ravishing," Collins said.

Oliver suppressed a head-to-toe shudder. He finally met the man's gaze, regretting it immediately. Collins was looking at him with far too much interest. He was supposed to be the unlikable Bennet sibling, but so far this was off to a terrible start.

Collins was an awkward man, with a shiny forehead already

slick with nervous perspiration, and whatever he had done with his short hair made it look so stiff Oliver would have believed it if someone told him it was actually a wig made of boar bristle. His cravat was frilly, like lace, which was falling out of fashion. The rest of his clothing was generally in fashion, but drab. White linen shirt, black overcoat, black trousers, black boots. The cut of the jacket and shirt was boxy, though, like it hadn't been tailored for him—or at least, not well.

Altogether, it created the impression of a young man trying to step into his father's too-large shoes.

"Good to see you, Mr. Collins," Oliver forced himself to say. "I understand you'll be visiting Longbourn tomorrow?"

"That's right. I realized recently that I haven't actually visited the estate yet, which struck me as preposterous as it will one day be my own. How strange that it hadn't occurred to me to visit earlier! But no matter, I'm very much looking forward to becoming acquainted with the property and with your family, of course. I think it will be good, indeed, important even—"

"Yes, I look forward to it as well," Oliver interrupted. "If you'll excuse me, I believe Mary is about to sit at the pianoforte and I really should stop her."

"Oh, don't you worry, dear," Mrs. Bennet said cheerfully. "I'll take care of Mary."

"It's really fine, Mama. I don't mind—"

"Actually, Miss Bennet, I was hoping you'd do me the honor of a dance?"

And there it was. Oliver stiffened, his forced smile slipping off his face as his mother glared at him with her most demanding stare. She arched her eyebrows at him, her message crystal clear: *You promised you would accept if someone asked.*

But Collins? he wanted to argue. *He's my cousin, not a gentleman!*

He didn't have to voice any of that to know that argument would go absolutely nowhere. His mother had, unfortunately, outmaneuvered him.

So, slowly, he turned back to Collins, who was still looking at him expectantly, his hand outstretched. "Of course," he said coolly.

Oliver took his hand. It was slick with sweat and slightly cold, like holding a fish that had been left on the counter for too long. This time he couldn't suppress the shiver that rolled down his spine, but somehow he managed to smile tightly at his cousin.

"You have such beautiful childbearing hips," Collins said the moment they stepped into the center of the room, apparently managing to think of the worst possible thing to say.

If a bolt of lightning ripped through Netherfield's ceiling and slammed directly into Oliver's heart, it would be a relief.

"Your cravat is . . . traditional," he responded stiffly.

Mr. Collins grinned. "Oh, you noticed!" Oliver fought to keep his expression straight. How could he *not* notice? The frilly monstrosity bursting from his chest reminded Oliver of an over-large doily.

"You could say I'm a traditionalist of sorts," Collins continued with a note of pride in his voice. "In the way I dress, of course, but also in life. I do think the world has continued on successfully for a reason, so we must as a society continuously learn from the past to better the future."

"How can you better the future if you continue mimicking the past?" Oliver retorted, unable to stop himself.

Collins blinked, clearly not expecting Oliver to actually challenge him on anything. "Well," he said, flustered, "that question presumes that we haven't as a society started falling into disarray by straying from the past. But surely you don't believe that."

"Surely not," he responded dryly.

Collins nodded, visibly relieved, evidently not understanding sarcasm. Then, perhaps made uncomfortable by the topic, he smiled as the music changed from a simple waltz to a line dance. "Ah! How wonderful, I do enjoy this dance."

Oliver was glad for the music change too, if only because a line dance meant less time spent practically on top of Collins. He stepped back into the line of women, ignoring the deep sense of wrongness as he did so. With women grinning on either of his sides, he was suddenly reminded of the way the rest of the world saw him. Looking at him right now, Collins saw a girl in a dress, like every other girl lined up for the dance. Oliver bit his lip, pushing the discomfort to the back of his mind. But every time he tried to ignore the twisting sensation in his gut that demanded he step out of line, the more difficult it was to force from his mind.

He suspected it wouldn't be long before he tried to shove away these feelings in the box in the back of his mind only to find the box bursting at the seams.

The music began and Oliver lost himself in the steps. He focused on his movements, on the push and pull of the dance with his partner, on pretending very hard that his partner wasn't Collins. When the time came to switch places with the girl to his left and dance with her partner, he found himself relieved to be away from his cousin, even if just for a few moments.

He stepped toward his new partner and, with a start, found Darcy moving toward him. They met with their palms not quite touching and circled each other as Oliver's heart thrummed in his chest.

"Good evening, Miss Bennet," Darcy said neutrally.

Oliver swallowed hard. "Good evening, Mr. Darcy."

"Enjoying yourself?"

"I'm not sure I'd say that."

Unexpectedly, Darcy smiled, just slightly, and Oliver found himself smiling softly in return. "Your partner seems to be rather chatty."

"An apt observation. Thankfully he seems to be the variety of chatty that only wants to hear himself speak."

Darcy arched an eyebrow. "That's a good thing?"

"It is when I have absolutely no interest in speaking to him."

"Ah." Darcy's smile grew. "Well, I hope that's not the case with me."

He . . . did? Oliver wasn't sure what to make of this change in demeanor. Every other time he'd interacted with Darcy dressed as a girl, he would have found a block of ice a warmer companion. But here Darcy seemed . . . almost pleasant?

"If you enjoy the discussion rather than the sound of your own voice, you're already a step ahead of my dancing partner," Oliver said.

Darcy opened his mouth as if to say something, but then the pattern of the dance was over and it was time to switch again. Oliver nodded at Darcy and stepped back to his right, swapping places with Darcy's original partner. It may have been Oliver's imagination, but the girl seemed relieved to be returning to Darcy.

Weaving in and out with Collins, Oliver found himself once again in the unenviable position of dancing close to his cousin for an extended period of time. Collins began rattling off immediately about *the questionable quality of women here* and for the sake of his own sanity, Oliver allowed his mind to wander. Collins's voice became distant, as if underwater, and the music swelled in his mind, carrying him through the hypnotic steps.

Oliver let his gaze drift, catching the swish of Darcy's tailcoats, the twist of his polished shoes as he turned, the cut of his dark trousers and well-fitting double-breasted outer coat. Darcy's clothes were tailored at the waist and shoulders, accentuating his enviable Y shape of broad shoulders and narrow waist, but the star piece was very clearly the coat. *Goodness,* that coat was beautiful—unlike many of the black coats in the room, Darcy's was a deep navy blue with a black velvet contrasting collar and sleeve cuffs. The buttons were silver and popped against the deep tones of the fabric. Oliver wanted one of his own immediately.

Oliver had a number of clothes for men, but he didn't yet have men's formal wear. He'd never really had occasion for it—after all, any event that required formal wear was generally attended by his family, and he couldn't very well pretend not to go and then show up in menswear. The general public may not notice that Oliver and Elizabeth were, in fact, the same person, but Oliver didn't doubt for a second that Mrs. Bennet would.

Now that he was here, surrounded by men dressed in their finest, he wanted more than anything to rip off his dress and put on a sleek pair of trousers, shiny leather shoes, a silk shirt, a cravat, and a perfectly tailored overcoat—maybe a burgundy or forest green with a contrasting black collar, similar to Darcy's. There was so much fashion to admire in this room—from overcoats like Darcy's, to beautifully colored vests contrasting with black waistcoats, to sleek black Hessian boots without all the frilly laces of women's boots. He could see himself wearing all of it, could imagine what it would be like to see his bound chest dressed to the nines. He wanted it so badly, but it seemed impossible that he would ever have the opportunity.

Pain in Oliver's left foot ripped him from his wandering thoughts. Oliver gasped and yanked his foot back, stumbling in the step of the dance.

"Oh!" Collins exclaimed. "I'm so sorry. This song trips me up sometimes—are you all right?"

Oliver stared at Collins, his foot throbbing. The pain wasn't excruciating, but it did hurt, and all at once Oliver recognized this unfortunate moment for the opportunity it was.

"I think I should go sit down," he said.

"Of course," Collins said quickly. "Of course. Do you need help getting to a chair?"

"No, no. I can do it. You must find another dancing partner. I'm very sorry for the inconvenience."

"Miss Bennet, please, it is I who apologize . . ." But Oliver was already turning away, so Collins let his apology fade.

Oliver stepped carefully, not having to fake a limp because his foot did genuinely hurt for the minute walk that it took him to find a corner with some chairs set out.

Once seated, Oliver closed his eyes and leaned his head back against the wall. This night may have been a disaster, but at least Collins had been kind enough to give him an out, even if accidentally.

"Excuse me, Miss Bennet, are you all right?"

Oliver groaned inwardly. Would this night never end? Reluctantly, he opened his eyes and with a start found none other than *Wickham* standing before him, concern etched into his brow.

"Uh, yes," Oliver said, hurriedly filling the awkward silence.

"My last dancing partner stepped on my toe, but I'm quite all right."

Wickham's brows shot up. "Stepped on your toe! What an oaf! Are you certain you're well?"

"Quite certain," Oliver responded firmly. "I assure you, there's no need for concern."

"I'm glad to hear it," Wickham said. "In that case, as your last dancing partner didn't injure you too grievously, would you do me the honor of a dance? I promise I won't step on your toes." Wickham smiled in a way he probably thought charming. It might have worked, if the manipulation weren't so obvious—and if Oliver hadn't already had an unpleasant interaction with him.

But what was he supposed to say? He couldn't very well feign injury now that he'd assured Wickham *twice* that he was fine. Wickham had artfully backed him into a corner—and he knew it.

Not trusting himself to keep the irritation out of his voice, Oliver took his hand wordlessly and stood. Which was how he *again* found himself in the unenviable position of dancing with a boy he had no interest in dancing with.

"You are so beautiful," Wickham said as he twirled with Oliver on the dance floor. "I think it's quite clear you'll make a very handsome wife for an exceedingly fortunate man one day. Perhaps even soon!"

Oliver balked at that. "Soon? I should hope not. I certainly haven't met anyone who I'd like to make my husband."

Wickham smiled slyly. "Perhaps you have and you just don't realize it yet."

Maybe if Oliver hadn't spent all his patience on Collins he would've been able to stop the distaste that showed clear on his face at Wickham's implication. As it was, he looked at the other boy like a jar of milk left out in the sun and said, "No. I don't believe so."

The smile vanished from Wickham's face in a flash, replaced with a stormy expression. They spent the rest of the song dancing in exceedingly awkward silence as Wickham barely concealed a glower. Logically, Oliver knew he should apologize, but he didn't want to encourage his flirtations.

Mercifully, the song eventually ended and Wickham stepped abruptly away from Oliver, bowed politely, and stalked back off into the crowd. As he watched the other boy walk away, Oliver found that he wasn't sorry. Not one bit.

CHAPTER 12

THE DAY AFTER THE NETHERFIELD BALL, OLIVER FINALLY FOUND an opportunity to go out on his own again. It was the day of Collins's scheduled arrival, so the energy permeating Longbourn was nothing short of chaotic. Mrs. Bennet was scurrying around doling out chores to the staff and her children as she fretted over the state of the home (which was, after days of cleaning, essentially immaculate) and the plan for supper.

Of course, Oliver had already spent days preparing Longbourn for the arrival of his esteemed cousin, so he was armed with an ironclad excuse when he announced he was going to visit Charlotte.

"Now?" Mrs. Bennet squawked. "You know very well who is arriving tonight, and you want to go out *now*? Are you trying to upset my poor nerves?"

"I think it's far too late for that, Mama," Oliver responded with a cheeky grin. "And anyway, I helped you prepare for Mr. Collins's arrival for the last three days. Don't you think I've earned myself a break?"

Mrs. Bennet opened her mouth, probably to deny his request, but Mr. Bennet looked up from his newspaper and said, "Oh, it's all right, dear. We have four other children to help prepare the final touches. I'm sure it won't take more than an hour's work to finish your preparations."

Oliver grinned. Mrs. Bennet's mouth snapped shut. She huffed furiously, then threw her arms up. "Fine! If you absolutely *must* visit Charlotte on the eve of your cousin's arrival—"

"I must," Oliver responded gravely.

"—then I suppose I must allow it, as long as you promise to return home before his arrival this evening."

"Thank you, Mama." Oliver pecked his mother on the cheek and grinned at his father, who winked at him before returning his attention to his paper. Jubilant, Oliver waltzed out the door before Mrs. Bennet could come up with any further requests.

Two hours later he was changed into more appropriate attire, fresh from the wardrobe he kept at Charlotte's, and taking his seat at an outdoor acrobatics show in a nearby park. The show was still setting up, but the pop-up stage was enormous, and Oliver had managed to find a seat in the third row, right in the center. It was sure to be an excellent performance—Oliver had seen this particular troupe perform once before, a year prior, and had been absolutely astonished by their fluid stunts.

"Is this seat taken?"

Oliver looked up.

It was none other than Wickham. Oliver froze, for a moment struck with terror that Wickham might recognize him—but slowly, he forced himself to relax. No one else had recognized him. Why would Wickham be any different?

"*I'm* not holding it for anyone," Oliver responded. "I can't speak for anyone else."

The boy shrugged and sat next to Oliver. "My name is Wickham," he said. "Yours?"

"Oliver Blake."

"It's a pleasure to meet you, Blake." He smiled brightly, and Oliver smiled tightly in return. He wasn't quite sure what to make of Wickham. Oliver hadn't exactly been impressed with him at the ball, but he could probably say that of most men in attendance. Darcy seemed to detest him, but then again by his own admission Darcy didn't like most people. So was it really so noteworthy that Wickham was someone who Darcy disliked? Probably not.

"Have we met before?" Wickham asked, frowning at him.

Oliver's heart all but stopped in his chest. He swallowed hard, forcing himself to breathe evenly as Wickham continued staring at him intently.

"I don't believe so," he responded, proud of how calm he sounded.

"We may not have been introduced, but I'm certain I've seen you somewhere," Wickham insisted.

Oliver felt faint. He'd done so well keeping his two lives separate—even Darcy, who had conversed with him at length in both, hadn't made the connection! How could Wickham recognize him when no one else had? He never should have agreed to that dance.

"Well, I do live in London so it's possible you've seen me walking around at some point," Oliver said. "Perhaps you attended the Bartholomew Fair earlier this year?"

Wickham shook his head. "No, that's not it. I haven't been to the fair."

Oliver just lifted a shoulder, maintaining an easy composure even as his hands shook. "I'm afraid I don't remember meeting you. Perhaps you're mistaking me for someone else?"

"Watier's!" Wickham exclaimed. "Of course! Did you go to Watier's recently?"

Oliver blinked, relief flooding through him. Wickham didn't recognize *Elizabeth*, he recognized *him*. Here he was, absolutely panicking over the thought of someone misunderstanding who he is and bringing scandal down on his family, and Wickham just recognized *Oliver*.

"Actually, I did." Oliver laughed, relaxing in his seat. "I don't think we were acquainted, though."

"No, I think not." He smiled and looked back at the stage. "Well! Mystery solved. Have you seen this troupe perform before?"

Oliver responded that he had.

"Splendid! This is my first time. I could use some amusement after the unpleasant week I've been having."

It was obvious Wickham wanted him to ask, but Oliver

wasn't entirely sure that he wanted to. Wickham seemed pleasant enough, but he was clearly trying to draw Oliver into a conversation he wasn't sure he was prepared to have. He'd gone out today with the intention of spending some time alone. Wickham, evidently, had gone out with the intention of finding someone to complain about his week to.

Still, the longer Oliver stayed quiet, the more awkward the silence became. Finally, he gave in and said, "I'm sorry to hear it."

"Thank you, that's very kind. Perhaps that was a bit of an exaggeration—I suppose if I really think about it, my week was going just fine until last night. But the unpleasantness that I experienced last night has overshadowed an otherwise perfectly average week."

Oliver may not have wanted to have this conversation, but now he'd been snared. An unwelcome thought unfurled in his mind: Was Wickham about to complain to Oliver about, well, *him*? He *had* been somewhat rude to Wickham the night before— but Wickham had been so grotesquely forward it seemed the only way to make his disinterest clear. Or had something else happened at the Netherfield Ball that he hadn't noticed? Perhaps he was referring to his staring contest with Darcy.

"What happened last night?" he asked against his better instincts.

"I made a terrible error in judgment, I'm afraid. I received an invitation for the Netherfield Ball and thought it completely benign, as one does. But I now fear my invitation was sent for much more sinister ends."

Oliver resisted the urge to laugh. Sinister ends? He was making it sound like he'd walked into a conspiracy to murder him. Wickham didn't elaborate, though, so evidently he intended to make Oliver an active participant in this strange conversation.

"What ends?" he finally prompted.

Wickham glanced around, as if whatever he was about to say was highly secretive information. Then he leaned toward Oliver and lowered his voice. "You *are* familiar with one Darcy of Pemberly, I believe? If I remember correctly, I think I saw you with him at Watier's."

Oliver discreetly shifted away from Wickham. "I am."

"I thought so. You aren't close, I hope?"

"That's a strange thing to hope."

Wickham smiled guiltily. "I just worry what I'm about to say may be upsetting if you have a close relationship with Darcy."

"I'm well acquainted with him, but I'm not sure he would call us close," Oliver said.

Wickham nodded. "Then it is fortunate that I happened upon you! Had you become any *more* acquainted with Darcy, you may have befriended a villain."

Oliver's carefully constructed facade of distant apathy almost broke. He choked down a laugh but couldn't stop the smile that came of it. "A villain?"

"Indeed," Wickham said somberly. "Darcy of Pemberly all but ruined my dear cousin's future. He's engaged to my cousin Genevieve, you see—we've always been quite close. They've been arranged to be married since they were children, and for a time all was well and good, until the two of them neared marrying age. For the past two years now, Darcy has treated my cousin most coldly. He won't see her of his own volition and never responds to her letters. When the two are brought together by outside parties, he treats her like a stranger. It's truly horrid and has been very upsetting for my poor cousin."

Oliver frowned. Darcy certainly had never mentioned being engaged. "If Darcy doesn't want to marry your cousin, why don't they break off the engagement?"

"You would think that a solution!" Wickham exclaimed. "But the villain refuses to break off the engagement, leaving my poor cousin to be alone and unable to court anyone else. Why, it boils my blood just thinking of it. But alas, I suppose I shouldn't be surprised—he's made his disdain for women clear."

Oliver's frown deepened. What Wickham described was cruel and cold, and Oliver wanted to deny that Darcy would be capable of such a thing. But the more he thought about what he knew of Darcy—about how Darcy had described himself, even—the harder it was to deny the capacity of such an act in his character. Though he'd had perfectly genial moments with Darcy when dressed as himself, the boy had been an entirely different person when Oliver was pretend-ing to be a girl.

"That's terrible," he said, and this time he didn't have to fake genuine concern. "I'm sorry to hear it."

Wickham nodded. "It's a reality not many are aware of, I'm afraid. The Darcys have always been well-connected, you see, so naturally they went out of their way to keep such an affair out of the public eye. But I assure you what I say is true."

Oliver wasn't really sure what to make of all this. He wasn't sure why Wickham would make up such a heinous story—after all, it wasn't like Oliver was someone important whose opinion of Darcy mattered on a societal level.

"I'm sorry," he said again, unsure of how else to respond.

"Would you believe there's more?"

Oliver's stomach churned. He wasn't sure he wanted to hear any more, truth be told. His mind was already spinning with this new information. Did Bingley know what Darcy had done to Wickham's cousin? He didn't think it was possible—Bingley and Darcy were practically connected at the hip, and the for-mer certainly didn't hide his affection for his friend. He couldn't imagine a sweet soul such as Bingley would associate with Darcy if he knew what he was capable of.

Oliver cast Wickham a wary glance, which only seemed to encourage him because he leaned even closer to Oliver.

"I've heard," Wickham whispered, his breath hot against Oliver's cheek, "that Darcy is a frequent visitor to a variety of

Molly Houses." He leaned back with a smug grin, crossing his arms over his chest.

Oliver blinked, hot prickles trickling down his face, into his neck and chest. The notion that Darcy may be attracted to other boys wasn't terribly surprising—that Wickham was sharing this hearsay with him, however, was. Given the obvious implications of someone frequenting a Molly House, this rumor was particularly dangerous. It was certainly enough to ruin someone's reputation, a reality that only infuriated Oliver. What business was it of anyone's who Darcy was attracted to?

"You know," Oliver said stiffly, "spreading a rumor like that could be incredibly damaging."

Wickham arched an eyebrow. "If it's true, people deserve to know."

"Why?" Oliver's tone was biting—perhaps suspiciously so, because Wickham's eyes narrowed. He forced some of the venom out of his voice. "I don't think that's something you should be spreading around, particularly because you don't even know if it's true."

"After what I've told you about his character, why should it matter to you?" Wickham asked, incredulous. "After what he did to my cousin—"

"I think," Oliver interrupted, "your insistence on repeating such toxic gossip knowing full well the harm it could do speaks more about *your* character than his."

Wickham's face shuttered, but it hardly mattered—Oliver

wasn't interested in spending a moment more having this discussion. He excused himself and stood, unable to control the tremble in his hands as he left the outdoor theater.

———

Oliver's mind was buzzing. After changing at Charlotte's, he walked home in a daze, trying to process everything he'd learned about Darcy. The news about his questionable behavior toward Wickham's cousin was upsetting, but if it *was* true that he went to Molly Houses, Oliver supposed he understood why Darcy didn't want to marry her.

If that was the case, though, why didn't he just break off the engagement? And in any case, it didn't explain Darcy's coldness toward Oliver when he was dressed as a girl.

Oliver wouldn't pretend a part of him hadn't hoped that Darcy might fancy other boys, especially after the night they shared at Watier's. Asking for such confirmation, however, would be dangerous, so he hadn't dared. But maybe he didn't need to ask. Maybe all he had to do was get the courage to visit a couple Molly Houses himself and ask if Darcy was a visitor. It *was* on his list of aspirations, regardless of Darcy's inclinations, so attending could serve dual purposes.

Then again, would such a discreet establishment share that information? Probably not. But how else could he find out for sure whether the rumor was true?

Oliver frowned. Lu had pointed out that particular Molly House that was especially for younger patrons. Maybe if he went there—

A snap of a broken stick somewhere behind him yanked him from his thoughts. Oliver looked over his shoulder, blinking at the empty walkway. Hedges along the path looked as undisturbed as usual, and even the muddy street was uncharacteristically empty save for the inevitable pile of horse manure.

He shook his head and continued forward, adjusting his uncomfortable dress. It was probably just a squirrel.

Oliver turned the corner and stepped onto the short walkway up to Longbourn. He moved past the two carriages in a near trance and walked all the way up to the front door before pausing.

Wait. *Two* carriages?

Oliver turned back to the carriages, and sure enough there were two. His gut twisted with anxiety. Was it later in the day than he'd realized? The sun was still high overhead—it couldn't be later than three o'clock. Collins had said he'd arrive in the *evening*, but Oliver didn't recognize the carriage. Who else could it be?

Biting his lip, he pushed open the front door and strode casually inside, closing the door as quietly as he could behind him. But it was for naught, because in the sitting room next to the foyer, Oliver spotted his sisters, mother, and Mr. Collins all together. Collins was sitting on one of the seats, as were most of his sisters, but Mrs. Bennet and Jane were standing. Spotting him, Jane's eyes widened and she hurried over.

"Mr. Collins arrived early," she whispered hastily. "He's been here for two hours already and his friend just arrived as well."

Oliver blinked. "Friend?"

"There was no way to hide you weren't here, I'm sorry—"

"Is that the missing Miss Bennet at last?" asked Collins, standing and walking over. Oliver barely had time to fix his face into a false smile before Collins rounded the corner and faced him. Though Oliver was smiling politely, Collins did not. He crossed his arms over his chest like a disapproving father, furrowed his brow, and shook his head, tutting condescendingly.

"My, my, Miss Bennet. Imagine my surprise when Mrs. Bennet told me you'd gone out on your own, without the company of a chaperone! Truly shocking behavior, indeed. I would certainly never allow *my* daughter to behave in such a way."

Miraculously, Oliver managed to hold on to his smile, even as a flush crept up his neck. "I suppose it's a good thing I'm not your daughter, then," he responded sweetly.

Collins's eyes widened, but before he could respond, a painfully familiar blond boy rounded the corner then froze, his eyes widening as he stared at Oliver. Oliver, for his part, stared right back, barely stopping his mouth from dropping open.

What on earth was *he* doing here?

"Oh," Wickham said. "Hello again."

Oliver couldn't believe his bad luck. What were the odds that

Collins's *friend* would be none other than the one boy Oliver had managed to offend as both himself and "Elizabeth"? Wickham must have gone directly here from the acrobatics show to arrive before Oliver did. If he hadn't stopped at Charlotte's to change, they probably would have awkwardly followed each other to Longbourn.

At a loss for words, Oliver just nodded politely at Wickham. Thankfully, Mr. Bennet rescued him from any further awkwardness.

"Lizzy!" he said, entering the room with a genuine smile. "How wonderful to see you. Mr. Collins was just telling us all the most enrapturing tale about his neighbor, Lady Catherine de Bourgh."

"Oh," Collins said quickly. "Well, I wouldn't say she was my *neighbor*, exactly, but it's true we do live nearby each other. I was telling your family about how blessed I've been to be permitted to frequent the premises of Rosings with some regularity. In fact, before I began my travels here, I had dinner with the esteemed Lady herself."

"Oh, how fascinating," Oliver said, trying somewhat futilely to keep the sarcasm from his voice as he pointedly didn't look at Wickham. "I must hear more. Shall we go sit together, then?"

Collins turned back to the room, launching into a detailed description of what they ate as Wickham followed closely behind. Oliver mouthed *thank you* to his father, who winked at him with a smile.

"Did you have a nice time?" he whispered.

"I did, Papa, thank you."

Mr. Bennet patted his shoulder, and with that they followed Mr. Collins and Wickham into the sitting room for another tale none of them were remotely interested in.

Dinner proved to be a similar affair. Oliver had the misfortune of being placed next to Collins and across from Wickham, but he supposed this was fair punishment for not being there for their initial arrivals. Kitty and Lydia sat at the farthest corner of the table away from them, whispering to each other between shooting furtive glances at Wickham, who was listening politely as he ate to Mr. Collins droning on endlessly. Collins didn't seem to notice the younger Bennet girls, which was for the best.

Partway through his story about a stray cat he found wandering the premises of Hunsford, his home, Collins abruptly lowered his knife and fork. "I must pause to thank you for your hospitality. I must admit, I was uncertain of what to expect upon my arrival, given the unusual circumstance of five unmarried daughters, all of whom are old enough to marry, but my expectations have been exceeded."

Everyone shifted uncomfortably. Oliver wasn't sure where to even begin with that. He certainly wouldn't classify *all* of them as old enough to marry—Lydia was only fourteen! Granted, he'd heard of girls getting married as young as fifteen, but it was absolutely not expected of someone so young, and for good reason. And what *expectations* did he have, for that matter? It certainly sounded like he was telling them he'd set a rather low bar for them.

"Actually, Jane is sure to be engaged very soon!" Mrs. Bennet chimed in, a little forcefully. "You may have seen her at the Netherfield Ball dancing with Mr. Bingley? He spent the entire evening with her and didn't look at another young lady even the once."

"I did notice that the other night," Wickham said. "Congratulations."

Jane's face reddened at the sudden attention, but she smiled softly. Though their mother was perhaps exaggerating slightly on the certainty of an engagement, what she said was generally true. Even Oliver expected Bingley would probably propose soon, though he didn't consider it already predetermined.

"That's wonderful news!" Collins responded. "Mr. Bingley is a fine fellow."

Mrs. Bennet nodded excitedly. "He and Jane get along splendidly. I really do expect they'll be married before the end of the year. It's very exciting."

"And how about you, Elizabeth?"

Oliver startled at the sound of that name on Collins's lips. Up until now his cousin had called him *Miss Bennet*, but he supposed there were many Miss Bennets in the room at the moment, so the switch to his given first name made sense. Still, the familiarity of it was uncomfortable.

"What about me?" he asked lightly, pointedly not looking at him.

"Have you caught the eye of a fine fellow as well?"

"I should hope not," he responded with a laugh. Awkwardly, no one else laughed. Oliver cleared his throat and tried again. "I don't believe so, no."

Collins nodded. "Well, perhaps you have and you just aren't aware of it yet."

Oliver glanced at Collins out of the corner of his eye, his polite smile slipping from his carefully composed facade. It was such a suspiciously similar setup to Wickham's line of questioning at the Netherfield Ball that Oliver couldn't help but wonder if the two had spoken about Wickham's interaction with Oliver that night. Was Collins trying to imply that Wickham was still interested in him? Unless . . . Surely Collins didn't mean *he* was interested . . . right?

Oliver focused on his food and continued eating, determined not to take the bait. It was then that Wickham turned to his mother and said, "Mrs. Bennet, I must commend you on your most handsome family. Why, I was honored to dance with Elizabeth at the ball the other night. To spend quality time with such esteemed company was the highlight of my evening."

Mrs. Bennet practically beamed with pride as Oliver's eyes narrowed. He knew for a fact that he'd been less than cordial

141

with Wickham, and that Wickham had taken it personally. What was he getting at?

"I am so delighted to hear that!" Mrs. Bennet crooned. "I do hope your experience was a pleasant one."

"With such a handsome dancing partner I do think that inevitable," he responded, which only served to confuse Oliver even more. And yet, though the man was complimenting *Oliver*, he was only looking at *Mrs. Bennet*. Did he think, perhaps, that it didn't matter if Oliver liked him as long as Mrs. Bennet did?

Oliver shivered at the thought that he might not be wrong.

As Collins launched into a new mind-numbingly boring story, Wickham continued to speak to Mrs. Bennet, making her laugh and blush with increasingly nauseating consistency. Eventually Oliver realized that he wasn't to be included in this conversation, and it did him little good to continue listening in, so he focused his attentions elsewhere. He let Collins's and Wickham's blended words wash over him, as if from a distance, as his mind wandered to kinder places.

Like taking a walk with a certain boy in the dark, side by side, so close their hands nearly brushed against each other. Whisper-thin space between them, under the moon and the stars, infinite possibilities laid out ahead of them.

CHAPTER 13

THE NEXT DAY, COLLINS INSISTED THEY ALL TAKE A WALK TOGETHER to "fully relish the start of a new month."

Mr. Bennet excused himself from attending, citing work he had to focus on instead. As Mr. Bennet was a man, Collins didn't protest.

Oliver didn't bother trying to get the same courtesy. In any case, last night—even after Wickham had left—Collins had kept them all up so late with his endless stories that Oliver hadn't had the opportunity to speak to Jane about what he'd learned. So as Mr. Collins led the group around a local park, Oliver caught Jane's eye and allowed himself to fall back.

Jane slowed as well, until they were several feet behind the rest of the group. Collins didn't notice—of course he didn't, he was far too absorbed in the story of the hour, this one having to do with the time he twisted his ankle on a walk to Rosings.

The park was full of wandering Londoners enjoying the temperate early spring air. Unlike some of the less favorable scents of the city, the park smelled of the sweet purple wisteria planted along the walkway, the aroma carrying on the cool breeze—strong, but not overwhelming.

Jane met his pace and quietly asked, "Is everything all right?"

"I think so," Oliver responded. "There's nothing urgent; I just heard something interesting about Darcy that I wanted to share with you."

Jane's arched eyebrow was all the invitation Oliver needed. He explained what Wickham had told him about his cousin, leaving out the part about Molly Houses—that rumor was too private, too volatile, to repeat. It still bothered him greatly that Wickham was sharing it with others at all.

"How terrible," Jane whispered after Oliver was done. "Do you think it's true?"

"I don't know," Oliver responded. "I'd prefer to think it isn't. I don't know if you noticed, but Wickham was at the Netherfield Ball and he and Darcy were glaring daggers at each other across the room."

"I can't imagine Bingley knows," Jane said with a frown. "He certainly wouldn't have such a close relationship with Darcy if he knew what he was capable of."

"*If* it's true," Oliver said. "I'm not sure I can trust Wickham either. He seemed rather determined to ruin Darcy's reputation however possible in our conversation. For all I know, the entire story is fabricated to smear his name."

Jane's frown deepened. "Do you think it's made up?"

Oliver didn't respond. He didn't want to think it could be true that Darcy would be perfectly content with ruining a girl's prospects, but put together with his coldness toward girls and the Molly House rumor . . . it seemed plausible. What if Darcy was using the engagement to avoid questions about his inclinations?

Oliver didn't know what to think, but the whole business left a sour taste in his mouth.

Collins's presence meant Oliver couldn't sneak out—not during the day, nor at night. He quickly learned Collins had the habit of going to bed extraordinarily late, and worse, tended to keep others awake with him. The one night Oliver had tried to sneak out, he'd ended up sitting by his barely ajar bedroom door, listening to Collins regale both of his parents with plans for how he'd take care of Longbourn once he inherited it.

So, by the time Collins was due to return to Hunsford three days after his arrival, Oliver was absolutely itching to leave. The morning of Collins's departure, he was in an exceedingly good mood. After all, he'd only have to deal with his exasperating cousin for a few more hours, then he could go "visit Charlotte" and get some air.

It was with this pleasant thought that he sat at the dining table, buttering a slice of freshly baked bread as his tea steeped in front of him. All the Bennets were present, but Collins hadn't yet joined them, which wasn't unusual. While he didn't sleep in terribly late, he did seem to get a later start to his day than the rest of them—probably due to his staying up late into the night.

Oliver had just bitten into the thick crust when Collins waltzed into the room, shoulders back and head held high. Rather than taking a seat, he cleared his throat.

"Good morning, everyone. I would like to request Elizabeth's presence alone."

The silence that fell over them was so jarring that for a moment it felt like time itself had stopped. Oliver's stomach swooped, his face hot. He couldn't imagine very many reasons why Collins would want to speak with him alone, especially after announcing it to the entire family in such a manner.

And the one reason he *could* think of made the bread in his mouth feel like wet sand.

Lydia dropped her butter knife onto her plate with a clatter, breaking Mrs. Bennet from her stupor. Their mother leapt to her feet, motioning for everyone to leave.

"Let's give them some privacy, girls," she said. "Up, up!"

Oliver grabbed Jane's hand as she moved to stand. "Don't leave me!" he hissed under his breath.

Jane looked at him apologetically as she untangled her fingers from his. "I'm sorry," she whispered. "You know Mama won't let me stay. I'll be nearby; don't worry."

And then she too was gone.

Oliver sat perfectly still in his seat, blood roaring in his ears as Mr. Bennet, the last to leave the room, paused at the door to meet Oliver's gaze, offering a small, reassuring nod before the door shuttered closed behind him. Collins nodded, cleared his throat again, then approached Oliver, stopping a few paces in front of him. He didn't sit, and thankfully he didn't kneel, but the way he stood towering over Oliver didn't feel much better.

"Elizabeth," he began, and Oliver flinched. Despite looking directly at him, Collins didn't seem to notice. "I'm sure you know why I summoned you here."

"I can't say that I do," Oliver said lightly as his palms grew slick with sweat. He pressed them hard against his thighs, desperate to hide the tremble in his fingers.

Collins raised his eyebrow. "Oh. Well, I suppose this will be a pleasant surprise, then. I came here to Longbourn with the intention of getting to know the estate that I will one day inherit, and the family currently inhabiting it. I had heard that the Bennet daughters were very beautiful ladies indeed, and I can now confidently say that I concur with that statement."

Oliver couldn't meet his eyes. He focused instead on Collins's forehead, which was gleaming with perspiration. When an awkward silence followed Collins's sentence, it occurred to Oliver that despite the sterility of his tone, that was a compliment he expected a response to.

"Thank you," he forced himself to say, even as the words *daughters* and *ladies* skittered down his back on spider legs.

Collins nodded once, the movement jerky. "As such, I've decided it would be in everyone's best interest for me to marry one of you. Originally I thought Jane would be the ideal wife, but after I came to learn she was already nearly engaged to another, I realized the second-eldest daughter was also perfectly acceptable. Given that, I believe that we should marry."

Oliver stared at him. Was he serious? A proposal was absolutely the very thing he was dreading, but even in his wildest nightmares he hadn't expected it to be like . . . *that*. Did he really just say he would have preferred to marry Jane but he would accept Oliver as a concession?

He couldn't begin to imagine how to form a response, but he didn't have to because Collins continued speaking.

"I would make an ideal husband for you, and you an ideal wife for me. You are handsome enough, well-bred, and the women in your family are clearly adept at having children. Furthermore, our marriage would mean a Bennet could always stay in Longbourn even after the passing of your father. This would ensure that, in a way, it remain a Bennet property for many more generations."

Horrifyingly, Oliver could see it. The picture Collins painted was one familiar to him, one that stalked him like a stubborn, looming storm. He saw himself trapped in a suffocating dress with a busk biting into his chest and drowning in petticoats; Mr. Collins, referring to Oliver as his *wife*, calling him *Elizabeth* endlessly, speaking to Oliver all day every day without any chance of respite; sharing a bed with Mr. Collins, bearing his children; his body contorting and changing in ways that made him sick to think about as he was forced to carry a child he never wanted to have. The prospect of such a life was dizzying.

Mr. Collins, incredibly, hadn't noticed Oliver's distress and was still speaking, but Oliver felt as though his head was stuffed with cotton. He couldn't marry Mr. Collins. He certainly couldn't be his wife. He would, Oliver realized without a hint of exaggeration, prefer far darker ends.

Strangely, it was that realization that cleared Oliver's mind. Mr. Collins's voice came back to him slowly, like the inevitable approach of the tide, washing over him and leaving him cold.

"I also believe I would make an ideal husband for you because of my status," Mr. Collins was saying. He wasn't even looking at Oliver at this point, which Oliver supposed wasn't all that surprising. Did Mr. Collins even see him? Or was Oliver just a vessel for him to continue to build his status in polite society? "I am well-respected," Mr. Collins said, "and my wealth would elevate your status as well. I am patient, intelligent, and I believe my firm hand will help steer you into an appropriate young woman and wife. I believe what you need is—"

"I'm sorry," Oliver said, no longer able to keep quiet as Collins's proposal became more horrifying by the second. "Do I get a say in this plan of yours? Or are you expecting me to accept your proposal by default?"

Mr. Collins blinked and looked at Oliver at last, wide-eyed.

He looked startled, almost as if he'd forgotten Oliver was in the room at all. "Oh," he said. "Well, of course you have a say in the matter, but I can't imagine any reason why you would refuse."

Oliver actually laughed. "You can't, can you?"

Mr. Collins's face reddened. "Of course not," he said, flustered. "As I mentioned, our union would improve your status in society and that of your family as well. It would also—"

"Mr. Collins," Oliver interrupted firmly, "contrary to what you may expect, I refuse to treat the course of my future as a business transaction. I cannot, under any circumstances, be your wife. We are not the match you believe us to be, and as flattered as I am by your proposal, I simply cannot accept."

Oliver wasn't in truth even remotely flattered, but it felt like a necessary addition to lessen the blow of the refusal, if only so Mr. Collins wouldn't hold it against him—or, more importantly, his family—for eternity.

But Mr. Collins didn't seem angry—he didn't even seem upset. He appeared confounded instead, for reasons Oliver couldn't fathom.

"I don't understand," he said after a painfully long pause. "Of course you can accept my proposal. It would be beneficial to us both, and as your sister Jane is already engaged, you're naturally the best choice for this union."

"Do you really think it flattering," Oliver said flatly, "to make it abundantly clear that even if I *were* to marry you—which I will not—I would only be a consolation prize because your first choice of my elder sister isn't available?"

Mr. Collins's brow furrowed. "I don't understand," he said again.

"No," Oliver said, standing. "I suppose you don't. No matter. All you need to understand is that I'm declining your proposal."

"But, Elizabeth—" That name screeched in his ears like nails on a chalkboard. "Don't you see how mutually beneficial this proposal would be? How happy it would make your family—your mother, particularly? Why, our children could grow up in the very same halls that you did! What union could be more appropriate? More suited?"

Oliver couldn't believe he was still arguing about this. How many times did he have to say no before Mr. Collins accepted it? How could he possibly be any clearer about his refusal? Something hot and itchy rose in his chest, flooding his mind and soul with the impulse to leave this room *immediately* before Mr. Collins trapped him in it forever. He needed out. He needed Collins to leave. And most of all, he needed to make it abundantly clear that he would *never* be anyone's wife—let alone Collins's.

"My answer is no," he said, fighting to keep his voice calm. "There is nothing you can say or do that will convince me otherwise. I will not wed you, Mr. Collins, not today, not tomorrow, not ever. I apologize for any misunderstanding between us and for any inconvenience my refusal has caused, but my answer will not change."

Mr. Collins stared at him for a moment, slack-jawed, before his mouth closed with a click. He nodded once, smoothing down his waistcoat, not that it was needed. "Very well," he said, at last. "I admit this wasn't the answer I was expecting or hoping for, but if you change your mind—"

"I will not."

"I see." Mr. Collins swallowed hard, his Adam's apple bobbing in his throat. "Well, in that case, I should be off. Thank you for your time, Miss Bennet."

And with that he finally turned away and strode out, the door swishing closed behind him with a resounding *thunk*. Oliver stood, shaking, alone, before he collapsed into a chair and pressed his face into his palms.

He wouldn't cry. Not over Mr. Collins. But he remained like that for many moments longer.

CHAPTER 14

IT DID NOT SURPRISE OLIVER TO FIND HIS SISTERS STILL WAITING IN the parlor outside the dining room when he finally emerged. He *was* surprised to find Mrs. Bennet wasn't there, until Jane spoke.

"Mama is speaking to Mr. Collins," she said with a small grimace.

Ah. Of course she was.

Oliver sighed and sat next to Jane on the settee. She placed her hand on top of his and squeezed his hand lightly. Oliver forced a small smile. "I do hope she isn't trying to change his mind. It required quite a bit of effort to convince him of my refusal to begin with."

"He seemed rather determined to marry you," Lydia said lightly.

"He was determined to marry *one* of us," Oliver corrected. "I don't believe he much cared which one of us it was once he realized it wouldn't be Jane."

"That's true," Kitty said. "He did say twice that he would have preferred to marry Jane."

Jane grimaced. Oliver turned to her with a small laugh. "You really did catch Bingley's eye at the perfect time."

Jane smiled softly, her cheeks turning pink. "It wasn't with the intention of turning Mr. Collins's attentions toward you."

"No, of course not." Oliver waved his hand. "It was just fortunate timing. I'm glad for you, truly. Bingley is a much more admirable match than Collins."

Though polite society would demand it, Jane did not deny it.

All at once, the door leading to the hallway opened and both Mr. and Mrs. Bennet entered the room. Mr. Bennet seemed oddly cheerful for a man whose child just embarrassed the guest set to inherit their home, whereas Mrs. Bennet looked every bit as furious as Oliver expected. Her face was blotchy, her eyes wide and wild. When she turned her heated gaze on Oliver, the instinct to flee was strong. But he remained in place, meeting his mother's gaze with every ounce of calm that he could muster.

"You," Mrs. Bennet said acidly, "will apologize to Mr. Collins and accept his proposal *immediately*."

Oliver pulled his shoulders back, holding Mrs. Bennet's gaze. "I *have* already apologized. But I won't accept his proposal. I made it very clear that I won't marry him, and I won't have a change of heart about it either. My mind is set."

"But you *must* marry him!" Mrs. Bennet exclaimed. "What are you *thinking* refusing a man of his status? A man set to inherit our home? How could you, Lizzy?!"

Oliver bit his lip. The nickname, while fine in his childhood, felt like a pair of ill-fitting shoes. An added discomfort on top of an already discomforting situation. "I must be a stranger to you entirely if you truly believe me capable of marrying *Mr. Collins*, of all people," he responded with a tremble in his voice. "I will not marry him, Mama. There is nothing you can say that will change my mind."

Mrs. Bennet threw her hands up. "How inconsequential my nerves must be to you! You cannot go on like this—if you refuse every man you meet, you will never marry at all!"

Oliver scoffed. "Rejecting *one* man is hardly dooming me to a life of loneliness."

Mrs. Bennet shook her head. "With the way you behave, you'll be lucky to ever see another proposal."

Oliver's mouth nearly fell open. With the way *he* behaved? He wasn't sure whether to laugh or cry—as far as he was concerned, he behaved perfectly well in front of his mother. She didn't even know about his nightly outings, his name, his— anything! And she *already* thought him so improper as to be destined for loneliness?

It would have hurt less if she'd slapped him across the face.

Mrs. Bennet turned to Mr. Bennet, who, until now, had been sitting quietly in his favorite chair with a steadily deepening frown. "Tell her, Mr. Bennet," she demanded. "She must marry Mr. Collins." She turned back to Oliver, her face red. "Why, if you refuse I shall never speak to you again!"

Oliver could barely believe his ears. Did she really think it so impossible that any other man would want to marry him? *She thinks it impossible already and she doesn't even know how much more complicated it is than she believes.*

It was a harrowing thought, but in the end it didn't change anything. Oliver didn't want to be alone, but if the choice was between being someone's wife and being alone, it wasn't really a question at all. It wasn't ideal, but Oliver had never minded his own company.

Now with the eyes of the entire family on his father, Mr. Bennet sighed and met Oliver's gaze. *Please*, Oliver pleaded with his gaze. *Don't force me to do this.* Mr. Bennet couldn't read his mind, of course, but something softened in his face nevertheless.

"I'm afraid an unfortunate ultimatum is before you," Mr. Bennet declared. "Going forward, your relationship with one of your parents will never be the same. Your mother will never speak to you again if you do not marry Mr. Collins, and I will never speak to you again if you do."

Oliver blinked. Did he just say . . . ?

Mrs. Bennet gasped. "Mr. Bennet! How could you? Does *anyone* in this family care for my poor nerves?" With that, she stormed out of the room, and as the door closed behind her, Oliver smiled.

With three quick steps he crossed the room and threw his arms around his father. "Thank you," Oliver said into his shoulder. "Thank you, thank you, thank you."

Mr. Bennet chuckled softly and patted Oliver's back. "You

know that all I care for is your happiness. I'll never force you to marry anyone you don't want to marry—even if it means you never marry at all."

Oliver closed his eyes, and though his cheeks were wet with tears, he smiled.

CHAPTER 15

"AND THE ENTIRE TIME HE WAS PROPOSING, HE SPOKE TO ME AS though my opinion on the matter was irrelevant!"

Charlotte frowned as she sipped her steaming cup of tea. As Oliver completed his recollection of the disastrous proposal earlier that morning, only the whistle of a spoon scraping porcelain filled the air as Lu stirred a sugar cube into her tea, her face devoid of the surprise he'd expected.

"How did Mrs. Bennet react?" Charlotte asked diplomatically.

Oliver groaned and slumped back into his seat, running his hand over his flattened chest for comfort. The backs of the wooden chair dug into his spine and he grimaced, sitting up. "She was furious, of course. Demanded that I apologize to Mr. Collins and accept his proposal, but when I refused, Father supported my decision in no uncertain terms, so she let it go." He paused. "Well, she stopped insisting, at any rate. She's still incensed."

"She'll forgive you over time," Lu said.

"She will," Oliver agreed, "but it doesn't sit right with me that I should be punished for refusing to marry a man guaranteed to make the rest of my life miserable."

Charlotte placed her teacup down on a nearby side table, her laced white boots digging into the green rug beneath them. "She's only concerned for your future," she said. "She wants you to marry so that you'll be secure financially when your father eventually passes."

"I'd rather be destitute than married to a man like Collins," Oliver grumbled.

Charlotte sighed. She looked at Lu, who lifted a shoulder in answer to an unspoken question.

"What is it?" Oliver asked.

With a slight nod, Charlotte turned back to Oliver. "You realize that if Collins asked me today to marry him I would accept without hesitation."

Oliver balked. "You would agree to marry *Collins*?"

Charlotte smiled softly. "He's a dull man, and rather full of himself, that's true. But he isn't cruel, and he has the capital to support himself and a family. It's a better situation than what's handed to many women."

"That may be so," Oliver agreed, "but you seem to be forgetting that I'm not a woman."

Charlotte grimaced and looked at Lu again, who met her gaze with raised eyebrows. "He's right on that point," Lu said.

"And I think it worth mentioning that you and I are fortunate, Charlotte, that we aren't put off by men the way some women who love women are."

"Yes, that's true," Charlotte said with another sigh, turning back to Oliver again. "You aren't a woman, Oliver. But your mother doesn't know that, and neither does Collins, nor most people."

Oliver shook his head, his gaze turning out the window to his left. It was a beautiful sunny day, and the streets below were full of horse-drawn carriages and people milling about. The cheeriness of the scene outside clashed with his dour mood, and Oliver pulled his gaze back to Charlotte and Lu, who were watching him with concern etched in their brows.

"I just don't believe any of us should have to accept circumstances that will stand in the way of our happiness," he said at last. "Including you, Charlotte."

"And in an ideal world where Lu and I were born into wealth, we wouldn't," Charlotte answered. "But the circumstances that have befallen us are quite different."

"Oliver," Lu jumped in. "Why do you think I chose to marry a man?"

Oliver hesitated. "Well, it . . . isn't possible for you to marry a woman."

Lu nodded. "That's true, but don't you think I would have preferred to remain unmarried and live with Charlotte permanently?"

Oliver nodded. Of course Lu and Charlotte would have been happiest that way. It wasn't even unheard of for two women to share a home without a man, though it was rare. But women who weren't born into wealth required a man for financial security and that, Oliver realized, was exactly Charlotte's point. The realization must have shown on his face, because Lu nodded.

"No one wants to deny themselves happiness, Oliver," she said. "But many of us have to choose a middle ground if we hope to survive."

She was right, Oliver knew. But marrying a man who would force him to pretend to be a woman, a *wife*, for the rest of his life didn't feel like survival at all.

———

"Oliver! Come swimming with me!"

Oliver's toes sank into cool mud as he stood at the edge of a large, placid lake. He'd removed his shirt already and stood in just his trousers with the sun warming his bare chest—flat from his clavicle down to his hips. The smooth expanse of his skin, like glazed ceramic, was so easy. Natural. His.

"Oliver!" The voice came from the lake, where Darcy was treading water. His long brown hair was dark and wet, his grin all but glistening in the light. He waved his arm over his head, water dripping down his forearm and over his bicep. "Come in! The water is so refreshing; you'll love it."

So, with a grin, he stripped off his trousers and leapt into the lake, his breath catching in his chest as the cool water enveloped him. He broke the surface with a laugh and swam toward Darcy, arms arcing overhead, feet kicking, chest rising and falling back into the water. He'd never swam like this—so easily, so carefree. It had never felt so natural to be in the water, to feel it kiss the bare skin of his flat chest. It was perfect. A dream.

He was dreaming.

Ahead, Darcy became blurred even as Oliver neared him. He blinked hard, clearing the water from his eyes. Darcy's face sharpened into focus, then slipped away again, like peering into a stranger's spectacles. Oliver swam harder, beating his legs faster, and he was *so close*, but Darcy was blurry and the water was luke-warm. He could barely feel it against his skin anymore. Even the strain in his legs faded, as the world around him became so blurred he could barely see anything at all. Oliver stopped, panting, treading water, squinting into an endless fog.

He couldn't see. Where had Darcy gone? Darkness was closing in on all sides, but he didn't want to wake up, he didn't want to wake up, he didn't want to—

Oliver sat up in bed, chest heaving. His hands leapt to his chest and the softness of his breasts curdled in his stomach like a glass of spoiled milk. The wrongness of it. His eyes burned with tears and he covered his mouth as a sob spilled out. The unfairness of it all twisted in his chest like a knife. It was so easy for most boys, so unthinkably simple.

Slowly, he lay back in bed, hugging his pillow to his chest and pressing his face against the fabric. Perhaps if he focused hard enough, he could place himself back in the dream, even if just for a few minutes. Those moments of standing at the shore, the sun's warmth spilling over his bared skin. His chest smooth, flat. He could imagine it. He replayed the moment, over and over, focusing on the easy relief of his body aligning with his soul.

It was with that careful concentration that he lay for some time on his tear-damp pillow, a small smile painted on his lips. Still, try as he might, he couldn't fall back to sleep.

He couldn't stop thinking about the freedom he'd felt in the dream, the euphoria of swimming without the burden of his chest. Of Darcy, calling his name and waving him over.

It ached, how badly he wanted it. But he couldn't begin to imagine how it would ever be possible to attain.

Oliver didn't have a large chest, a fact for which he was extremely grateful as it made it much easier to use his chest flattener. But without the constricting fabric reshaping his body, he wasn't flat. Even now, lying in the dark with only the light of the moon sweeping in through the window, he could see it beneath the blanket, the small hill that formed a pit in his stomach every time he looked at it.

Most of the time, he just tried *not* to look at it.

But the dream had broken through his fragile resolve, like a hand brushing away spider's silk.

Oliver knew what he needed, and he wasn't going to get it lying awake in bed. He slipped out from beneath his bedsheets with practiced ease, placing his bare feet on the not-creaky spot of the floorboards. Across the small room, Jane was fast asleep in her own bed. While his sister never protested when he woke her up sneaking out—or back in—in the dead of night, he still tried to be as quiet as possible as he lowered to his knees. Ducking his head, he peered beneath his bed, lifted the trunk hidden there, and carefully pulled it out and placed it on top of the bed.

The trunk was locked, but even in the dark Oliver hurried through grabbing the key tucked beneath his mattress and slipping it into the keyhole with ease. Once open, he pulled out a pair of carefully folded trousers, his chest flattener, a shirt, waistcoat, cravat, hat, and an overcoat. He dressed quickly, the tension in his muscles easing as he tightened the flattener around his ribs, pushing his chest into the proper shape. He worked fluidly in the dark: buttoning his white linen shirt, tucking his tight-fitting trousers into his Wellington boots, getting his deep-green cravat just right, buttoning his black double-breasted waistcoat, tying his hair into a tight, high bun and hiding it beneath the hat, and finally donning his coat—an elegant thing with a cutaway front and long tails behind.

Then, at last, he was ready.

There were few places still open this late. But Avery's Tavern certainly was.

When Lu had first pointed out the Molly House to him, the thought of attending had been exciting. But now that he was standing outside the unassuming tavern, his gut curled nervously. How did this work, exactly? Maybe this was a bad idea. He could still turn around and go home . . . but then what? Lie awake in bed for several more hours, regretting his decision not to even try to enter?

No, that wouldn't do. He would go in, even if just for a few minutes. Just to see what it was like.

Biting his lip, Oliver pulled his shoulders back and entered the tavern.

If Oliver didn't know this tavern housed a secret Molly House, he never would have guessed it. It looked rather like every other tavern he'd ever entered—dimly lit with gas lamps, a long bar counter at the back of the room with a rack of alcohol behind the bartender, some tables and chairs scattered about, and relatively muted conversation for the surprisingly full room. Oliver wove his way through the crowd, heart slowly climbing into his throat as he approached the bar.

The bartender looked up at him and smiled. He was handsome. Distractingly handsome, really, with dimples and a sharp jawline and a corded neck—

"What can I get you?" the bartender asked with that broad, dimple-marked smile.

And now he had a decision. This was his last chance to back out. He could order an ale and leave. Or just return home now.

But he'd be kicking himself if he didn't try, so he leaned forward and lowered his voice.

"I'm . . . looking for the coffeehouse?" Oliver's voice broke slightly at the question, and he winced. But the bartender didn't seem to notice, or if he noticed he didn't care. Instead, his smile somehow grew even wider.

"First time?" he asked softly, and heat crept up Oliver's neck. Was it really so obvious?

Oliver laughed slightly and smiled apologetically. "Yes."

"Not to worry," the bartender responded cheerfully. "You'll have a great time. Head to the left side of the room, where you'll find the stairs up to the lodging rooms. The one you're looking for is at the very top, the last door on the right. Knock three times and ask for a coffee."

It was all so clandestine, which, oddly, crowded some of his anxiety with excitement. He thanked the bartender, then followed his instructions, through the oblivious crowd, up the creaky stairs, down an even creakier hallway and to the last door on the right. Soft, unintelligible murmurs of voices leaked from beneath the door. Oliver swallowed hard, ignoring the way his heart all but pummeled his ribs, and knocked three times.

The door opened almost immediately. A reedy young man stood in the entryway, peering down at Oliver through half-moon spectacles.

"Um," Oliver stammered. "Could I, um, have a cup of coffee, please?"

The man grinned. "Please, eh? How polite."

Oliver wasn't sure what to say to that, but he didn't have to come up with a response because the man laughed and opened the door wider, stepping out of the way. Oliver entered, stuffing his trembling hands into his pockets.

The room was larger than he expected—and lit better than the tavern below. About two dozen people milled about the room—some in lavish dress and others in more casual attire. Oliver spotted two girls wearing trousers and button-down shirts in the back corner of the room, speaking with their faces very close to each other. A few boys and androgynous teenagers sat at a table in the center, playing a game of cards. And sitting just ten feet away on a comfortable-looking green sofa, reading a book was—

Oliver's mouth dropped open. "Darcy?"

Darcy's head jerked up, eyes wide before their gazes met. He arched an eyebrow, then slowly his face relaxed into a hesitant smile. "Oliver! I've . . . never seen you here before."

Oliver sat on the sofa next to him, his anxiety melting away like snow in the spring. "It's my first time. Do you come here often?"

Darcy hesitated. "Not . . . *often*. But I do enjoy the company here, when I can make the trip."

Those sitting at the card table broke into uproarious laughter. The air was full of happy chatter—Oliver had never seen so many smiling people in one place before. The buoyant mood of the room was infectious.

"I can see why. I'd been nervous about coming here, but I'm glad I did."

"I'm glad you did too," Darcy said without missing a beat. "I hadn't realized you . . ." He hesitated again.

"Fancy men?" Oliver supplied for him. "Yes, I do."

Darcy closed the book and placed it on a nearby side table. Oliver wasn't familiar with the title, *Dalliances of a Young Man.*

"I come here sometimes to read books that might be . . . frowned upon in larger society." Darcy gestured to a small white bookshelf Oliver hadn't noticed in the back of the room. The bookshelf was not very large, but it was absolutely packed—not only was every shelf full, but there were books stacked on top of one another and on top of the bookshelf as well. Most of the books seemed bound, but a number of them appeared to be unbound manuscripts as well.

Oliver's eyebrows raised. "All these books are for people like us?"

Darcy paused. "Probably half are. The other half are, erm . . . rather more explicit than the norm? In any case, most of them are from very small publishing houses or bound by hand."

"Ah." Still, Oliver hadn't even known there were any books for people like him at all, let alone enough to fill a whole bookshelf. Slowly, he turned back to Darcy with a wry smile. "So you come here to read?"

"Mostly." Darcy's cheeks pinked and he smiled sheepishly. "Does that surprise you?"

He almost said yes, but then he remembered Darcy's behavior at Netherfield, and of course at the Temple of Muses. Between the two, he'd almost always had a book in hand whenever Oliver had seen him, so maybe it wasn't so surprising after all.

"Come to think of it," he responded, "it suits your character. So maybe not a surprise, but it *is* endearing."

Darcy's smile turned to a grin. "Can't say there are many who would agree with you on that front, but I'm pleased that you are. You should look at the shelf—some of the books are actually quite good."

"Any recommendations?"

And that was how Oliver was drawn into a lengthy conversation on books about men who fancy men, women who fancy women, people who are neither a man nor a woman, and, to Oliver's true shock, even a couple books about boys who were mistaken for girls and the other way around. (That Darcy recommended *those* books to Oliver filled him with a fuzzy lightness, if only because it meant Darcy knew boys like him existed.) They were titles that Oliver absolutely could not bring home—he didn't want to even begin to imagine how Mrs. Bennet might react if she ever caught him with one—but now he certainly had to return as many times as necessary so that he could read them.

Darcy had just pointed out six books that Oliver would absolutely come back to read, when someone sat at the pianoforte on the opposite side of the room and began to play a waltz. Darcy's eyes lit up and he grinned at Oliver.

"Would you care to join me for a dance?" he asked, his eyes gleaming and hand outstretched.

Oliver blinked. Dance with Darcy? Dance with Darcy *as himself*? He'd never imagined it possible, but pairs of people of all genders had already begun dancing. It was safe here, Oliver realized, to completely be himself.

And unlike every other dance Oliver had seen Darcy at, the other boy looked genuinely happy at the prospect of dancing with him.

So, Oliver found himself grinning back. "Why, Darcy, I thought you'd never ask."

When Oliver took Darcy's hand, a shock ran down his arm like lightning to his nerves. Darcy's hand was warm, soft, dry. It enveloped his easily, and Oliver followed the other boy to the center of the room feeling as though he were floating. By the time they reached the area where others were dancing, Oliver felt as though he were in a daze. Dreaming.

And then Darcy took his waist with one hand and his hand with the other, and he *had* to be dreaming, didn't he? How was he actually here, fully himself, dancing with *Darcy*, of all people? His entire body felt as though it were vibrating—he was impossibly aware of his entire being, of his closeness to Darcy, of the warmth emanating from his dancing partner.

They were two boys dancing together for all in the room to see, and Oliver had never felt happier.

"And here I thought you didn't like to dance," Oliver said with a breathy laugh.

Darcy arched an eyebrow. "What made you think that?"

Oliver's heart froze in his chest. Had he and Darcy never spoken about dancing before when he was himself? "Bingley mentioned it," he answered smoothly, even as his pulse pounded in his ears.

"Ah." Darcy laughed, and the tenseness in Oliver's shoulders melted away. "Well, Bingley's right that I don't generally enjoy dances, but that's because it's generally frowned upon for boys to dance together."

Oliver found himself laughing. In hindsight, it all made perfect sense. Darcy's sour mood at the Meryton Ball took on a new light—of course he was unhappy. He was in a space where he had to pretend to be someone he wasn't. Where he had to flirt with a future that would never—could never—make him happy. Even his *not handsome enough* comment, rude as it was, took on a new meaning. Of course "handsome" was used to refer to men, women, and everyone else alike, but Darcy had been thinking of a man when he'd said it.

"Is that really so funny?" Darcy asked with a confused smile.

"What's funny," Oliver responded, "is that now all those rumors of your infamously sour mood at a variety of balls make perfect sense."

"Ah." Darcy's face went pink. "Is it really so infamous?"

"I'm afraid so." Oliver smiled, but softly. Darcy's hand tightened ever so slightly at his waist, and Oliver squeezed his hand gently in response. "From what I can tell, though, no one important suspects why."

"I should hope not," Darcy grumbled. "I certainly put enough effort in keeping this side of myself private." Oliver's smile faded. Darcy frowned in response. "What is it?"

Oliver shook his head. "It's nothing. I just . . . I wish we didn't have to hide. Can you imagine what it would be like, dancing together like this at a public ball?"

The corners of Darcy's lips quirked up. "I imagine I would be far too terrified to enjoy it."

"But if it were allowed," Oliver pressed. "If we were in a society where our dancing together wasn't frowned upon, where it was accepted. Unextraordinary."

"I can't imagine," Darcy said, "that you could ever be unextraordinary."

Oliver's breath caught in his chest. Warmth crept up his neck and into his face, and it occurred to him all at once just how close his face was to Darcy's. The other boy's eyes were dark and so full of warmth. And his lips—they looked so soft. Darcy's breath was warm on his skin, and all it would take was for Oliver to lean forward. To close the gap.

It would be so easy.

"Oliver," Darcy whispered, his breath hot on Oliver's mouth.

He swallowed hard. "Yes?"

"I very much want to kiss you."

Oliver shivered. His heart was pounding so loudly in his ears that he could barely hear his own breath. "Then I think," he said, his voice trembling, "you should kiss me."

And so he did.

Darcy's mouth was every bit as soft as he'd imagined. His lips brushed featherlight against Oliver's, a taste at first, then again with slightly more pressure. Kissing Darcy was like sitting in the sun on a perfectly temperate day, eating a fresh plate of strawberries dipped in sugar. Kissing Darcy was like jumping off a cliff into a pool of refreshingly cool water. Kissing Darcy was like sinking into the warmth of his favorite blanket in front of a fire. Kissing Darcy was like drinking mulled hot apple cider, the steam making his face flush as the hot, spiced liquid warmed him from the inside out.

Kissing Darcy was everything.

It was only when they broke apart that Oliver realized the song had ended. Couples were breaking apart, but no one seemed to notice—or mind—the two boys kissing in the center of the room. Oliver stared at Darcy, wide-eyed, his mouth still tingling with the echo of Darcy's lips.

"Wow," Oliver whispered.

And then Darcy released him and took a step back. His expression was closed off—something had shifted in his gaze. The warmth he'd seen there just moments prior was gone, replaced with something unreadable.

"I'm sorry," Darcy said stiffly. "I don't know what I was— something came over me. I should go."

Oliver blinked. The shift in Darcy's mood couldn't have been more shocking if he'd dumped a bucket of ice water on Oliver's head. "Darcy—"

But Oliver couldn't finish because the other boy turned away, grabbed his coat, and rushed out of the room, leaving Oliver alone in the middle of the dance floor.

CHAPTER 16

Oliver woke bleary-eyed in the late morning light the next day with a renewed determination and sense of self. After washing his face and dressing, he bounded down the stairs, shoulders pulled back and a stubborn smile set upon his face.

It was Mary who saw him first. She looked up from the pianoforte she was already plunking away at. Her eyes widened at the sight of him, and she stumbled on the scales she was playing. Oliver forced his smile to remain as he strode confidently past her and into the dining room.

He'd woken late, so most everyone had eaten already, but Mr. Bennet was still at the table, reading the paper. Unfortunately, Mrs. Bennet was also present. *Maybe*, Oliver thought, *it's actually fortunate. Now I'll get the worst part over with.*

Mrs. Bennet was drinking tea. When her gaze fell upon Oliver, she dropped her teacup, which hit the edge of the table and tumbled over onto the floor with an overdramatic crash. Oliver startled at the sound, his smile faltering. Mr. Bennet's head snapped up, but his gaze was set on the shattered teacup now on the floor in a thin puddle of tea. Having determined the source of the noise, his gaze rose to Mrs. Bennet, who was still staring at Oliver, color leaching from her cheeks. At last, he followed her gaze to Oliver—and merely arched an eyebrow.

"What," Mrs. Bennet said in a tremulous warble, "are you wearing?"

"Trousers, of course," Oliver responded cheerily. He'd paired the trousers with a linen shirt, and though he'd wanted to wear his chest flattener, he'd opted to skip it if only to avoid uncomfortable questions from Mrs. Bennet. He mildly regretted that decision and mostly tried to avoid looking down at his chest as a result. "Is anyone going to clean up that tea? I can fetch a broom and washcloth if—"

"And *why*," Mrs. Bennet interrupted, "are you wearing trousers?"

Though Oliver's heart was drumming against his chest wildly and his palms were damp with anxiety, he kept his tone light. "Because I want to. They're quite comfortable actually. I see no reason why I shouldn't dress the way I wish in the comfort of my own home."

Mrs. Bennet's face reddened so deeply Oliver was momentarily concerned she might burst a vessel. She opened her mouth in likely protest, but Mr. Bennet lowered his newspaper and peered at Oliver over the edge of his spectacles.

"I think you look quite fetching," he said with perfect calm. He met Oliver's gaze with warmth and his lips twitched into a small smile.

Oliver couldn't help but smile back. The realization that Mr. Bennet was really *seeing* him, that he saw his son beneath the misleading exterior, would never grow old. It filled him with warmth and energy that began in the center of his chest and spread to his extremities.

"Mr. Bennet!" Mrs. Bennet exclaimed, her hand flying up to her forehead. "Do you have any care for my nerves at all? How could you encourage her like this? The impropriety—"

"Oh please," Mr. Bennet interrupted. "We're home. I think we can allow our children to dress in the way most comfortable to them within the safety of our home, don't you think?" He lifted his newspaper again, making it all too clear his question was rhetorical and the conversation was over.

Mrs. Bennet looked furious, but she wouldn't contradict her husband. Honestly, Oliver could hardly believe how well this had gone—he'd expected much worse. Arguing certainly. Begging, maybe. But none of that was needed—Mr. Bennet had made his approval clear, ending any argument before it began.

It was impossible for Oliver to hide his smile as he sat at the table and grabbed a roll from the bread basket. As he bit into the soft bread, he found himself thinking maybe being himself wouldn't be so difficult after all.

<hr />

Two days passed in relative quiet. The Bennets all adjusted to Oliver's new style at home rather quickly—save for Mrs. Bennet, who still shot him silent, unapproving glares, but Oliver found it relatively easy to ignore. It was easier to ignore than the discomfort of wearing dresses and skirts at least, and for that Oliver chose to deal with her disapproval.

Oliver was chatting with Jane in the living area, their voices barely audible over Mary practicing the pianoforte, when Mrs. Bennet entered the room looking very severe indeed. Her lips were pinched, her face taut. Oliver frowned, his voice trailing off in mid-sentence as Mrs. Bennet cleared her throat and placed her hand on the pianoforte.

"Mary, dear, if you could pause for a moment."

Mary frowned but stopped playing as requested.

"Is something the matter, Mama?" Jane asked.

"I'm afraid I've just received terrible news," Mrs. Bennet responded somberly. "The Bingleys and Mr. Darcy have departed from Netherfield, and it does not appear they intend to return."

The silence that fell over the room was heavy. Even Kitty and Lydia, who had been giggling in the corner, went quiet. The Bingleys and Darcy left? But why? Oliver had seen Darcy just a few nights ago, and he hadn't mentioned—

Unless.

Oliver's stomach swooped. Could Darcy have left *because of him*?

"I don't understand," Jane said carefully. "Why would they leave without saying goodbye? Are you quite sure they don't intend to return? Perhaps they're just off visiting somewhere."

Mrs. Bennet's face softened. "I'm afraid not, my dear. Mrs. Daley spoke to Mrs. Hughes, who heard from Mrs. Morris that the Bingleys have opted not to renew the lease. Bingley mentioned to the landowner that they were returning to the countryside for some time."

Oliver's head swam, the room rocking in dizzying waves. Had he scared Darcy away by kissing him? Darcy had initiated it and *kissed him back*—but then he'd left so abruptly that night, and now more abruptly still. But why? The connection between them had been clear; their conversation flowed so easily. Oliver had never seen Darcy so animated as he'd been that night, crouched in front of the bookcase, pitching Oliver his favorite books. And the kiss—it had been so tender. Sweet, even. So why was he running away?

And even if that night *was* the reason Darcy had taken off, why would Bingley leave as well? He couldn't begin to fathom an explanation, but he couldn't shake the feeling that this was, somehow, his fault.

"I see," Jane said softly, and though she remained composed, the heartbreak in her face was all too clear.

It didn't make any sense. Bingley had courted Jane repeatedly. They were all so sure that the two of them were soon to be engaged. And Oliver had seen the way Bingley looked at Jane, as if she were the only star in the vast expanse of the night sky.

So why would he just leave?

When Oliver arrived at Charlotte's to change into his full

ensemble, his friend stopped him from immediately going to her room to switch his outfit.

"Actually," she said, gently touching his arm. "There's something I need to speak to you about first."

Oliver frowned. "Can I change my clothes before we do?"

"I . . . think it'd be best if we spoke first."

That couldn't be good.

His frown deepening, Oliver followed Charlotte down the hall and into the sitting area. There, she had a steaming teakettle on the small table, with two teacups set out on saucers, one on either side. Oliver's stomach knotted as he sat in a lounging chair, flattening his skirts beneath his palms, feeling absurdly like a child about to be reprimanded.

Charlotte poured tea for each of them, only the hush of hot water filling porcelain breaking the tense quiet. It seemed Lu wasn't around this time, and Oliver realized it'd been a little while since he'd spent time with his friend alone. Maybe Charlotte wanted to take the opportunity to speak with him privately. But of course, if this was just a casual discussion, why insist on having it before he changed?

Oliver couldn't take the uncertainty anymore. "Is something wrong?" he asked. "Are you all right?"

"Oh!" Charlotte blinked and looked at him, wide-eyed, as if it hadn't occurred to her that he might interpret this strangeness with foreboding. "I'm perfectly all right and nothing's the matter—I apologize for worrying you. I actually have some happy news to share." She smiled and offered Oliver one of the steaming teacups. He took it gratefully and placed it on a small side table to cool, his shoulders relaxing a little.

"Well, that's a relief," he said with a small laugh. "I was beginning to think you were about to tell me someone had died."

"No! Not at all." Charlotte sat in the chair opposite him and pulled her shoulders back, her face splitting into a grin. "I'm excited to share that I'll soon be getting married."

Oliver blinked. "Married?"

"Yes!"

Charlotte seemed to be happy about this, so Oliver pushed his own feelings about marriage aside and forced himself to smile. This was, after all, what Charlotte had told him she'd wanted—or perhaps needed, in any case. Though Oliver hadn't expected it so soon, if his friend was happy, then it was his duty to share in her happiness.

"Congratulations! To whom?"

At this, Charlotte's smile faltered. She laughed a little, perhaps nervously, and said, "Well, that's the part that may come as a surprise . . . It certainly was to me."

Oliver arched an eyebrow. "Do I know the fortunate individual?"

"You do." Charlotte took a deep breath, then sighed, her shoulders relaxing. "Well, I suppose I might as well say it. I'm engaged to marry Mr. Collins."

Oliver, who had just taken a sip of hot tea, choked. He

coughed hard, lowering his cup to the table as Charlotte leapt to her feet in alarm.

"Oliver! Are you all right?"

Oliver nodded, red-faced and eyes watering as he caught his breath and tried to process what she'd just said. "*Collins?*" he rasped. "As in, the man who proposed to me *a few days ago?*"

Charlotte winced. "The very one. I didn't think you'd be upset, as you'd made your feelings clear about the man, so I hope you don't consider it a betrayal of our friendship."

"I—no, of course not, but . . ." Oliver's mind reeled. Charlotte had agreed to marry Collins. *Collins!* And she was happy about it! Part of him felt foolish for being so surprised—after all, hadn't she directly told him if Collins asked her she would accept? But it had never occurred to him that it was actually a possibility.

"Doesn't it bother you that he's treating you like a consolation prize?" Oliver finally asked.

Charlotte frowned. "I don't see it that way."

"But he asked *me* a few days ago and *I* was a consolation prize."

"And how well do you know him?"

Oliver grimaced. "I barely know him at all. We danced once and had a couple unpleasant conversations."

Charlotte nodded. "Then I know him as well as you do. It doesn't bother me that he asked you first, Oliver, because you were the logical choice. As he's going to take over Longbourn,

182

it made sense that he'd try to keep it within the family. But you rejected him, and we'd had a lovely conversation at the Netherfield Ball, and again two days ago when he visited. So when he asked me yesterday, of course I said yes."

"But—Charlotte, you could do so much better!"

His friend looked at him pointedly. "I could also do much worse. I told you this is what I want, Oliver. Marrying a respectable man who will care for me while I continue my friendship with Lu is the best I could ask for."

"But you aren't *friends* with Lu!" Oliver protested. "How will you ever be happy pretending to love someone you never could? You're *in love with Lu*, not Collins!"

"But I can't marry Lu, can I?!" Charlotte cried. Oliver's mouth snapped closed as his friend wiped at her glassy eyes. He'd never seen Charlotte cry before, and he'd certainly never imagined the first time would be because of him.

"Of course I would marry Lu if I could, Oliver, but it's impossible!" she went on. "And even without marriage—which, by the way, would be crushing to me in and of itself—we'd never survive on our own. I can't—" Her voice tightened with emotion, tears spilling down her cheeks. "I can't live in a fantasy that will never happen. It's time to grow up. *This* is the best I could possibly hope for."

Oliver was frozen, his friend's pain blazing hot in his chest, mingling with his own. It wasn't until he tried to speak that he realized his own voice was strangled with the tears he was fighting to keep at bay. "I can't accept that," he said. "I refuse to settle for a future that will deny me the happiness I deserve—the happiness we *both* deserve."

"Then don't," Charlotte said, her voice frosting over. "But if it never comes to pass, don't say I didn't warn you."

CHAPTER 17

Oliver kicked a rock down the footway as he strode back home. London was well and truly awake now, the air full of the rattle of horse-drawn carriages and the murmur of conversations constant as people passed him by. Though the sun was bright and the spring breeze pleasant, it did little to buoy Oliver's stormy mood.

He'd never before gone to Charlotte's with the intention of changing into his boy clothes and *not* done just that. The missed opportunity compounded with his argument with Charlotte left him with a sour taste in his mouth.

Before he'd left, Charlotte explained that she'd be moving to Hunsford with Collins immediately after the wedding, and that Lu would take Oliver's clothes in her stead. Lu lived a walkable distance as well—though it tacked an extra ten minutes to his already fifteen-minute walk—so that wasn't a problem, but Oliver would have to learn an entirely new schedule to dodge her husband. And what would happen if she ever had children?

He shook his head with a sigh. He supposed that didn't matter—at least, not right now.

Oliver turned the corner onto the pathway up to the town house he called home. Now with Collins gone and without any other impending guests, at least Oliver could relax at Longbourn, even if not in the way he'd wanted to.

Stepping past the small garden out front where bees hovered over the flower bushes, Oliver walked up to the front door and let himself in. He nearly walked directly into Mr. Bennet.

His father's eyebrows rose as he stopped in his tracks. "That was a quick outing. Is everything all right?"

Oliver opened and closed his mouth. In truth, nothing was *wrong*—in fact, he should be happy for Charlotte. *She* seemed happy about it, even if Oliver couldn't fathom why. But he didn't want to speak the reality aloud. If he didn't mention it, then at the very least it would delay Mrs. Bennet learning the news. It was inevitable that she would hear about Charlotte's engagement, of course, but once she did . . . Oliver grimaced.

Best not to think about it for as long as possible.

"I'd prefer not to discuss it," he finally said.

Mr. Bennet frowned but didn't push the matter further.

———

A month passed in relative quiet before Jane departed Longbourn to visit their aunt and uncle at Gracechurch in the countryside. They had extended the invitation to help Jane escape the stresses city life had brought upon her, but Oliver suspected Jane accepted at least in part because of their proximity to Pemberly, where the Darcys resided and the Bingleys were sure to frequent given the nearness of their own estate.

It was a long shot, hoping Jane might cross paths with the Bingleys while visiting, but Oliver supposed it was better than staying home and knowing they'd certainly *never* cross paths in London.

Jane hadn't shed a single tear, but Oliver knew she was hurting. How couldn't she be? Whether she'd admitted it aloud or not, there wasn't any question that she'd developed feelings for Bingley. For him to up and leave like that . . .

Well. Oliver could imagine exactly how it felt, because his own heart was still smarting from Darcy's sudden departure.

He'd pored over the question of why for weeks. He'd all but convinced himself that Darcy's departure was a direct result of their kiss that night. After spending a full week wallowing in self-pity, Oliver decided a better course was to acknowledge the cowardice of such a move. Darcy had kissed Oliver. Several times, no less. He'd held Oliver's face in his soft, soft hands and kissed him, open-mouthed, for several minutes.

There wasn't any question as to whether Darcy had actually wanted to kiss Oliver—he'd even said so. *I very much want to kiss you.* But when he'd pulled away, the fear that iced over his face was clear. Darcy was running, Oliver surmised, from his own feelings. He'd realized just what it meant that night to kiss another boy, and it had scared him.

The fear was understandable, excusable even.

The cowardice of running without so much as acknowledging what had happened between them was not.

Jane's departure meant the morning was a whirlwind of packing, prepping the coach, and eating, so that when she did leave, the quiet afterward felt deafening in comparison. Oliver poured himself a second cup of tea as he sank into a chair, intent on actually enjoying his cup while it was hot this time without Jane's preparations to distract him. Though it felt somewhat odd to sit at the empty dining table scattered with mostly eaten scones and emptied mugs, the solitude was also nice, in a way. It was a rare thing to come by at Longbourn, and Oliver wouldn't squander it.

Or at least, he wouldn't have if Mrs. Bennet hadn't burst into the room with all the grace of a deer running on ice. "Oh!" she exclaimed. "*There* you are! I was looking everywhere for you!"

Oliver smiled softly, careful to hide the disappointment from his face. "You found me."

"I have the most excellent news," Mrs. Bennet proclaimed, resting her hands on the table as she beamed. Oliver wasn't sure what it said about him that his mother's unabashed happiness filled him with the deepest suspicion.

"All right," he said carefully, lowering his mug to the saucer with a clink.

"Mr. Wickham has asked to come by this morning and requested the honor of your attention! It seems he'd like to become better acquainted with you, so of course I accepted. He'll be arriving within the hour."

Oliver's mouth dropped open. "What?"

"Yes, isn't it wonderful? Of course, this means you must dress immediately. You certainly can't be seen wearing *that*." She gestured to his trousers and shirt with a grimace, leaving Oliver cold. She was right, of course, but the weeks that he'd been dressing *mostly* as himself at home had been so freeing. Forcing himself into a dress now was an unwanted regression that filled his stomach with sand.

It's only temporary, he reminded himself. *Once Wickham leaves, you can change back into your trousers and shirt.*

Grimacing, Oliver stood as Mrs. Bennet hurried him out of the room and up the stairs to change.

So much for enjoying his cup of tea.

Wickham arrived at eleven o'clock on the dot.

After the usual harried introductions, Mrs. Bennet went off to fetch some tea and biscuits, while Oliver and Wickham sat in the sitting room. Wickham took his place on the settee next to a low table in the center of the room. Perhaps he expected Oliver to sit next to him, as the settee certainly had more than sufficient room for two, but Oliver did nothing of the sort. Instead, he sat in the single chair opposite him. With the table serving as a barrier, it was the most space he could place between them without being rude.

"I thank you for your attention, Miss Bennet," Wickham said with a handsome smile. "After my last visit at Longbourn, I realized I'd never really had the opportunity to become better acquainted with you that evening. Now that Collins has returned to Hunsford, I thought it a good opportunity to remedy that."

Oliver clenched his jaw. He thought he'd made his disinterest in the other boy clear at the Netherfield Ball, but it seemed Wickham was more persistent than Oliver had given him credit for. "I see," he said, forcing himself to smile.

"May I add, you really look so handsome in that dress. The shape and color are very flattering to your feminine nature."

Oliver wanted to scream. This right here was his nightmare. Oliver couldn't bring himself to thank the boy for the comment that felt like rubbing his face against a grater, so instead he forced himself to maintain his tight-lipped smile.

Wickham, evidently oblivious to Oliver's discomfort, pushed on ahead. "I've heard that several of your close acquaintances have become engaged—or are expected to be soon—as of late."

Oliver frowned. Wickham knew about Jane, of course—he'd been there at the dinner with Collins where Mrs. Bennet shared the expected news about Bingley and her eldest daughter. But that had fallen apart, apparently. The only other person Oliver knew who'd become engaged was Charlotte, but Wickham didn't know Charlotte, not really. So had he heard from Collins, then?

And if so, had he *also* heard that Oliver had rejected Collins's proposal first?

"Not a great many," Oliver said in response.

"Nevertheless, I imagine it has brought your prospects to mind as well."

Oliver looked at Wickham appraisingly. The blond boy was handsome—that was undeniable. Oliver imagined in another world, one in which he really was a girl—and Wickham wasn't spreading rumors about people's private lives—Oliver may have found himself attracted to him. But that wasn't the world he lived in. In this reality, while the physical attraction was there, it was dulled by the memory of Wickham's cruel gossip. That the other boy leered at his chest and drew attention to Oliver's so-called *feminine nature* made any chance of attraction that was left wither before it could bloom.

Charlotte and Jane would most likely marry and become wives, and probably one day mothers, but though that was clearly the future Wickham envisioned for Oliver—the future that *most people* envisioned for Oliver—it wasn't one he could accept. It would destroy him, he was sure, if not physically then spiritually. And what kind of life could one have with a crushed soul?

But Wickham didn't know that. So maybe Oliver was being

too harsh. Maybe Wickham just needed to understand that what he wanted would never be possible with Oliver.

So, with a sigh, Oliver met Wickham's gaze and said, "You should know that I intend to never become someone's wife."

Wickham blinked, his face frozen for a moment in shock. Then he laughed. It wasn't a mere chuckle either, it was a full-body laugh that made Oliver's stomach curdle.

At that moment, Mrs. Bennet returned with a tray, a steaming teapot, and four saucers, two ceramic cups, a half loaf of bread, a ramekin of butter, and a butter knife. She placed the display on the low table between them, smiling as she turned to Wickham.

"It sounds as though this meeting is developing fortuitously," she said.

"Absolutely," Wickham responded with a grin. "Elizabeth just said something very funny."

Mrs. Bennet's eyebrows rose in surprise. "How wonderful! It's just occurred to me that I left the cheese and jam in the other room. I'll return shortly."

With that, she strode out and Wickham shook his head with a smile, his gaze settling back on Oliver as he ripped a piece off the loaf.

"It . . . wasn't a jest," Oliver said at last. "I won't do it."

"How old are you?" Wickham asked as he buttered his slice of bread.

Oliver frowned, uncertain what his age had to do with any-thing. "Seventeen."

Wickham nodded. "I may only be a couple years your elder,

but believe me when I tell you you'll outgrow such childish notions. Of course you'll marry, and of course you'll become a wife and, one day, a mother. It's the natural inclination of all females, yourself included."

Oliver stared at him incredulously. "I won't *outgrow* this, Mr. Wickham. It's central to who I am. I won't become anyone's wife, not ever."

But Wickham didn't seem bothered. He waved his hand, as if brushing away Oliver's concerns. "I'm certain you'll change your mind once you have a husband."

Oliver's eyes widened. "Once I—"

But Mrs. Bennet interrupted with a flourish as she placed a new tray full of sliced cheeses, cheese knives, and a small bowl of fig jam beside the bread tray. "There we are!" she said cheerily. "I must say, Mr. Wickham, Elizabeth and I are truly so happy to have you here."

Wickham smiled. "And I couldn't be happier to be here myself. Why, we're having a jolly good time, aren't we, Elizabeth?"

Oliver forced his mouth into a shell of a smile. He hoped it looked like a snarl.

"Ohhh Mr. Wickham, you're so handsome!" Kitty crooned.

Lydia fell into her sister's arms in a mock faint, her arm thrown over her forehead as she cried, "Won't you dance with me, Mr. Wickham?"

Oliver rolled his eyes. Of course, his younger sisters' teasing only worked under the assumption that Oliver *wanted* to be with Wickham, which he most certainly did not, so the whole performance rang false. Nevertheless, it hadn't stopped them from immediately jumping into false crooning over the blond boy the moment he'd left Longbourn.

"Clearly," Oliver said, "you two heard absolutely nothing of our conversation, or you'd know I'm not remotely interested in him in that way."

Kitty and Lydia looked at each other skeptically. Oliver wasn't sure why it was so difficult to believe that he was truly uninterested in the boy. Sure, he was handsome, but he was also arrogant. Although, he supposed arrogance, to some people, could be interpreted as a positive quality.

Unfortunately, Mrs. Bennet had walked into the sitting area the moment Oliver had declared his disinterest in Wickham. She stopped in her tracks, her face first pale, then reddening as she turned a heated stare onto Oliver.

"Elizabeth!" she admonished. "How could you say such a thing? Mr. Wickham is a handsome boy, of the appropriate age, and very well-mannered! What is there to dislike?"

Oliver froze, uncertainty tightening around his throat like a vise. He couldn't exactly explain to his mother that there were multiple things he disliked about Wickham—namely the way he treated Oliver not just like a girl, but an insipid one at that, and his lack of care for other people's reputations. He couldn't do that without giving himself—and Darcy—away. So he chose what he could say from the truth.

"He . . . doesn't value my opinion or intelligence," Oliver said carefully. "He treats me like a young girl in need of his guidance. It's infantilizing."

Mrs. Bennet tutted. "That's hardly reason to discount him, dear. Why, if you turn away every man who thinks himself superior to women, you'll find yourself a spinster. And we can't have *that*."

Oliver balked. "You're suggesting that I shouldn't expect a man who I'm considering as a husband to treat me with respect?"

"I'm *suggesting*," Mrs. Bennet said tersely, "that men have very different standings in society that cannot be ignored. Men *should* expect to guide their wives, and women should expect to defer to their husband's authority, even when it vexes them. It's the way of things."

Oliver grimaced. "Perhaps I'd prefer my future husband to treat me as an equal partner, rather than a child in need of *guidance*."

Mrs. Bennet shook her head, her face pinched. "You're suggesting that your future husband should treat you as a man, but that will never happen, Elizabeth. You are a young *woman*. It's long past time you behave like one."

Tears blurred Oliver's vision as he forced his gaze away from his mother, turning the room into blobs of green and brown.

I am not *a young woman*, he thought, the back of his throat aching with restrained emotion, *but even if I were I'd never want to be treated as an inferior*. And yet, that desire was incompatible with the society he'd been born into. What he wished for, what he *yearned* for, was to be seen as a boy—and one day, a man—by his future husband, and to be treated accordingly.

But sitting in a room with his giggling sisters and his terse mother, that wish felt like an impossible dream, and Oliver began to wonder, with a despair that made him feel hollow, if Charlotte was right about settling after all.

CHAPTER 18

LATER THAT AFTERNOON, OLIVER WALKED TO LU'S FEELING AS though he'd swallowed a bucket of rocks. It was well after noon, so unlike his usual morning walks, the city was alive around him. He passed countless others along the familiar route, breathing shallowly to avoid the unpleasant but familiar stench of horse manure. He passed rows of town houses and a street full of shops, all the while the prickling sensation of being watched grew on the back of his neck.

Slowing to a stop, Oliver glanced around with a frown. There were plenty of people about, of course, but no one was directly looking at him. People were busy with their own errands, some herding children, others laden with bags full of fresh produce. Oliver even spotted someone carrying several bolts of cloth.

But none of this explained why he felt like he was being watched.

Frowning, Oliver continued walking. He was only five minutes away from Lu's at this point, but he sped up his pace, just in case. And yet, despite the bustle around him and the familiar crowded streets, Oliver couldn't shake the feeling that someone was directly behind him, trailing his steps.

He carried this discomfort the rest of the way, ignoring the note of fear that trilled in the back of his mind. As he knocked on the front door to Lu's home, he looked back over his shoulder, almost certain he'd spot someone watching him from behind.

But no one was there, and as Lu opened the door with a smile, Oliver found himself feeling foolish for being afraid of his own shadow.

———

Once he was dressed appropriately, Oliver sat for tea with Lu.

Lu's home was larger than Charlotte's, and the seating area was twice the size of Charlotte's former bedroom. This wasn't really a surprise as Lu was married, and up until recently, Charlotte had been living on her father's meager salary. But it was strange, nevertheless, to be sitting dressed as a boy in a home that was entirely new to him.

The floor was a deep hardwood, still gleaming with fresh polish. Much of that was obscured, however, by the large blue rug patterned with various flowers. The fireplace to the left of Oliver was unlit, and daylight streamed in from the large window opposite him onto a beautiful black pianoforte.

"Do you play?" Oliver asked, nodding to the instrument.

"Oh, that old thing?" Lu snorted, waving her hand dismissively. "No. It's mostly an aspirational piece. Charlotte would play at times when she came to visit, though."

Oliver smiled. "I hope you aren't expecting *me* to play it, because you'll find yourself quickly disappointed."

Lu laughed. "No, of course not. Here." She poured him a steaming cup of tea, to go with the plain scone he'd already started picking at.

Lu's mention of Charlotte was meant to be casual, but Oliver felt as though it had sucked the life out of the room. Neither of them had spoken about her since her departure for Hunsford, and given how they'd left things, Oliver had preferred not to think of her at all. He wasn't *angry* at her, not really, but she'd certainly seemed cross with him at the conclusion of their last interaction. And given that her new husband was *Collins*, of all people, the pompous but awkward traditionalist . . . Oliver didn't really know what to think. He struggled to imagine *any* woman being happy with that man, but Charlotte seemed to believe otherwise.

He hoped she was right.

"Have you written to her?" Lu asked casually, stirring sugar into her tea.

Oliver shook his head. It'd been two weeks since Charlotte had married—and a month since their disagreement—and Oliver . . . didn't know what to think. He'd attended the wedding, of course, but it had been full of so many people he hadn't had the opportunity to speak to Charlotte, even if he'd wanted to. What did it say about Charlotte that she was happy to marry a man such as Collins? And what did it say about him that even now, two weeks later, he still couldn't find it in himself to be happy for his friend?

"I don't think she much wants to hear from me," he responded.

Lu arched an eyebrow. "What makes you say that?"

Oliver glanced at her, frowning. "Well . . . you know our last conversation wasn't . . . the most pleasant that we've had."

"I'm aware. But I don't see why that would make you think she wouldn't want to hear from you. You two have been friends for how long?"

Despite himself, Oliver's lip quirked into a small smile. Oliver and Charlotte had met when he was twelve years old, after her father became acquainted with Mr. Bennet. Mr. Bennet had invited Mr. Lewis to come by Longbourn for supper one evening, and the man had brought his only child, Charlotte. Despite the slight age gap, the two of them had hit it off instantly.

"Five years," Oliver answered.

"Five years," Lu repeated. "And you think because of one argument she never wants to hear from you again? Please. You know Charlotte better than that."

Oliver sipped his still-steaming tea. The hot liquid was a balm for the roiling emotions stewing in his chest. Lu was probably right. He supposed it wouldn't hurt to send a letter to congratulate Charlotte, even if his heart wasn't entirely in it.

"She's happy, you know." At this, Oliver met Lu's gaze. She watched him with knowing, kind eyes. "I visited her a few days after the wedding. Life as a married woman has come naturally to her, and Collins has been a kind and oblivious husband. You should visit with her and see for yourself."

Oliver frowned. "I don't know if that's such a good idea."

"Why not?"

Oliver's frown deepened. Lu knew what had happened between Collins and him. "What makes you think I would be welcome?"

Lu made an impatient sound. "Did you not just tell me you've been friends with Charlotte for five years?"

"Well, yes——"

"And are you not Collins's cousin?"

"His cousin who refused to marry him, yes."

"And did they not both invite you to their wedding?"

Oliver shifted in his seat. "They invited the family, not me personally."

"Please." Lu rolled her eyes. "Do you really believe Collins is still upset about your rejection now that he's happily married? If anything, he may even thank you—if you hadn't rejected him, he wouldn't have married Charlotte."

Oliver thought any gratitude from Collins at all, for any reason, was far-fetched, but he supposed Lu might be right about his cousin no longer being cross with him.

"I'm still not sure Charlotte would want to see me," Oliver hedged.

"She wants to see you," Lu responded without missing a beat. "She asked about you when I visited with her. Believe me when I tell you that she isn't upset with you."

Charlotte had asked about him? And so soon after their argument? Oliver found himself surprised but . . . perhaps he shouldn't be. Charlotte had never been the vindictive type.

"So?" Lu asked. "Will you visit her?"

"I'll . . . consider it."

Lu looked at him so incredulously Oliver couldn't help but laugh. "What? I said I'd consider it!"

"That's hardly sufficient," Lu said, but the corners of her lips were smiling.

Oliver groaned. "Has it occurred to you that perhaps I just really don't want to see my cousin?"

Lu arched an eyebrow. "So, that's it, then? You'll never see your friend again because you'd prefer to avoid your irritating cousin?"

If Charlotte hadn't been such a close friend, Oliver would have said yes. But he supposed Lu had a point. There was no way to uncouple his friend from his cousin, not anymore. So unless he planned to write Charlotte out of his life forever, he'd have to deal with Collins.

And if he was being honest with himself, no amount of arguing would change that Charlotte was, and always would be, his closest friend.

"Fine," Oliver grumbled with a huff. "I'll go visit her."

Lu's face brightened immediately. "Wonderful! Let's write her to let her know, shall we?"

CHAPTER 19

OLIVER ARRIVED AT HUNSFORD IN THE EVENING, THE EARLY SUM-mer night already cooling. The air smelled different out in the country—fresher, wilder. Oliver spent a moment just closing his eyes and listening to the utter quiet, the lack of carriage wheels and horses and the constant hum of movement and voices. He wasn't sure he'd ever want to live so far from the city and all of the amenities London provided, but this was undeniably nice.

"There you are!" Charlotte strode quickly down a stone pathway to the driveway, her face aglow. As soon as she reached him, she threw her arms around him and Oliver smiled, pulling her close. Charlotte had been married for less than a month. He hadn't realized how much he'd missed her presence.

"It's good to see you, Oliver," Charlotte whispered.

He smiled. "And you as well, dear friend."

"Ah! Miss Bennet, how wonderful to see you." Mr. Collins approached them with a genteel smile. "How was the carriage ride? Smooth, I hope? I insisted on giving the carriage a once-over before it departed to pick you up. The wheels are new and the axles greased, but I still wasn't entirely convinced we'd done quite enough—"

"The ride was very pleasant," Oliver interrupted, holding in a laugh.

"Excellent," Collins responded. "What did you think about the upholstery?"

After enduring further pleasantries with Collins and feigning interest in a conversation about the texture of the carriage seat fabric that went on for far longer than Oliver would have thought possible, Charlotte graciously interrupted to suggest they go inside before the bugs ate them alive. From there, Charlotte whisked Oliver away to the guest room where he'd be sleeping during his stay. As soon as the door closed behind them, Oliver sighed heavily.

"Thank you," he said with a small laugh.

Charlotte smiled with a giggle. "You seemed about ready to fall asleep mid-conversation, so I thought it a good time for a break."

"Had it gone on for much longer I may have seriously considered bursting my own eardrums." Oliver laughed and sat on the carefully made bed. The room was small but beautifully decorated. The walls were lilac, the floors freshly waxed, and a small white bookcase near the large curtained window was full of—Oliver squinted—Bibles?

He shook his head and looked back at his friend. She was

all smiles—Oliver had to admit, it'd been quite some time since he'd seen her looking so buoyant.

"You seem happy," he said. "I take it the life of a married woman is suiting you well?"

Charlotte grinned and sat beside him. "Oh Oliver, I love it. Hunsford is such a nice estate, and the countryside is so peaceful. It really does feel fulfilling, maintaining a household I can take pride in and accompanying Mr. Collins to social events. I know the two of you haven't historically gotten along perfectly, but he really is a sweet man, believe it or not."

"I'm glad to hear it," Oliver said, suppressing a shudder at the thought of being trapped in the same house as Collins forever. "You seem genuinely happy. That's all that matters, in the end. As long as he's treating you well, that is."

"He is," Charlotte reassured him. "I would tell you if I was unhappy, but I promise you everything is well. The financial security has lifted such a weight from my shoulders, and Lu visits often, for extended periods of time. Mr. Collins loves playing host and made it clear Lu is welcome to stay whenever she'd like, for however long she'd like. I feel so fortunate to be here in this position."

Oliver nodded. Sitting here, his dress skirts splayed out over his legs and his busk forcing him to sit upright, Oliver had the unpleasant sense of being a dressed chicken ready to be presented to a table of starving men. He wanted nothing to do with these clothes, with this life that Charlotte had fit herself into.

And he was glad for her, of course (and, selfishly, glad for himself, if only because it meant Collins had well and truly forgotten the notion of marrying him), but it left him feeling alien. This was the life everyone expected him to want, but he couldn't bear the thought of it.

Sighing, Oliver pulled his gaze away from his skirts and met Charlotte's eyes again. "I . . . *am* sorry, by the by. For upsetting you, when you told me about your engagement. You needed my support and I didn't provide it."

Charlotte's face softened. "Thank you. I apologize as well. I shouldn't have implied that you'll never find happiness if you don't compromise who you are. I hope it won't come between us in the future."

"Never," Oliver responded, tension melting off him. Charlotte squeezed his hand, and Oliver squeezed back.

"Oh!" His friend stood and crossed the room to a small writing desk pushed up against the wall. She swiped a closed envelope from the surface and turned back to him, extending the envelope to him. "This letter arrived from Jane this morning. It's addressed to you."

Oliver smiled and took the letter. He'd been writing with Jane since she left and mentioned his upcoming trip to visit Charlotte, so she'd know to write to him here. The name on the envelope was, unfortunately, Elizabeth Bennet, but it had to be so long as Oliver was around people who didn't know who he truly was.

"I'll give you a minute to settle in, shall I?" Charlotte asked. "Supper will be ready soon as well."

"Thank you, Charlotte," Oliver said. "I'll be right down."

Charlotte nodded and left the room, closing the door behind her. Oliver slipped his finger beneath the edge of the envelope's closure and opened it.

Oliver,

I hope your trip to Hunsford was uneventful and easy. I expect Charlotte will be very happy to see you, and I imagine even Mr. Collins will be glad for a guest, if only to show off his home and status in society.

Things here at Gracechurch are mostly uneventful. Our aunt and uncle have continued to be wonderful hosts, of course. But that won't surprise you. What will is that I ran into the Bingleys yesterday—Charles wasn't present, but his two sisters were. We exchanged pleasantries, but they didn't seem particularly surprised or happy for the coincidence. Louisa was rather cool in demeanor, and though I mentioned I'd be staying with our aunt and uncle a few weeks more, neither of them extended any invitation.

I couldn't bring myself to ask after their brother. It seemed so clear to me that they were eager for the end of the conversation, so I didn't prolong what was quickly becoming an unpleasant interaction for the three of us. Oh Oliver. It really does seem I've lost favor with the Bingleys entirely. It burns me to know the Bingleys have seemingly been aware of my presence this entire time and haven't once reached out. I'm afraid things between Charles and I are truly over, forever.

But enough of sad news. You know I'll be all right—I always am. I ask that you not worry after me. Have a wonderful time with Charlotte and please give the two of them my best.

Love,
Jane

Oliver put the letter down, his stomach sinking like a boulder dropped into a lake. His poor sister! The Bingleys' behavior was truly so odd—it wasn't as if something had happened between Jane and Bingley before the latter had departed. What on earth could have caused the sudden change of heart?

CHAPTER 20

OLIVER HAD SPENT HALF A DAY WITH CHARLOTTE AND MR. COL-
lins before the latter announced with a puffed-up chest that
they had all been invited to dine with Lady Catherine de
Bourgh at Rosings. This meant very little to Oliver. He'd heard
of Lady Catherine de Bourgh, of course—she was a woman
of status and wealth, well-known in English polite society—but
he didn't have the predisposition to be known by those born
into wealth.

Mr. Collins, however, was over the moon. "Have you ever been
to Rosings?" he asked Oliver immediately after his announcement.

"I can't say that I have," Oliver responded.

"Never been to Rosings!" Mr. Collins threw his hand over
his heart and gasped with far more drama than the situation
warranted. "Why, you're in for a special treat, then! Rosings is
absolutely beautiful—I've been fortunate enough to be invited a
number of times now. I do believe Lady Catherine de Bourgh

has taken a liking to me, and I am honored to have her attention, of course. She really is a remarkable woman—surely you've met her at one time or another?"

Oliver was certain Mr. Collins knew the answer to that, but given that he was currently a guest here at Hunsford, he forced himself to play along anyway. "I have not."

"Oh lord! Lady Catherine de Bourgh is an *incredible* woman—I feel as though I leave every conversation with her cleverer than when I entered it. She's accumulated quite a bit of wisdom over her years, and she has the most fascinating stories. Miss Bennet, you are absolutely in for a treat. I'm delighted I'll be there to witness your first experience there."

Oliver smiled tightly.

They departed shortly after midday, via carriage even though Rosings was less than a ten-minute walk away. But, being the countryside, Mr. Collins insisted on taking the carriage so Oliver and Charlotte didn't risk getting dirt on their skirts.

As they exited the carriage, Oliver had to admit that Collins was right about one thing: Rosings was certainly impressive, at least from the outside. The estate was a tan, two-story brick building with ivy artfully grown over the face of it and trimmed around the white-framed windows. Two large wings of the building jutted out like arms reaching forward. The grounds were enormous and meticulously manicured. Oliver didn't think he spotted a single leaf out of place in the hedge walls lining the very long driveway up to the massive house.

It seemed like an awful lot for one person to live in, but Oliver supposed Lady Catherine must have company with frequency. *You would need a lot of company to fill that house*, Oliver thought. *You could fit an entire battalion in there.*

Of course, Oliver was all too aware homes of this size weren't usually intended to actually house a lot of people as much as they were to impress a lot of people. Rosings was a status symbol, not a home.

Inside, they were led down a long hallway with shiny marble tile floors to a large room with gleaming hardwood floors. Oliver nearly stopped in his tracks taking in the size of the sitting room—it was at least one and a half times the size of the sitting room at Netherfield. Like Netherfield, bookcases lined the far wall, and a piano was placed in the center of the room. Several small tables with comfortable-looking chairs were spaced out along the walls, and closer to the piano area were larger upholstered chairs, big enough to fit two people in each.

In the center of the room, standing by the piano, was an elderly woman dressed in finery and an almost comically large hat. She clapped her hands as they entered the room.

"There you are!" she exclaimed. "How wonderful to see you again, Mr. Collins."

Collins dipped his head and removed his hat. "It's an honor as always, Lady Catherine."

Lady Catherine turned her appraising gaze onto Oliver and Charlotte. She nodded at Charlotte with stiff familiarity, but her eyes narrowed as her gaze settled onto Oliver. "I don't believe we've been acquainted," she said sharply.

"Ah, of course," Mr. Collins said quickly. "This is Miss Elizabeth Bennet. She's visiting with us this week—a good friend of Mrs. Collins, you see. And my cousin."

Oliver forced himself to smile and curtsy, no matter how it twisted his stomach. "It's a pleasure to meet you, Lady Catherine."

"Yes, it is," Lady Catherine responded.

Oliver bit back an incredulous smile.

"Miss Elizabeth Bennet," Lady Catherine murmured in thought. "I've heard your name recently. Ah! Yes, of course. You recently became acquainted with my esteemed nephew."

Oliver blinked. "Did I?"

"I believe she means Mr. Darcy," Charlotte jumped in.

"Indeed," Lady Catherine responded dryly.

Oliver's eyebrows shot up. He supposed it made sense—the Darcys were known to be wealthy, even more so than the Bingleys. Still, physically at least, he couldn't say he saw the resemblance.

More importantly, though, how did Lady Catherine know he had met Darcy? Did Darcy mention him to her? He couldn't imagine it would have been in a flattering light, given his limited interactions with Darcy as "Elizabeth."

"Well! Come, sit, all of you. I have some tea being prepared as we speak; it should be here any moment now." Lady Catherine gestured to the comfortable-looking chairs near the piano. Mr. Collins took the seat to Lady Catherine's right, and Charlotte sat on the largest chair, patting the seat next to her and smiling at Oliver invitingly. Oliver sat beside her, grateful for the company.

At least he didn't have to endure alone what was sure to be a trying couple of hours.

"Miss Bennet," Lady Catherine said, turning her hawkish eyes onto Oliver. "Do you play the pianoforte?"

Oliver hesitated. "I . . . took some lessons as a child, but I wasn't really suited to the instrument. So no, not very well."

Lady Catherine gasped so theatrically Oliver immediately suspected Mr. Collins had learned it from her. "Why, knowing how to play an instrument is vital to a lady's education! Do you play a different instrument, then? Violin, perhaps?"

"I do not."

"Such a shame! Do you have any siblings?"

Oliver could already see where this conversation was going and he didn't like it. "I have four sisters."

"And do *they* play the pianoforte?"

"We all took lessons as part of our education. Out of all of us, Mary took to it best—she plays all the time."

"But the rest? No other instruments?"

Oliver paused. "No."

Lady Catherine tutted, shaking her head. "And drawing?"

Oliver frowned. "Drawing?"

Lady Catherine nodded. "Do you and your sisters draw?"

"Oh. I've dabbled in it here and there, but I can't say I really took to it."

Lady Catherine turned to Mr. Collins, her hand flying to her heart. "No instruments *or* drawing!" Her eyes turned back on Oliver, who was already very much ready to leave though they hadn't even been here long enough to have tea. "It is truly shocking that your governess didn't teach you to draw *or* play instruments. These are vital skills for any woman, as I'm sure you're aware. Such a shame to lack such important skills. Who is your governess, dare I ask?"

Oliver bit his lip as dull pain bloomed at his temples. He could already imagine Lady Catherine's inevitable reaction to his answer, but there wasn't really a way around it short of lying. And given the way Lady Catherine spoke to him, he strongly suspected she was a gossip who would certainly catch Oliver out in any lie he attempted to save face.

"We don't have a governess," he said at last.

The choked gasping noise Lady Catherine made may have been appropriate if she was having a heart attack in front of them all, but alas he wasn't so fortunate. This time the back of her hand flew up to her forehead, as if she felt faint. It was clearly put on, and Oliver clenched his jaw with the effort to keep his face neutral. How on earth was he going to survive remaining polite to this woman for *hours*?

"No governess!" Lady Catherine squawked, gripping Mr. Collins's forearm like a lifeline. "No governess! You poor dear, I'm very sorry to hear it. Very sorry indeed."

"There's no need to be," Oliver responded lightly. "We've received a perfectly fine education without one. We're all quite content with our present circumstances."

"Of course you are, dear," Lady Catherine cooed, like one might at a cat or a deluded child. "Of course you are. I must say, if I were your mother all five of you would have been educated by the best governess in all of England. Piano, violin, drawing, sewing—every skill a woman needs, I am certain you would have received the best of it. Why, I near raised my nephew and niece, and they are both very well educated and prepared to thrive in polite society. It won't be long before my nephew takes on a suitable wife indeed, if he takes my advice as he should."

"How nice for them," Oliver gritted out through a carved smile, even as his mind stuttered on that last sentence. He *knew* Darcy wasn't interested in women, and the other boy had certainly never mentioned courting someone, even to save face . . . unless this was the young woman who Wickham had told him about? But Wickham had said Darcy was ignoring her.

Oliver couldn't think on it for much longer, because Lady Catherine wasn't done. She went on to describe the exact specifications of her niece's education, down to the manner of her dress and her daily practice of the pianoforte, but somewhere along the line her voice drifted into the background. Oliver felt as though he were floating away, carried by the increasing volume of his own pulse.

Every woman. Every lady. Miss.
Miss.

Miss.

Oliver had thought himself used to the mischaracterization, but Lady Catherine's insistence on Oliver's supposedly lacking education around *becoming a woman of proper society* was absolutely suffocating. He'd always thought Mrs. Bennet to be stringent in her ways, but Lady Catherine made Mrs. Bennet appear lackadaisical in comparison. He struggled to imagine a world in which Mrs. Bennet accepted him as her son, as Oliver, a boy preparing to enter the world *as a man.*

If it was going to be a difficult transition in manner of thinking for Mrs. Bennet, it would be impossible for Lady Catherine.

What will people like her say about the family once I tell them the truth? Oliver didn't know, but sitting in front of Lady Catherine as she ranted about their lack of a governess, he could begin to imagine. It was a reality that was dizzying in its unpleasantness.

The discussion around him faded entirely as the room blurred. His chest was tight, his pulse racing, his palms cold with sweat. An impossible heat surrounded him, and while his face burned his head felt light. Lady Catherine was still speaking, and both Charlotte and Mr. Collins seemed very interested in whatever she was saying, but it felt as though Oliver were underwater. He was underwater and he couldn't breathe.

Oliver abruptly stood. Lady Catherine balked at him in midsentence, her eyes wide as she stared, incredulous, at the interruption.

"Apologies," Oliver said quickly. "I need . . . air."

And with that he turned on his heel and walked quickly out of the room. The hallway was long and looked identical on either side. He couldn't remember which way led to the front door, to outside. A maid who was tidying a nearby table frowned at him.

"Are you all right, miss?"

"Outside," Oliver said, fighting to keep his voice calm. "I need some air."

The maid nodded and put the dusting wand in her hand into her bag. "Right this way, miss."

Miss. No one will ever see you, a voice in the back of his mind whispered viciously. Oliver forced his legs to move as he followed the maid, his steps clacking on the hard marble tile. He just needed some air. He just needed a break, away from Lady Catherine, away from people who looked at him and saw someone Oliver didn't recognize.

He needed to stop pretending to be someone he wasn't, but the impossibility of it all was a crushing weight threatening to grind his bones into dust.

CHAPTER 21

TWO DAYS AFTER THE ILL-FATED VISIT AT ROSINGS, OLIVER SAT AT the desk in the guest room penning a letter to Jane when Charlotte appeared with a knock at the open door.

"Sorry to interrupt," she said with a small, confused smile. "You have a visitor?"

Oliver blinked. "A visitor?"

There were only a handful of people who even knew he was at Hunsford. Oliver frowned, lowering his pen as he stood. "Is it Jane?"

Charlotte shook her head. "It's . . . Well, you should come see for yourself, I think."

That was . . . ominous. Oliver's frown deepened, but he followed Charlotte out of the room and down the stairs to the waiting room where—

"Darcy?" The name fell out of his mouth before he could stop it, forgetting all propriety for a moment. Darcy smiled thinly at his address and bowed his head.

"Good morning, Miss Bennet," he said, and Oliver flinched. "I apologize for the intrusion. If you don't mind, could I have a few moments of your time?" His gaze slid from Oliver to Charlotte, still standing next to him. "Erm, alone, if possible? Perhaps outside?"

Oliver couldn't begin to imagine what Darcy had come to tell him—and the request for privacy only confused him further. How did Darcy even know where he was?

He supposed there was only one way to find out.

Charlotte was frowning at the request, but Oliver nodded nevertheless. "Very well. Charlotte, I'll just be a moment."

She nodded slowly, without protest, as the two of them stepped through the front door. Darcy wandered a few feet away from the door to a bench near a rosebush. Oliver followed him and, unsure how to behave during this exceedingly awkward interaction, sat. The stone bench was cold beneath his skirts.

He despised being like this, like "Elizabeth," in front of Darcy. He hated having to pretend he didn't know Darcy the way he did, pretending he hadn't *kissed* Darcy just a couple months past. Pretending he didn't know the softness of Darcy's mouth, the warmth of his soft hands on Oliver's face. It was unbearable, watching Darcy pace in front of him in silence, pretending.

He was exhausted of it. But how was he supposed to tell him?

"Mr. Darcy," Oliver finally managed, slowly, "is everything all right?"

Darcy stopped pacing and faced him at last. He pulled his hands behind his back and straightened his shoulders. "Yes, apologies. I've been thinking all morning about how to begin to say this, but I can't say I ever settled on an appropriate opening. So I suppose I'll just jump right in. Miss Bennet, I've come here today to ask for your hand in marriage."

Oliver's mouth fell open. He closed it quickly, blinking hard, as warmth flooded his chest and up his neck. When Lady Catherine had said she expected Darcy to take on a *suitable wife* soon, there wasn't a chance she'd been thinking of *Elizabeth*.

What on earth was Darcy doing?

"I . . . don't understand," Oliver choked. "I'd heard you were already engaged to someone."

Darcy's expression was a painting of confusion. "Engaged? To whom?"

"I don't know her name. And in any case, I was under the impression you weren't fond of me."

Darcy's eyes widened. "Whatever would make you think that? I think very highly of you, Miss Bennet. In fact, I once believed I would never find the appropriate girl for myself, but shortly after meeting you I realized we had an opportunity laid out before us."

Oliver wasn't sure whether to laugh or cry. *You thought you'd never find a girl to match you because you don't like girls!* he wanted to say. *You kissed me, a boy*, he wanted to say. And the irony of it all was Darcy had apparently decided that he found a "girl" he could live with, and Oliver wasn't even a girl! It was truly incredible.

And yet, despite the irony of the situation, it cut deep nevertheless. Darcy had kissed him, had kissed *Oliver* and—what? Decided that his next step had to be to quickly find a woman to marry? Was he really so terrified of his own emotions?

"I have heard," Darcy continued, "that like myself, you too are being pressured to marry by certain members of your family."

Oliver frowned. "You could say my mother has been disappointed in my lack of interest in the topic."

He had hoped that admission would discourage Darcy from pushing the matter further, but on the contrary he actually *smiled*.

"Yes, precisely. I've been experiencing the same with my aunt, Lady Catherine de Bourgh. I believe you've been acquainted?"

Oliver grimaced. "We have."

"Then you understand the situation at hand."

Oliver did not, in fact, understand. Yes, they were being pressured to marry, but that was hardly a new turn of events. And it wasn't as though Oliver and Darcy were unique in being in that position—he imagined most unmarried people of their age were beginning to encounter the pressure of familial expectations. Darcy could have asked any girl his age and found the same.

"I don't believe you truly have feelings for me, Mr. Darcy," Oliver said stiffly. "In fact, I'm quite sure you don't."

Darcy blinked, a frown etching over his brow. "I don't under-stand. What would make you believe you know my emotions better than I do?"

Oliver wanted to scream. *You kissed a boy! You kissed a boy and you liked it!* Instead, he asked, "Why did you run?"

Darcy frowned. "How do you mean?"

Oliver hesitated, choosing his words carefully. He couldn't give away that he knew about the kiss, but . . . "The Bingleys and you left Netherfield so abruptly. Bingley didn't even say goodbye to Jane before he left. Your friend never struck me as one devoid of manners, so why?"

Darcy's frown deepened. "Why would Bingley say goodbye to your sister?"

Oliver scoffed. "Don't pretend you weren't aware the two were courting."

"I was aware," Darcy responded stiffly, "that Bingley was courting your sister, yes. But it was also painfully obvious to me that your sister didn't reciprocate the depth of my friend's feel-ings, so I advised him to walk away before suffering emotional injury."

Oliver's mouth nearly fell open. "You had no right!"

"I don't see why it should concern you. Your sister was so clearly unaffected by Bingley's affections—"

"Jane is shy!" Oliver knew he shouldn't shout, but he couldn't help it. Rage surged in his chest like an overboiled pot, spilling out to his extremities. Oliver couldn't say he'd ever felt violently angry before, but right now he could wrap his fingers like claws into Darcy's shoulders and shake him. "It's true that she doesn't outwardly show affection in public, but in private she is the sweetest, kindest person I know. And she's in love with Bingley! She was *devastated* when the lot of you took off. She still is!"

Darcy's eyes widened slowly as Oliver spoke. "I didn't realize—"

"Of course you didn't! You don't know Jane. And you had no right meddling in your friend's relationships."

"I was only trying to protect him—"

Oliver laughed harshly. "From what, Jane? From love? Happiness? All you've accomplished is ripping your friend away from the person by your own admission he was falling in love with. Well done. I suppose I shouldn't be surprised, seeing how averse you are to anything resembling happiness."

Darcy scowled. "I can't even begin to fathom what would make you think that."

"You just proposed to *me*, didn't you?" Oliver asked. Darcy opened his mouth in response, but Oliver pushed forward. "Do you really believe you'd be happy living with a woman for the rest of your life? Do you really believe you could love *me*?"

Darcy froze, eyes widening as color drained from his face. "What—I don't understand. What do you mean?"

"You know exactly what I mean." Oliver stood, crossing his arms over his chest. "Answer the question, Darcy. Look me in the eye and tell me *that* could bring you happiness."

Darcy took a step back, as if struck. "I don't believe it's always possible to find happiness, Miss Bennet," he said. "And I don't believe we all have the privilege of marrying the person we love. But I *do* believe I could find some semblance of happiness with you, yes. Perhaps it wouldn't be love, not today, and perhaps not in a year. But eventually?" He shrugged.

Oliver shook his head, fury and hurt and despair swirling in his chest like a hurricane. He'd been so foolish. He'd really believed, even if only for a moment, that there was something between him and Darcy. That Darcy saw something in Oliver that he liked. But how could that be true, when he was here proposing to—as far as he knew—someone else entirely?

He really was so afraid of who he was that he would throw away any future happiness by running from it.

"You don't want this," Oliver said, his voice shaking.

Darcy sighed. "Perhaps not, but all my other realistic options are even less desirable. So believe it or don't, but this arrangement is enough for me."

But Oliver shook his head, the world blurring with hot tears. "It isn't enough for me. I won't agree to circumstances that are all but guaranteed to saddle me with misery. And you shouldn't either. You're a coward, Darcy. I can't stand to look at you any longer." He turned around, wiping furiously at his eyes.

"Who told you?" Darcy's voice was low, so quiet Oliver almost thought he'd imagined it altogether. Oliver wiped his hand across his face, banishing the tears before turning around to face Darcy again. The other boy looked defeated, shoulders slumped, face blotchy. But there was something raw in his gaze, something wounded. "Who told you?" he repeated, his voice breaking.

You did, Oliver wanted to say.

Tell him, something inside Oliver whispered. *Tell him who you are.*

But how could he ever face Darcy as Oliver again when he'd been so clearly rejected—so decisively that he was ready to marry someone he barely knew just to get away from him? Oliver couldn't tell him, not now. Not ever.

It'd be best, he told himself, if Oliver and Darcy never crossed paths again. It hurt so deeply to think it, but he held it in his mind, burned it behind his eyes. He couldn't keep doing this with Darcy. He couldn't fall for a boy who would never love him the way he needed—openly, and genuinely, as a boy.

"Wickham," Oliver said at last, and it was true. Wickham *had* told Oliver that Darcy goes to Molly Houses—which more or less meant announcing to the world that Darcy fancied other boys.

Darcy's face darkened.

"He had quite a lot to say about you," Oliver added. "And your character."

Darcy barked out a single, humorless laugh. "*My* character! That's rich, coming from him."

Oliver didn't know what Darcy could mean by that. "Do you

deny that you are engaged to his cousin and refuse to break off the engagement, regardless of the coldness you exhibit toward her?"

Darcy's eyes widened and his lips parted, but he didn't speak.

It was enough of an answer for Oliver. He shook his head, his eyes burning from the strain of holding back tears. "My answer is no," Oliver said quietly.

Darcy snorted. "Yes, I believe you've made that abundantly clear."

Oliver nodded once, started to turn, then paused. "And I . . . won't tell anyone. About . . . your leanings. Wickham never should have said anything to me about it at all."

"No," Darcy said stiffly. "He shouldn't have."

With one last nod, Oliver turned around and walked away, leaving the boy he was falling for behind.

CHAPTER 22

THE DRESS WAS HOT AND SUFFOCATING, WRAPPED AROUND HIS RIBS like the ever-tightening grip of a boa constrictor. Oliver winced and wobbled on the stool he stood on as Mrs. Bennet yanked at the stays down the back. In front of him, Lady Catherine glowered at him, shaking her head with a disapproving frown.

"A lady must always appear petite, delicate," Lady Catherine said. "You must pull in your waist to accentuate your hips."

"She's right," Mrs. Bennet said behind him, giving the stays another rough tug.

The corset cinched tighter around his ribs, threatening to crack. The room rocked dizzyingly. Oliver reached behind himself, trying to find Mrs. Bennet's hands. "It's too tight," he wheezed. "Mama, I can barely breathe."

"Nonsense," Lady Catherine said. "Take shallower breaths. It's of utmost importance that you look ladylike at the ball. Do you want to be known as the *mannish* Bennet sister? I think not. Tighter."

"No!" Oliver gasped, but the stay pulled tighter nonetheless. Pain flared across his ribs and black spots dotted his vision.

"This is necessary, Elizabeth," Mrs. Bennet said behind him. "I won't have a daughter who thinks herself a boy."

Oliver was going to throw up. Or pass out. Possibly not in that order. The room rocked like the deck of a ship in a storm. "I'm not a daughter," he wheezed. "I'm not a girl. Please."

Lady Catherine laughed, and to Oliver's horror, so did Mrs. Bennet behind him. The echoes of their laughter ricocheted across the room, sending a wave of gooseflesh over Oliver's arms. "I'm a boy," he said, his voice so small against the riot of their laughter. "I'm a boy. My name is Oliver. Please."

The women laughed harder. The stay cinched tighter. The edges of his vision darkened. He couldn't breathe. He couldn't breathe.

"Please," he whispered, but if either of the women heard him they didn't show it. Their laughter was cold, empty, piercing in his ears. The room was darkening. He felt light-headed. He couldn't breathe. "Oliver," he wheezed. "My name is—"

Oliver jerked up, heart pounding, pulse throbbing in his temples. Their bedroom was still cloaked in night, and Jane was fast asleep in the bed across the room. Slowly, he lowered himself back to his bed, his head hitting the pillow with a soft thump. He pulled the sheets up over his shoulders, shivering despite the heat. It was just a nightmare. A horrible nightmare, and it was over.

But was it really?

A hot tear slipped down Oliver's cheek and he pressed his face to the soft fabric of the pillow. Of course Mrs. Bennet and Lady Catherine didn't know about Oliver, didn't know who he was or how he was trying to reclaim his life. But Mrs. Bennet would certainly know eventually, and Oliver suspected in time Lady Catherine would as well. It terrified him, thinking of the whispers, the stares, and what that might do to his family's reputation. But even more terrifying than the thought of society's disapproval was the thought of his mother's rejection.

Oliver just couldn't imagine a world in which Mrs. Bennet would embrace him with a smile and a word of encouragement. He couldn't imagine telling his mother that he was a boy, that he was her son, and being met with unconditional love. Mrs. Bennet loved him, of course she did, but she loved a version of him that he could never be, not forever. She loved an act, a painting she'd built up in her own mind of who Oliver was.

But Oliver wasn't Elizabeth Bennet. He never was. And he couldn't go on pretending to be for much longer.

———

Oliver picked at his breakfast, pulling the sultana scone apart one crumb at a time. His cup of tea sat cooling on the saucer, untouched. Though he'd joined the family for breakfast, mostly out of obligation, he didn't have much of an appetite after that nightmare. He'd slept fitfully afterward, repeating snippets of the nightmare over and over until he gave up all pretense of trying to sleep and watched the bedroom turn from dark gray to dusky purple.

It was his first full day back from Hunsford, and he should have been energized and fresh from the holiday. Instead, he sat morosely as Kitty and Lydia spoke animatedly about some attractive soldiers they'd met downtown.

"Lizzy, you still haven't told us about your trip. How was Charlotte?" Mrs. Bennet asked.

It took a moment for Oliver to register that Mrs. Bennet was, in fact, speaking to him. He looked up at once, a sultana half squished between his thumb and forefinger. He dropped it onto his plate and sat up.

"She's well," he said, trying to sound as casual as possible. "Very happy, well settled into her new life."

"Good!" Mrs. Bennet exclaimed. "What a lucky girl she is. And to think, that could have been *you*."

Oliver shuddered.

"I hope you learned something, Lizzy," Mrs. Bennet continued. "Charlotte is a perfect example of what you should be striving for. She married to increase her station, and now she's running *Hunsford* of all places! And with its proximity to Rosings, I'm sure she's become well acquainted with Lady Catherine de Bourgh as well. That's precisely what you should be looking for—a man to increase your station in society."

Ordinarily Oliver might have argued, but he was too exhausted to have this conversation yet again. The life Mrs. Bennet described was so unpleasant it was dizzying, but a single thought grounded him: He'd turned down two proposals for marriage already. Nothing was stopping him from doing so until the men stopped asking.

But was that really what he wanted? To be alone? The truth was that the thought of living here, with his mother, forever was almost as unpleasant as the thought of being someone's wife. But if neither option was desirable, what was left? Was there any point in hoping for an alternative, a life where someone might take him as a *husband*, might recognize him as a *boy* and one day a *man*?

Oliver wanted to believe it was possible. But right now, with the sting of Darcy's rejection of his true self still smarting, it all felt so hopeless.

"Don't you think?" Mrs. Bennet said.

Oliver was suddenly aware of the gazes of all his siblings and his mother on him. He'd clearly missed something while wallowing in self-pity. "Sorry," he said. "I missed the question."

Mrs. Bennet sighed heavily, clearly affronted. "Honestly, Lizzy, how can you expect to ever find happiness with a man if you can't learn to listen?"

Thankfully, Oliver didn't have to figure out a way to respond to *that* because at that moment Mr. Bennet lowered his newspaper and cleared his throat. "There's a letter for you, Lizzy. Did you see it?"

Oliver blinked. "A letter? No, where is it?"

"I left it on the coffee table in the sitting room. I think you should go read it—it seemed important." His eyes twinkled with a smile, and it occurred to Oliver that his father was giving him an out.

He stood. "I'll do that, then. Thank you, Papa."

With that he turned and waltzed out of the room before Mrs. Bennet could protest. He was halfway into the sitting room before it occurred to him there might not actually be a letter at all, but then he spotted the envelope sitting exactly where Mr. Bennet had said. Oliver picked it up with a frown and gasped at the return address.

The letter was from Darcy.

Miss Bennet,

Please don't worry, I'm not writing you to repeat the humiliations of our last encounter. I write without any intention of hurting you or dwelling on the incident I'd rather we both forget. I apologize for demanding your attention like this, but I ask that you indulge me for just a moment longer for the sake of uncovering the truth.

That night you accused me of two egregious offenses that I feel compelled to clarify. The first was that I separated Bingley from your sister, and the second was that I ruined the prospects

232

of Mr. Wickham's cousin. If you'll allow me, I'd like to address both.

I was not in London long before it became obvious that Bingley favored your eldest sister over anyone else. But it wasn't until the dance at Netherfield that I began to worry about any serious attachment. I've seen Bingley in love before, you see, but never in the deep, encompassing way he so clearly was with your sister. When I observed your sister, however, though she seemed pleased by his attention, it didn't seem to me as though she reciprocated the depths of his feelings. From what you've told me, it sounds as though I was wrong, and given how well you know your sister, that seems likely to be the case. As such, your resentment is warranted for the pain I inflicted upon her, and for that I am sorry.

As for Mr. Wickham and his cousin, I hope that by revealing the truth of our relation that I will banish any doubts about my character in regards to my treatment of them both.

To begin with, I must mention an incident I'd rather forget and I had hoped to never share with another person. Still, I trust your discretion. Last summer my younger sister, Georgiana, was taken from school in Ramsgate—where Mr. Wickham attended as well. There, Mr. Wickham made Georgiana, who was fifteen at the time, believe she was in love with him and agree to an elopement. Thankfully, Georgiana told me about the elopement before it occurred and I was able to put a stop to it and forbid Wickham from ever seeing my sister again. It was abundantly clear Mr. Wickham's aim was my sister's fortune of £30,000—a fact to which he admitted during our argument. Georgiana quickly understood how she had been deceived, for which I am grateful.

As for Liliana, Wickham's cousin, it's true that our families matched us as children and strongly encouraged us to become engaged when we reached a marriageable age. Despite the pressure of our families, no such engagement ever occurred, though it does not surprise me to hear some claim otherwise. Liliana is as interested in marrying me as I am in marrying her—which is to say, not remotely. As for why she hasn't become engaged to someone else, that is not for me to say.

Finally, I hope you can see for yourself how it doesn't speak well of Wickham's character to be apparently sharing with others the rumor you mentioned to me the other day. While I won't address it further, and I believed you when you promised your discretion, I don't think I have to explain how such a rumor could destroy my reputation should it befall the wrong ears.

In any case, I hope this letter brings you clarity and that you won't hold against me our discussion. Though I think you are probably right that happiness would be elusive should we marry, I hope you know that I meant what I said about your character. I do think if I were ever to find a modicum of happiness with any woman, it would have been with you. I hope that one day we could put this behind us and perhaps even be friends.

Darcy

CHAPTER 23

Oliver had no sooner finished reading the letter and stepped into the hallway than Mrs. Bennet opened the front door just fifteen feet ahead of him. He couldn't see who had knocked from where he was standing because Mrs. Bennet was in the way—which, thankfully, also meant whoever was at the door couldn't see him properly either, but his stomach dropped to his toes at the sound of Wickham's voice.

"Mrs. Bennet! I apologize for coming by without notice," he said. "I just happened to be in the area when I remembered Longbourn was nearby, and I thought how wonderful it would be to spend some time this morning with Miss Elizabeth. That is, if it's not any trouble."

Oliver's eyes widened. Did this boy have no shame? He thought he'd made his disinterest in Wickham quite clear, and yet here he was, *again*, trying to court him.

"Oh!" Mrs. Bennet said, her voice near shrill. "It's no trouble at all; I'd be happy to fetch her."

It all happened too quickly. Mrs. Bennet turned around, and

in doing so shifted away from Wickham, which meant, all at once, Oliver was staring at Wickham. And the blond boy looked right back at him. Ordinarily this may have been slightly awkward, but generally fine except for one thing: Oliver was wearing trousers.

Wickham stared, wide-eyed, at what he certainly perceived to be a girl wearing trousers. Oliver's heart hammered in his chest as he willed his legs to move, but he was paralyzed. Wickham was here. He was here, and he was staring at Oliver, who was wearing trousers.

Mrs. Bennet, perhaps perplexed by Wickham's expression, turned around and gasped upon seeing Oliver. She widened her eyes at him and jerked her head toward the stairs, which finally broke the spell. Oliver darted up the stairs and around the corner to his room, closing the door perhaps a little too forcefully behind him. He leaned his head back against the door, closed his eyes, and groaned. How would he ever explain this away before Wickham made the connection between Oliver and the boy he'd first seen at Watier's?

When Oliver joined Wickham in the sitting room, he was eating a crumpet slathered in jam. Oliver's hands were clammy as he sat across from the other boy, the cool air around his legs as the fabric of his skirt settled, making him feel naked, somehow.

"I apologize for the wait," Oliver said lightly. "I hadn't realized we'd have any guests today."

"That *is* partially my fault, I suppose," Wickham said. "I should have sent a calling card ahead of me. I apologize for the intrusion—I just became so enamored with the notion of seeing you again that when I realized how close I was to Longbourn, I couldn't resist coming by. I hope you'll forgive any inconvenience."

Oliver smiled thinly. "May I ask why you're here?"

Wickham arched an eyebrow. "To see you, of course."

"I thought it had become quite clear during our last conversation that our visions of the future are incompatible."

"Incompatible!" Wickham laughed. "Nonsense. You have some unrealistic fantasies of the future, certainly, but what young girl doesn't hold fanciful notions? It is a weakness of your sex to struggle to differentiate between flights of fantasy and reality. All the more reason why you need a strong husband to guide you."

If he hadn't been so outraged by Wickham's statement, he might have laughed. Instead, Oliver gaped. "Weakness of my sex?!"

Wickham nodded gravely. "One of many, as I'm sure you're aware."

"Have you really come all this way just to insult me?"

"Insult you!" Wickham looked aghast by the suggestion. "Quite the opposite. Why, I'm here because I think you're beautiful, and more importantly, *interesting*. I'm certain you'll make a diverting wife for a husband of superior intellect."

Oliver snorted. "Is that what you are? A man of superior intellect?"

"Of course," Wickham said with all the confidence of a boy who had never in his life heard the word *no*.

Oliver shook his head. "Allow me then to clarify the situation. I have no interest in being courted by you, Mr. Wickham, and even *less* interest in one day becoming your wife. I will not agree to marry you, not if you ask today, or tomorrow, or next month, or next year. In fact, I don't wish to ever see you again."

Wickham's face slackened. "Really," he said, and though it wasn't a question, Oliver responded all the same.

"Really."

"Well." Wickham stood, adjusting his cravat and donning his hat. "I suppose I have no further reason to stay, then."

"I suppose not," Oliver said coolly.

"Very well. I shall be going, then." Wickham paused to straighten his topcoat—which was already straight—and glanced at Oliver as if to make sure the other boy wasn't about to protest his sudden departure.

Oliver, who was doing all he could to mask his pleasure for the sake of propriety, merely met his gaze with an unaffected stare. With a huff, Wickham strode out of the room, around the corner, and out the front door.

As the thump of the front door's closure broke the quiet, Oliver fell back into his seat and smiled.

CHAPTER 24

IT'D BEEN NO MORE THAN A HANDFUL OF MINUTES AFTER WICKHAM had left that the storm that was Mrs. Bennet blustered into the sitting room, where Oliver had remained. As she turned on her son, her face was red and her hands were shaking at her sides. Oliver was familiar enough with the shades of her mood to know before she even spoke a word that he was in trouble.

"What were you thinking?" Mrs. Bennet cried. "You are so fortunate that another man expressed any interest in you at all after the way you treated Collins—and you treated him just as abhorrently! How *could* you?"

Oliver opened his mouth to respond, even as his face prickled with suppressed emotion, but Mrs. Bennet didn't give him the chance to speak.

"If I didn't know better, Elizabeth, I'd begin to believe you *want* to live the rest of your days alone! You can't expect acceptable suitors to continue pursuing you if you keep rejecting them, you know!"

"I don't want to be alone, Mama," Oliver said softly, his throat aching as he fought back tears. "But—"

"He saw you in *trousers*!" Mrs. Bennet cried, shrill. "It was a miracle he didn't leave immediately, but he still entered, waited for you to change, and courted you *anyway* and what did you do? You sent him away!"

"Mama—"

"I never should have allowed such deviancy in my home! I don't know *what* your father is thinking, Elizabeth, but you are a *girl* and you will dress like one in our home!"

The tears burst out of him unexpectedly. Oliver stared, open-mouthed, as tears streamed silently down his cheeks. *She doesn't know*, he reminded himself. *She thinks you're her daughter. If she knew the truth . . .*

But Oliver couldn't finish the thought, because he didn't know what she would do. What he knew right now, as her words cut deep into his chest, was the thought of losing the one freedom he had at home made it hard to breathe.

"Mama, that has *nothing* to do with Wickham," Oliver forced himself to say, his voice trembling as hard as his hands. "If anything, that he was still interested after seeing me in trousers should be encouraging. If Wickham didn't mind, maybe—"

"No husband wants his *wife* to dress as a *man*, Elizabeth!"

"Well, maybe I don't want to be anyone's wife!" The words exploded out of him before he could stop himself. Oliver had never yelled at his mother before, not since he was a child, but now with the tears unstoppable and the pain in his chest burning through him in the hollow spaces between his ribs, lungs, and heart, he couldn't bring himself to care.

Mrs. Bennet's face was taut, red, livid. She opened her mouth, but before she could speak Mr. Bennet entered the room, his frown deepening as his gaze shifted from Mrs. Bennet to Oliver.

Oliver, who stood trembling, barely containing the sobs racking his body.

"What is happening here?" Mr. Bennet asked. Then to Oliver, "Are you all right?"

Oliver couldn't trust himself to speak. He shook his head, but with every passing second the iron grip on his control was slipping.

"Is *she* all right?" Mrs. Bennet screeched. "Are my nerves not important? She has no reason to be upset, not after sending yet *another* suitor packing—"

"Mrs. Bennet," Mr. Bennet said tersely, "that's quite enough. I'll speak to our child alone now."

As Oliver's mother stormed out of the room, Mr. Bennet crossed it to wrap him in a tight embrace. Oliver's face pressed into his father's chest.

And he broke.

———

When Oliver calmed enough to breathe without gasping sobs, Mr. Bennet brought him to his office. At first Mr. Bennet left Oliver to compose himself in the office for a few minutes while he fetched some tea. Wiping at his eyes, Oliver drifted from Mr. Bennet's small bookshelf—packed with mostly law books—and crossed the deep-green rug set between the bookshelf and the desk.

Distracting himself from his turbulent emotions, Oliver allowed his gaze to wander over the letters and papers stacked in neat piles on his father's desk. One envelope was pulled aside—a letter from Dr. Henry Marsh.

That gave Oliver pause. Dr. Marsh was an odd older gentleman—what one might call eccentric. He also happened to be the man who helped deliver Oliver, as well as all the other Bennet children. Oliver had long suspected the physician *also* attended Molly Houses, but of course that was hardly a topic the man could ever speak freely about, so Oliver would probably never know. Still, he had a second practice in Paris, where the laws were much more lax, so he spent about half the year there.

But what was he doing writing to Mr. Bennet?

The door opened behind him and Oliver's gaze snapped to his father, who was carrying a tray with a steaming pot of tea, two saucers, and two teacups. Using his backside to close the door behind him, Mr. Bennet set the tea on his desk.

After taking a steaming cup gratefully, Oliver sat on one of the two chairs in front of his father's desk, bringing the cup close to his face to savor the hot steam over his mouth and nose.

Mr. Bennet sat opposite him with his own cup of tea and

smiled softly at him. "I know you're not all right, so I won't ask. I'm very sorry for what your mother said to you. I think it's time I have a conversation with her, but . . . I'm not certain how much you'd like me to tell her."

Oliver stared into his teacup, uncertainty warring in his chest. After what she had said to him, he didn't think his mother was ready to hear the truth. But a part of him worried she may *never* be ready, and if that was true, what was he to do? He couldn't go on like this for the rest of his life just because his mother didn't want to hear the truth. But after today, he was even less prepared to tell her than he was before.

"I'm not ready to tell her everything yet," Oliver said softly. He forced his gaze up from the steaming black tea and found his father watching him with warmth. It was reassuring in a way he'd once never dared to hope for.

"That's perfectly all right," Mr. Bennet said. "In that case, perhaps I'll focus my energies in discouraging her from pressuring you to marry before you're ready."

Oliver's shoulders relaxed. "That would be incredibly helpful."

"Good." Mr. Bennet nodded. "In the meantime, I suspect you could use some time away. Why don't you visit your aunt and uncle at Gracechurch this afternoon and spend some time with them? A couple of days, or a week, even. I'm sure they'll be happy to have you, and it'll give you an opportunity to be yourself for some uninterrupted time."

Oliver paused, considering. "That . . . would be perfect, actually."

"Excellent." Mr. Bennet smiled. "I'll write to them immediately to alert them of your visit. You should go pack. I'll take care of your mother."

Just the notion of being able to spend multiple days as himself made Oliver feel lighter. He finished his tea and stood, the heaviness of his argument with his mother melting away at the prospect of his upcoming visit. "Thank you," he said, his voice cracking with emotion. "For everything. I—I don't know how I would have handled all of this without you."

The warmth in his father's face alone made Oliver misty-eyed all over again. "I know you didn't tell me perhaps the way you'd imagined, but I'm so glad to know you, son. No matter what, I will always fight for you."

CHAPTER 25

D{.sc ETERMINED NOT TO THINK OF HIS MOTHER}, O{.sc LIVER SPENT MUCH} of the ride to his aunt and uncle's focused on the letter he'd received from Darcy two days prior.

Darcy's explanation made all the sense in the world, and as for Wickham's character, well—he *was* spreading a rumor he had no business telling. Oliver couldn't begin to imagine how he would feel if Wickham knew who he was and began to tell all the world about it. It was despicable.

So, given his evident capability of such an act, and, frankly, his rudeness as he'd attempted to court Oliver, he supposed the rest of Darcy's explanation about what had actually gone on between them wasn't such a stretch.

But what Darcy hadn't said was *why* he'd proposed to Elizabeth. He'd admitted in the letter that he agreed he probably wouldn't be happy marrying a woman, so why had he proposed to someone he believed to be a girl? And why *then*? Darcy had mentioned they were *both* being pressured to marry. And his disappearance after the kiss seemed far too coincidental to not be related, so the only explanation Oliver could think of was that Darcy had reacted to kissing a boy by trying to immediately marry a girl.

It wasn't the most reassuring of conclusions.

It was with this in mind that the carriage pulled up to the Gracechurch estate and Oliver stepped out of the carriage to greet his aunt. When she wrapped her arms around him and asked how he was, something inside him cracked. The tears surprised them both, but once he'd started retelling the recent events, Oliver found he couldn't stop.

───────

When Oliver's uncle suggested they go visit the grounds at Pemberly the next day, Oliver protested—but only until his aunt reassured him Darcy wasn't home. Reluctantly, Oliver agreed, if only to avoid questions from his uncle about why it should matter whether the lord of the house would be present.

Once there, Oliver had to admit the grounds were every bit as beautiful as he'd heard—especially now that the trees and shrubs were in full bloom. The estate itself was a massive tan brick building with columns on either side of the entryway. And though the building was impressive to look at, the estate was nothing compared to the land it sat on. Directly in front of the mansion was an enormous, placid lake that rippled with the manor's reflection. A walking path was carved out around it, artfully decorated with perfectly manicured hedges, trees, and flowers.

"Isn't it gorgeous?" his aunt asked. "I love coming here to take a long walk. It's so peaceful—there truly isn't anywhere else like it in all of England, I'm convinced."

"It's nice," Oliver admitted.

What was even nicer was taking a walk with his aunt and uncle as himself. Hearing *Oliver* from his family, strolling alongside his uncle, both dressed in their finest, the comfort of the chest flattener hugging his ribs and the soft silk cravat tucked beneath his chin—it all felt so *good*. So right. He wished it could be like this all the time. More than anything else, *this* was what he wanted. To be himself, in the open, unabashedly.

It could be so easy, but the world made it so difficult.

They walked along the lake's perimeter in silence, only the crunch of their shoes on the white pebbled pathway disturbing the quiet. Birds chirped overhead and a warm temperate breeze tousled the strands of Oliver's hair peeking out beneath his hat. After ten minutes they'd walked not even a quarter of the pathway, and Oliver found himself glad that he'd let his aunt convince him to join them. The grounds here were so calm. He couldn't help but wonder what it would be like, being there every day, having that idyllic walking path literally steps from your front door. And Oliver hadn't even gone inside yet—he could only imagine the decadence within.

The muted crunch of wheels on gravel somewhere behind him drew Oliver out of his thoughts. The three of them paused and turned back as a carriage pulled up to the front of the estate and out stepped—

Oliver's stomach dropped to his toes. Out of the carriage stepped *Darcy*. The very person his aunt had *insisted* wouldn't be here.

Oliver turned to his aunt, wide-eyed, and she stared open-mouthed before pursing her lips. With an apologetic shrug, she said, "I was told he was spending time with the Bingleys all this week. He must have returned early."

Oliver groaned and his uncle frowned. "Is there a problem with Mr. Darcy being here?"

"I'll explain later, dear," his aunt said lightly.

Any hope Oliver had of slipping away unnoticed evaporated as Darcy strode forward, onto the well-manicured path. Directly toward them. Oliver bit his lip, uncertain of whether to keep walking or wait for Darcy to catch up. Most of him wanted to keep moving forward in the hopes that Darcy hadn't yet realized who the three of them were, but he also knew that would be impossibly rude and there wasn't a chance his aunt and uncle would agree to it.

So instead, he watched with growing dread as Darcy approached. He knew the exact moment that Darcy had come close enough to spot him—he paused, then suddenly began walking more quickly toward them. Oliver's mind whirled with what he would say. As far as Darcy knew, the last time they'd seen each other was when Darcy had kissed him, then run away. He supposed with that in mind it was maybe encouraging that Darcy was approaching them quickly rather than turning away, but it didn't ease the anxiety building in his chest.

Darcy had proposed to him—to "Elizabeth." They'd argued, and Darcy had sent that letter, and he had no idea Oliver was present for all of it. How was he supposed to act normal? How was he supposed to pretend he didn't know Darcy had proposed to a girl—then admitted his fault afterward?

He'd never imagined living a separate life as himself would crash so spectacularly into his life pretending to be a girl, but here he was, mere minutes away from confronting the collision of the two.

"Mr. Gardiner, Mrs. Gardiner, it's a pleasure to see you," Darcy said as he approached. Then his gaze settled on Oliver, heavy and full of warmth. "I didn't know the two of you knew Oliver."

Oliver's aunt smiled brightly and placed her hand on Oliver's shoulder. "He's our nephew," she said cheerily. "Are you two well acquainted?"

Darcy's face flushed, just a little, and Oliver couldn't help but bite back a smile. He knew *exactly* what kind of *acquainted* Darcy was remembering.

"You could say that," Oliver responded.

"Actually," Darcy said, "would it be all right if I spoke to

Oliver privately? I do have something important to discuss with him."

Oliver's pulse roared in his ears. Prior to that moment, he'd been envisioning an awkward but bearable walk with Darcy and his aunt and uncle. He wasn't prepared to talk to Darcy *alone*.

But his uncle said, "Absolutely. Mrs. Gardiner and I will continue on our walk, shall we?" He offered his wife his arm, who took it with a smile. And without another word, the two of them continued forward, leaving Oliver with lead in his stomach and heat creeping up his neck.

Once his aunt and uncle had distanced themselves enough to be out of earshot, Darcy sighed heavily. "I hadn't expected to find you here."

"I could say that as well," Oliver responded with an awkward laugh.

"Well. I *do* live here." Darcy smiled wryly. It was far too handsome on his already handsome face.

"I was . . . reassured, falsely it seems, that you wouldn't be here."

Darcy frowned. "Were you trying to deliberately avoid me?"

Oliver arched an eyebrow. "Does that surprise you after our last interaction? If anything, I was under the impression *you* wouldn't want to see *me*."

Darcy flushed and ran a hand through his hair. With a sigh, he nodded toward the path ahead of them. "Walk with me?"

Oliver nodded and the two of them ambled slowly forward.

They followed the pebbled pathway for a few minutes before Darcy broke the silence.

"I shouldn't have run," he said. "I apologize. I can't imagine how that must have made you feel after—after we—"

"Kissed," Oliver said flatly. "We kissed."

Darcy swallowed, his Adam's apple bobbing in his throat. "Yes. We kissed."

"Was it really so bad that you felt the need to escape?" Oliver asked.

Darcy's eyes widened. "No! No, not at all. It was . . . the opposite, in fact."

Now it was Oliver's turn to frown. "The kiss was so good you had to run away?"

Darcy laughed, the sound dry and brittle. "If the confirmation that you enjoy kissing other boys didn't frighten you, you're braver than I am."

It was as he'd thought, then. For Oliver, that night was terrifying, but kissing Darcy had been perhaps the least scary part of it. It was scary going out in public dressed as himself, as Oliver—it was terrifying presenting himself to a world that would scorn him if they knew how he'd been born. It was terrifying being himself with the ever-nagging fear that someone might recognize him as "Elizabeth," might ruin everything he'd worked for months to achieve. Just the prospect of someone telling the world that Oliver and Elizabeth were the same person made him want to throw up.

So kissing Darcy had been scary, yes, but in the moment the only fear he'd had was Darcy's rejection—not society's. In the moment, he was in the only safe place in the world that wouldn't attack him for who he was, that would see a boy kiss another boy and smile. So compared to the fear of being outed that he faced every time he left his home as Oliver, the fear of kissing Darcy had been nothing.

Still, Oliver imagined that for Darcy, who didn't have to worry about the world thinking him someone he wasn't, kissing Oliver probably *was* the scary truth that he worried about someone discovering.

So no, kissing him hadn't been so scary. But he understood why it could be for Darcy.

"I . . . understand," Oliver said at last, a new fear blooming in his chest. This was, he knew, the perfect opportunity to tell Darcy the truth. They were alone, and the topic of conversation was so close to the truth already. But once again, he found himself fearing Darcy's rejection—and this time the thought of it was nearly as terrifying as the thought of being outed. He bit his lip.

Darcy frowned at him. "Are you all right?"

Oliver's pulse thrummed in his ears. He should tell him. He should tell him now. *Darcy won't tell anyone, even if he doesn't react well*, he reassured himself. *Darcy wouldn't. He knows what it's like for someone else to reveal his identity to the world.*

Still, a small part of him wondered if he might be wrong with that supposition. But even if he was, what else was he going to do? He couldn't keep courting Darcy without being honest with him. He couldn't keep living two lives like this. It would rip him apart.

He stopped walking and faced Darcy, pulling his shoulders back and taking a deep breath. "I have to tell you something."

Darcy frowned and stopped walking as well. Slowly, he faced Oliver and nodded. "All right."

Oliver swallowed hard, unsure of where to begin. What was he supposed to say? How was he supposed to explain? For as long as he'd known that he'd have to one day explain this to Darcy if he wanted their relationship to continue, he'd never actually figured out the words.

But Darcy was patient. He watched Oliver with a soft, warm gaze. A cool breeze shifted the dark hair framing his handsome face. Birds chirped nearby, filling the air with light song. Oliver wanted to stay here, in this idyllic moment. He wanted to freeze time and feel the breeze against his cheeks and the soft ground beneath his boots. But if he didn't tell Darcy the truth now, he never would.

So, slowly, carefully, he pulled out the words. "When I was born, the name given to me wasn't Oliver."

Darcy arched an eyebrow. "No? Was it something terrible?"

Oliver laughed, just a little. "It was . . . ill-fitting." He chewed on his lip, trying to calm the racing of his heart in his chest. "My parents made a mistake when I was born. They . . . they mistook me for a girl. And raised me as one."

Darcy blinked. The ghost of a frown crept over his brow.

Oliver pushed forward. "But I'm *not*. I'm a boy, and it's only been in the last year that I've finally been able to start living my life as one. But . . . most of my family doesn't know yet, including my mother. Only a handful of people know, so I've had to continue living a—a second life. A false life. Where I've had to pretend to be a girl."

Darcy didn't interrupt, which Oliver felt was as promising a sign as any. He listened, the frown deepening, but nodded slowly, as if in thought. "That sounds . . . terrible," he said softly. "You said only a few people know who you are?"

Oliver nodded. "My eldest sister, two close friends, my aunt and uncle, and most recently my father. That's it. It's just—I think you can imagine how difficult it would be if . . . if people who wished me ill knew."

"Of course," Darcy said quickly. "I understand why you wouldn't want others to know. Thank you for trusting me with that." Oliver nodded, just slightly, worrying his lip. Darcy hesitated. "Is there more?"

Oliver took another long, shaky breath. Darcy had taken the first part well, but that didn't mean he'd be understanding about this. But there was no hiding from it. "You've . . . met me. When I've had to pretend to be a girl."

Darcy blinked, his eyebrows raising. "I have?"

"Several times, actually." Heat crept up his neck. "Um. The name my parents gave me when I was born . . . it was Elizabeth."

Darcy's brow furrowed. ". . . Elizabeth?"

Oliver grimaced. "Elizabeth . . . Bennet."

Darcy's mouth dropped open and he took a step back. "*Bennet?*" He stared at Oliver, wide-eyed, as Oliver's pulse pounded in his ears. This was the moment. The moment Darcy either accepted him or—

Darcy laughed. Hard. And Oliver wasn't sure what to do with that. A small, nervous smile crept over his lips as Darcy doubled over laughing, wiping tears from his eyes.

"Is it . . . really so funny?" Oliver asked with a slight chuckle.

"Elizabeth Bennet!" Darcy exclaimed, looking up at Oliver at last. "As in the—the person I proposed to just a few weeks ago?"

Darcy was still smiling, and still laughing, which Oliver felt was as good a sign as any. He didn't seem angry, which was the reaction he'd been scared about. But he wasn't sure he quite understood this reaction either.

"Ah yes," he said. "You, uh . . . You did do that."

"So you're telling me," Darcy said, sitting in the grass, "that in my panic about kissing a boy, I ran off to ask a *boy* to marry me. Out of every possible *socially acceptable* person I could have asked in England, I chose the only one who wasn't actually a girl."

The thought *had* crossed Oliver's mind. Now, with some distance between himself and that disastrous proposal, even he had to laugh as he sat beside the other boy. "Yes. I suppose you did."

"It makes so much sense," Darcy said. "I never understood why I was so drawn to—to *Elizabeth*. I'd never in my life met a girl who caught my attention like that, and it's because Elizabeth wasn't a girl at all!"

Oliver blinked. The thought was . . . oddly affirming. It was as though Darcy had seen right through his forced disguise. As though somewhere, deep down, he'd known Oliver was a boy all along.

The two of them laughed until Oliver had tears in his eyes too. They laughed until his middle hurt, until their faces were red. The relief of being accepted, of being seen, of his building fear of Darcy's reaction evaporating like mist—it filled him with light.

When they settled at last, Darcy was grinning ear to ear. "Thank you," he said again, "for trusting me with the truth. And thank you for telling me—everything makes so much more sense now."

Oliver was all smiles. "I'm just so happy to finally tell you all of it. The longer I waited, the more terrifying it became. Honestly, when you proposed I thought I'd never be able to tell you."

"I'm glad you did." Darcy ran his hand through his hair and sighed. "So, what now?"

"Well," Oliver said slowly, "I *did* enjoy kissing you."

Darcy grinned. "And I enjoyed kissing you."

Oliver wanted to return the smile, but a far more terrifying thought weighed on his shoulders. "I can't go on pretending to be a girl for much longer. I have to tell my family."

Darcy's face sobered, and he nodded. "I expected as much. I wouldn't want you to have to pretend to be someone you aren't for eternity anyway. That would be . . . miserable."

Oliver glanced at him. "Even if it means we'd never be able to be open about the nature of our relationship?"

"I'd rather be secretly happy with you than openly living a lie."

This made Oliver smile at last. And when Darcy slid his fingers through the grass and touched Oliver's hand, he didn't pull away. Emboldened, Darcy eclipsed Oliver's hand with his own, their fingers twining together. And so they sat, hand in hand, for some time.

CHAPTER 26

Eventually Darcy suggested they go inside for a respite from the hot sun, and Oliver agreed. They'd just stepped inside when a maid approached them with an envelope in her hand.

"Mr. Blake?" the young woman asked.

Oliver startled. How did she know the false last name he was using? He was certain he hadn't spoken his full name all day . . . "Yes?" he asked hesitantly.

"A runner just arrived with this letter for you, sir." She extended her hand. "He said it was quite urgent."

The thrill of being called *sir* warred with his confusion and anxiety. He took the envelope and his frown deepened, wondering who even knew he was there and what could be so urgent. The letter was from Wickham, which made some sense as *he* knew the name Oliver used—but how on earth had Wickham known where he was? It was addressed to his aunt and uncle's estate, so Oliver could only assume the runner had gone there first, only to be told that they were all at Pemberly today.

Anxiety roiled in his stomach as he looked back at the maid and thanked her in as calm a tone as he could manage. The woman nodded and walked away as Oliver slid his finger beneath the envelope's opening and pulled out Wickham's letter.

The very first line made him dizzy with terror.

Elizabeth (for that, not Oliver, is your name),

He knew. Wickham knew who he was. But *how*? Oliver shook, the letter trembling in his hand as he forced himself to read.

I will not faff about with pleasantries. I thought it odd that the boy I'd met visited a married woman, and stranger still that he never seemed to emerge from her home after entering—but you did. When I saw you in trousers the other day, however, my suspicions were confirmed. That you have deluded yourself into believing that you're a boy is laughable, but easily corrected. What you need is a strong husband to remind you of who you are and who you always will be: a woman in need of serious guidance.

If you wish to keep your secret safe you will meet me, alone, at the statue of Alfred the Great in two days' time at noon. Should you fail to attend, a visit to Longbourn will be in order.

Wickham

Oliver felt as though he'd swallowed a bucket of rocks. His breath caught in his throat, his heart raging in his ears. "Oh God," he whispered.

"What is it?" Darcy asked with a frown. "Is your family all right?"

Oliver swallowed hard, forcing himself to lower the letter. "It's Wickham," he said, his voice faint. "He knows."

CHAPTER 27

OLIVER'S SUITCASE PACKED FULL OF BOY CLOTHES HIT THE ground with a thump. He stepped out of the carriage parked in front of Longbourn, his skirts rustling around his ankles. After reading the letter, he'd rushed home immediately. His uncle had said something about connecting with Mr. Bennet and swore to help however he could. Oliver barely remembered packing his things and saying goodbye to his aunt and uncle.

And Darcy—he'd barely said a word. What was there to say? Any attempt to intercede on Oliver's behalf carried the heavy risk of exposing himself. Oliver couldn't—*wouldn't*—ask that of him. The power Wickham held over them both made Oliver's blood run cold. The thought that one boy could so thoroughly alter the course of Oliver's life was sickening.

Leaving Darcy behind felt like saying goodbye to his only chance at happiness.

Oliver would find out what Wickham wanted from him in

two days, but he couldn't shake the feeling that he would ask for more than he could give.

﹏﹏﹏﹏﹏

Oliver had expected Jane to be horrified, fearful even, upon reading Wickham's letter. What he'd not expected was to see her look up with an expression of pure rage.

Come to think of it, Oliver wasn't sure that he'd ever seen Jane properly angry before.

"That right bastard," Jane hissed.

Oliver's mouth fell open. "Jane!" he exclaimed, his shock turning to a laugh. He'd *certainly* never heard Jane swear before.

"I apologize, Oliver," Jane said, her face pink, "but the audacity of this man! Who is he to tell you who you are? He barely even knows you! And he's all but admitted to *following* you. That he thinks it appropriate to behave this way is incredible." She shook her head, slapping the letter down onto her bed. "You know what he said is rubbish, don't you? You're not a woman, and you certainly don't need a man to try to force you to be one."

Oliver sighed and sat next to his sister, his stomach churning with anxiety. "I know," he said softly, even as Wickham's vile words burrowed more deeply into his mind. "But he could so easily ruin our family's reputation if he were to expose me. And Mother . . ."

Oliver's face heated as that terrifying possibility played out in his mind. What would he do if she refused to accept him as her son? The conflict would tear their family apart.

And yet, there was nothing to do but press forward. He couldn't masquerade as a woman forever.

"I think," Jane said, "if Wickham insists on continuing on this path, you should consider telling the family before he can. It wouldn't be completely on your terms, which isn't fair. But it'd allow you to introduce yourself in your words—rather than Wickham's."

Oliver bit his lip and nodded. Jane was right. But the necessary words eluded him.

The next morning, Oliver sat in the front garden. A small white bench was placed there among the flowers, more for decorative purposes than anything else, but Oliver enjoyed coming out here to think.

And he certainly had plenty to think about.

Oliver was gently touching the tiny purple buds of a lavender plant when the crunch of nearing wheels on dirt pricked his ears. He stood and turned, frowning as an elaborate black carriage pulled up. He couldn't imagine it was Wickham—their meeting wasn't until tomorrow, and it wasn't at Longbourn. In any case, Oliver couldn't imagine Wickham would be able to afford such an extravagant carriage.

Then the door opened and out stepped Lady Catherine de Bourgh, of all people.

Oliver's eyebrows shot into his hairline, and he only barely managed to keep his mouth from dropping open. He was quite certain she'd never visited before—and even more certain she wasn't acquainted with either of his parents. Was she . . . lost?

But she didn't seem surprised to see Oliver. Instead, her gaze homed in on him immediately and she nodded, pulling her shoulders back as she strode directly toward him.

Oliver curtsied politely, forcing a pleasant smile at their surprise guest. "Lady Catherine, how unexpected. Can I get you a cup of tea?"

"No need," Lady Catherine said stiffly. "I won't be here long."

Oliver wasn't sure what to do with that, so he just nodded and said, "Can I help you, then?"

"Actually, yes. You're exactly the person I came to see, in fact."

"I see," Oliver said, utterly bewildered. "How can I help?"

"You can *help*," Lady Catherine seethed, "by reassuring me that the rumors around your engagement with my nephew are absolutely false."

This time, Oliver couldn't stop his mouth from falling open— but he recovered quickly, even as his face twisted with confusion. He couldn't imagine who would have spread such a rumor, or why.

"If I am engaged to your nephew," Oliver said carefully, "that's the first I've heard of it."

"So you deny it?" Lady Catherine snapped.

Oliver frowned at her aggressive questioning. "I do," he said, trying to ignore the prickle of anger creeping up his spine. "I'm not engaged to your nephew. I'm not engaged to anyone at all."

"Good!" Lady Catherine said. "I'll have you know my nephew's future has been arranged since he was a young babe. He will marry a *respectable* woman of his station, one who has been waiting many years to do so. In fact, I'm certain they'll be married before the year's end."

Oliver could only assume she was referring to Wickham's cousin, but he didn't bother correcting Lady Catherine's assumption. "I see."

"I hope you realize if my nephew was going to marry someone *else*, it certainly wouldn't be someone of your station. It was absolutely foolish if you ever believed otherwise. These rumors are ridiculous and insulting. I will be sure to put them to rest *immediately*."

Oliver gritted his teeth. Did she really come all this way just to insult him and his family *on their own property*? "Is that all?" he forced himself to ask.

Lady Catherine bristled. "It is *not* all. You must promise me that if my nephew has a moment of clouded thinking and he *does* ask you to marry him that you will refuse."

Oliver couldn't help it—he laughed. The irony, of course, was that Darcy had *already* proposed and Oliver had *already* declined—but if Darcy asked again, if he asked *Oliver* instead of *Elizabeth*? There wasn't a chance that Oliver would refuse him again.

"I don't see what's so funny!" Lady Catherine exclaimed. "Does this seem to be a jest to you?"

"I can't promise that," he said flatly.

Lady Catherine gasped. "Do you really think yourself qualified to marry him? To become a *Darcy*? *You?*"

"I think," Oliver said, "that I'll trust Darcy to make the decision about who he wants to marry on his own."

"The arrogance!" Lady Catherine threw her hand over her heart. "You must refuse him! You *cannot* marry him!"

Oliver shook his head. "Are you so certain he will come here to ask me that my refusal to meet your demands upsets you? Perhaps you haven't noticed, but as far as I can see Darcy isn't here. I'm not engaged to him, but if he *does* ask me, I'll make whatever decision I'd like to without your influence, thank you very much."

Lady Catherine gasped again, the sound choked with outrage. Oliver barely resisted the urge to roll his eyes.

"If that's all, Lady Catherine, I have business to attend to." Oliver turned to the front door.

"You have not heard the last of me, Elizabeth Bennet!" Lady Catherine screeched at his back.

Oliver didn't bother dignifying that with a response.

CHAPTER 28

DRESSED AS HIMSELF, OLIVER ARRIVED AT THE STATUE OF ALFRED the Great.

The statue was carved out of white stone, depicting the old king in his fine robes and a crown upon his head. It was an ancient thing, stained with weather and time, placed in the center of a stone walkway that branched around it, surrounded by shrubbery and trees on all sides. In a city of a million people, it was as good a place as any to have a private conversation.

Wickham was already there, waiting for him. He looked up and scoffed upon seeing him. "Incredible. You are certainly bold to arrive here dressed like *that*, Elizabeth." Wickham said Oliver's former name like a curse. Oliver felt it like a knife tip slipped between his ribs.

"What's incredible," Oliver countered, "is that you think it your duty to meddle with my life. Is your own truly so uninspiring that you feel compelled to involve yourself in matters that do not concern you?"

Wickham snorted. "You think too highly of yourself. The strange choices you make with your life wouldn't have concerned me at all, had your cousin not made it my concern."

That gave Oliver pause. His eyes narrowed. "My cousin?"

Wickham nodded. "When I mentioned your foolishness to Mr. Collins, he handed me an opportunity that I intend not to waste. In exchange for ensuring you stop this ridiculous charade, I have been offered a significant sum. I will not allow you to ruin this for me, Elizabeth. You will marry me and stop fighting the role you were born to fulfill."

Oliver actually laughed. The entire situation was so absurd that had Wickham not been looking at him so seriously, he would have been certain it was all a jest. Marry *Wickham*?

"This is no laughing matter," Wickham chided, which only made Oliver laugh more loudly.

"I have been subjected to a number of terrible proposals this summer," Oliver said, "but I must say, Wickham, this is truly the worst of them all."

Wickham went red-faced. "How *dare* you?!"

"I would sooner marry a lamppost than take you as my husband," Oliver said acidly.

Wickham's reddened complexion turned an ugly shade of purple. "If you refuse to marry me, I will be left with no other option but to inform your family of your deviancy."

That made Oliver near dizzy with fear, but he forced himself to meet Wickham's eyes with a flinty gaze of his own. "Go on, then," he said, slipping his trembling hands into his pockets. "See if my cousin still pays you after you've informed my family there is a Bennet son, after all." It all fell into place as Oliver spoke, the connections fitting together in his mind. "Because that's what this is about, isn't it? Collins has paid you to force me to live my life as a woman so that I won't get in the way of Collins's plan to inherit Longbourn."

A muscle in Wickham's jaw twitched, but he didn't deny it. "You're a fool if you think your family will ever accept this nonsense."

"Maybe so," Oliver said, turning away. "But I still won't marry you."

Oliver walked, his mind buzzing and exhausted, until he found himself at Westminster Bridge.

He strode to the center of it and leaned against the rail, smiling softly as a cool breeze kissed his face. The quiet lapping of the water below, the hum of conversation and foot traffic, and the squeak of carriages somewhere behind him—it was all oddly soothing. Ahead and to the right lay the Palace of Westminster with its many pointed spires reaching to the clouds. Westminster Abbey's twin western towers overlooked the gothic church, the tallest structure on the horizon.

He could stay here for hours. He wanted to. Clouds were

rolling in over the sun, darkening the sky. Oliver just hoped no one went looking for him in his room. He supposed he probably should have told Jane so she could cover for him if needed, but it was too late for that now.

Part of him didn't care if someone noticed his absence. Part of him wanted to be discovered, to be seen. He was so exhausted of pretending, of putting everyone else's needs before his own. He was tired of trying to make everyone else happy, to his own detriment.

Soon it may not matter anyway. Wickham would go to his family and tell them who he is, in the most unflattering terms possible. His mother would be outraged. Lydia and Kitty would enjoy the scandal at least.

The rain began all at once—Oliver blinked and his clothes were soaking up water like a sponge. He laughed, and the sound was as cold as the rain's chill. Perfect. Now he'd walk home sopping wet and weighed down by drenched clothing. It'd be a miracle if he got back in unnoticed.

Oliver considered returning home, but he couldn't bring himself to move. When he went back home he'd have to face a choice: continue pretending, accepting a life of silent misery and denying Wickham's accusations, or do the far more terrifying thing and be honest with his family.

He knew what he *wanted* to do, what he *needed* to do, but the risk of an unenviable reaction was so terrifyingly high. It would be worse to have a mother who knew who he was and rejected him wholly, he decided, than to suffer through her continued obliviousness.

Someone leaned against the banister next to him, and Oliver jumped at the movement. He hadn't even heard the other boy approach—the rain hit the stone of the bridge so hard it was a constant clattering in his ears. The other boy turned to face him, and Oliver blinked for several stunned seconds, sure his mind was playing tricks on him, or his eyes were too rain-drenched to see properly.

But there was no mistaking Darcy standing next to him on the bridge.

"Hello," he said cautiously, with a slight smile. "Lovely weather for a walk."

Oliver laughed, shaking his head even as a smile grew on his face, unbidden. "It wasn't raining when I initially went out."

Darcy's smile softened. "I assumed not."

"How did you find me?"

"Well," Darcy said. "When you weren't home, I remembered what you told me about where you went to get some air. I thought this was as good a place to try as any."

Oliver's eyes widened. "My family knows I'm not home?"

Darcy cringed, just slightly. "I'm afraid so—entirely my fault, I apologize. But if it helps, I told them I'd just forgotten that we'd agreed to meet in town. At any rate, I'm sure Bingley has thoroughly distracted them by now, so I wouldn't worry."

Oliver didn't think his eyes could widen further, but they did. "Bingley is with you?"

"We traveled together, yes. He's currently with your family and Jane, of course. I believe he had much to say to your sister after I explained to him the error of my initial judgment and reassured him I do now believe your sister reciprocates his feelings."

Oliver didn't know what to say. It was, of course, Darcy's fault that Bingley had walked away from Jane to begin with, but if Darcy admitted his mistake to his friend and encouraged him to go back to her . . .

"Is he . . ." Oliver was almost too nervous to finish his question. "Is he proposing?"

Darcy smiled and looked over the river. Rain plastered his dark hair to his forehead and dripped over his nose onto his soft lips. "I do believe so, yes."

Oliver grinned, his mood turning so suddenly he felt as though he might just float away. "Darcy, that's—" He laughed, this time genuinely. "Thank you. You'll always have my gratitude."

"I'm not sure I deserve that," Darcy said, though he still smiled faintly. "After everything I did to cause you and Jane so much unhappiness to begin with . . . being honest with Bingley was the least I could do."

"Whether you believe you deserve it or not, I'm grateful all the same."

"If you *must* thank me," he said, turning his gaze back to

Oliver, "I won't deny that my desire to make you happy was the strongest of my motivating forces. I thought only of you."

Warmth crept into Oliver's face as he bit back a smile. Here Darcy was, sitting in the unrelenting rain, declaring the importance of Oliver's happiness. He didn't know how to respond, but he didn't have to because Darcy wasn't finished.

"My aunt returned home recently in a most sour mood, but it gave me hope. I know you well enough to be sure that if you had been completely decided against me, you would have said so to Lady Catherine."

The warmth in Oliver's face became a furnace and he laughed. "I suppose you do know me well, as I can't deny that's true."

Darcy just smiled.

Oliver hesitated, then said, "I spoke to Wickham earlier today. Collins had apparently offered to pay him to marry me, and when I refused he . . . didn't take it well. He's determined to tell my family about me."

Darcy scowled. "That is truly vile. Do you know when he intends to do this?"

Oliver shook his head. "He didn't say. Soon, I imagine."

Darcy's frown deepened. "Are you all right?"

"I don't know." Oliver sighed, running his fingers over the wet stone of the bridge. "I was terrified at first, but . . . now I'm starting to wonder if it might be time to tell them myself."

Darcy nodded. "I'd be happy to go with you to offer some support, if it would help."

The gesture was so kind, Oliver found his throat aching with emotion. "You would do that for me?"

"Certainly." Darcy hesitated, then, as if deciding something, nodded and said, "I have struggled for some time, and I won't allow it any longer. If your feelings are still what they were earlier this month, please tell me so, but I can no longer contain my own. I admire you, Oliver Bennet. Your spirit, your wit, your open honesty—I have thought of nothing else since we first met."

Tears blurred Oliver's vision, spilling hot over his cheeks and cooling in the rain. "Darcy—"

"I love you, Oliver," Darcy said. "Most ardently."

It was everything Oliver had ever dreamed of hearing. Everything he'd been so afraid he would never hear. It was every dream he dared have wrapped in a bow and presented with so much warmth in those brown eyes that Oliver couldn't deny their legitimacy.

Oliver blinked hard through the pouring rain. With the deluge unceasing, most others had retreated indoors, leaving just Oliver and Darcy on the bridge. So, before Oliver could think better of it, he leaned forward, closing the distance between them. Then his lips were on Darcy's, and the other boy cupped Oliver's face in his soft hands. They kissed, with rain pattering their faces, with their hair wet and heavy on their foreheads, with their rain-slicked skin slipping against each other. They kissed as Oliver's tears mingled with the rain, as his heart filled with so much happiness he thought it might just burst, as warmth bloomed in his chest and spread across his body, like a mug of steaming tea in the dead of winter.

Oliver pulled away, just slightly, the warmth of Darcy's breath spreading over his nose and mouth. Darcy opened his eyes, his heated gaze searching Oliver's.

"I love you, Fitzwilliam Darcy," Oliver said. "With my whole heart, I love you."

The grin that lit up Darcy's face in response would live in Oliver's memory forever. This time, when Darcy closed the distance between them, Oliver was not the first to pull away.

He had never been happier.

CHAPTER 29

IN THE END, IT WAS DARCY WHO CONVINCED OLIVER TO USE THE front entrance. After a quick stop at Lu's to get out of their drenched clothing and into dry menswear, they rushed over to Longbourn. Together they stood on the stoop, the maroon-painted door closed and oblivious before them. Oliver bit his lip, his insides absolutely trembling, his shivering fingers clenched tight at his sides. He could do this.

He had to do this.

"If you're not ready," Darcy said, "it's all right. We can always do this at another time."

Oliver shook his head. He knew now there would never be a good time, never be a *right* time. There would always be a reason to wait, to put it off, to torture himself just a day longer. He could survive today. He could survive tomorrow. But a lifetime of pretending he couldn't abide.

"No," he said at last. "I want to do this. Get it over with."

Darcy nodded and, so gently, placed his hand at the small of

Oliver's back. The touch was warm, comforting. He leaned forward, his lips brushing Oliver's ear. "No matter what happens, I'm here. I'll always be here for you."

Oliver smiled, despite the situation. It was such a relief, having Darcy at his side. He would face his family, and he would tell them the truth, and if they didn't like it . . . well. At least he wouldn't be alone.

So, rolling his shoulders back and taking a steadying breath, Oliver knocked on the door.

The *thunk* of his knuckles against the wood reverberated through his body. Oliver held his breath. Then, after a moment, Mr. Bennet opened the door.

Oliver's breath caught in his chest, but then Mr. Bennet's face melted into a smile. "Well," he said brightly. "Don't you look fetching?"

Oliver's face warmed, but he cleared his throat and forced himself to speak. "Papa, this is Mr. Darcy."

"We've met," Mr. Bennet said, still smiling. "Welcome back, Mr. Darcy." He stepped out of the way, inviting the two of them into the entryway.

Darcy nodded and entered, Oliver following while anxious energy buzzed in his stomach like an entire hive of bees. But Mr. Bennet was still smiling, and that took the edge off, at least.

"You've missed Jane and Mr. Bingley's big announcement," Mr. Bennet said. "It seems the two are engaged at last."

Despite the nerves making his bones vibrate, Oliver burst into a full grin. "That's incredible news!"

"It is!" Mr. Bennet agreed. "Mr. Collins and Mr. Wickham have also just arrived. I believe they have something to discuss with the family, though they haven't said what yet."

Oliver's stomach dropped to his toes, but slowly, stubbornly, he pushed back the panic clambering up his throat. It didn't matter that Collins and Wickham were here because *he* was going to tell his truth first. He was ready. It was time.

But before he could say anything, a new figure strode over. "Mr. Bennet, who is—" Her words died on her lips as Mrs. Bennet's gaze fell on Oliver, her eyes wide as carriage wheels.

All at once, Oliver found he couldn't breathe. He'd been about to say he was ready to tell the family, but he hadn't been prepared for Mrs. Bennet waltzing in like this. Still, did it really matter if she learned the truth now instead of a few minutes from now?

Forcing a deep breath, Oliver said, "Mama, there's something I need to tell you."

Mr. Bennet clasped his hands behind his back and nodded encouragingly. He was still smiling and his eyes glinted happily. *If nothing else*, he reminded himself, *Papa will support me.*

And that reminder gave him the strength he needed to continue.

"*Why*," Mrs. Bennet said haltingly, "are you dressed like—"

"My name is Oliver," he interrupted, and though his voice trembled, he forced himself to finish, "and I'm your son."

For a long moment nothing happened. Mrs. Bennet stared at him, open-mouthed, while Oliver's heart slammed against his chest so hard it hurt. Mr. Bennet was smiling rather pointedly at his wife, his eyebrows raised as if to say *I'm happy about this, and so should you be.*

Then Darcy's hand clasped Oliver's and squeezed tight. The pressure was reassuring, and warm, and Oliver held on to his hand like a guardrail while descending icy stairs. Mrs. Bennet's gaze flickered down to their clasped hands as the shock on her face morphed to confusion.

"Also," Oliver added, his voice tight with tension. "Darcy and I are, erm, courting, I suppose."

Mrs. Bennet turned her moon-eyed stare onto Darcy. "Is this true?" she asked at last, as if there were any other way to interpret Darcy holding Oliver's hand.

"It is," Darcy said cheerily. "I've been quite fond of your son for some time."

"How wonderful!" Mr. Bennet exclaimed. "Oliver, I'm so happy for you." Then to Darcy, he added, "Be good to my son."

Son. Oliver suspected it would never get old.

"Always," Darcy said. He met Oliver's gaze with a warmth Oliver wanted to weave into his soul.

"Thank you, Papa," Oliver said softly. Then his gaze settled back on Mrs. Bennet as he searched his mother's face for clues as to her reaction.

Mrs. Bennet looked at Oliver, then Darcy, then back to her son before throwing the back of her hand up to her forehead and exclaiming, "My! This is most unexpected." Her hand fell back to her side, before she added thoughtfully, "I suppose your vehement distaste for dresses makes all the sense in the world now."

Oliver couldn't help it—he laughed. "I hope now that you know the truth you won't require me to wear them."

Then the strangest thing happened. Mrs. Bennet actually *smiled* and said, "Require my son to wear a dress? Well, that wouldn't be proper at all."

Oliver burst into tears. He hadn't meant to—hadn't expected to—but hearing those words, *my son*, from his mother was so unexpected but so *needed* that it broke the dam of anxiety within him. He frantically wiped at his face as he fought to catch his breath. "I'm sorry," he said quickly. "I'm all right, I was just—so scared I'd never hear those words from you."

Mrs. Bennet's face softened and in oddity upon oddity, she crossed the distance between them and pulled him into a hug. Oliver couldn't remember the last time he'd embraced his mother, but it felt so *good* to be in her arms, to be held, to be *accepted*. She'd called him her son. She'd called him *her son*! He'd been so terrified for so long of her rejection that her acceptance lifted a weight from his shoulders he hadn't realized he'd been carrying.

Mrs. Bennet pulled back from the embrace, but she was still smiling. Oliver grinned back so hard his cheeks hurt.

Mr. Bennet beamed. "Now, shall I reintroduce you to the family?"

Oliver nodded. The notion of presenting himself to the rest of the family was still terrifying, but maybe less so now that Mrs. Bennet knew. Furthermore, the thought of Mr. Bennet doing it, of him presenting Oliver as his *son* to the family, of his support made clear from the beginning—it was a better scenario than Oliver had dared dream of.

"Thank you," he said softly.

"Of course, son."

Darcy slipped his fingers between Oliver's, sending sparks scattering across his skin. "Are you ready?"

Mr. Bennet said, "The family is in a good mood right now thanks to Jane's engagement, so I think the reception may be warmer than you fear. Although, if you'd prefer we can wait until Wickham and Collins have left."

Oliver bit his lip. "I actually know why they've come. Wickham threatened to . . . *expose* me to the family in an effort to force me to marry him. He said Collins paid him to marry me so that I would . . ." He swallowed hard, not even wanting to speak the words. "So that I would be forced to live the remainder of my life as his wife."

Mrs. Bennet's eyes widened as Mr. Bennet's face grew stormy. Oliver couldn't say he'd ever seen his father truly angry before, but there was no mistaking the flush in his face and the dark look in his eyes for anything else. "This is about the inheritance, isn't it?" He shook his head, his tone reinforced with steel. "No. That won't do at all."

It was then that Collins and Wickham entered the room. Upon seeing Oliver, Collins's eyebrows shot up and Wickham smirked.

Collins threw his hand over his heart. "Is that *Eli*—"

"His name," Mr. Bennet interrupted darkly, "is Oliver. But I suspect you already know that, don't you, Mr. Collins?"

Collins blinked, his eyes widening. Even Wickham's smirk slid off his face. "I don't understand what you mean," Collins spluttered.

"I think you understand perfectly," Mr. Bennet said. "Furthermore, I think it would be best if you both left immediately. Mr. Collins, you should know I'll be updating my will forthwith to ensure that my *son* inherit Longbourn as is his due."

Oliver could hardly believe his ears. Mr. Bennet was actually going to update his will? Longbourn would be his? In all of his considerations of what living as a Bennet son would entail, Oliver had never once believed it possible that he'd ever be able to inherit Longbourn. But if there was a chance . . .

"I've already spoken to the physician who delivered him," Mr. Bennet continued, "who has assured me he will vouch in court, if needed, that Oliver is in fact my son."

Oliver's eyes widened. That must have been the letter from Dr. Marsh he'd spotted in Father's office. How long had Mr. Bennet been working on this?

Wickham and Collins, evidently, couldn't believe it either.

"This is absurd!" Wickham cried.

"Mr. Bennet," Collins said quickly, "there's no need to be rash."

"No," Mr. Bennet agreed. "Being rash would be paying your friend to entrap my son in a loveless marriage. Or would you like to deny that wasn't your aim with your arrival today?"

Collins's mouth opened and closed like a fish out of water. Wickham was as pale as the dead. Mr. Bennet just shook his head, something like disappointment creasing his brow. "Should you insist on taking this to court, the combination of my testimony, along with the rest of the family, and Dr. Marsh's testimony should be more than sufficient. I wouldn't advise wasting your resources fighting it."

"And *you!*" Mrs. Bennet said, shrill, pointing at Wickham. "Attempting to swindle my son into an unhappy relationship *for money*? Have you no shame?"

"It wouldn't be the first time," Darcy said, leveling his gaze on the blond's reddening face. "He attempted to do the same to my sister as well, to take on her inheritance."

"As if *you're* an angel," Wickham seethed. "I know all about your dalliances at Molly Houses!"

Mrs. Bennet gasped, but rather than turning to Darcy, she directed the full force of her fury on Wickham. "I'll have you know I have the ears of *many* influential people. Speak an ill word of my son, or of Mr. Darcy, to anyone, and I assure you you'll soon find your social capital worthless."

As Wickham paled, Mr. Collins frowned. "You aren't the only one with social connections, Mrs. Bennet."

"You mean Lady Catherine de Bourgh?" Mrs. Bennet crossed her arms over her chest. "Interesting that you should mention her. I don't suppose *she* knows your friend tried to swindle her niece out of her fortune?"

"She does not," Darcy responded evenly.

"Interesting," Mrs. Bennet said. "And, knowing your aunt, how do you think she'd react to such information?"

"I imagine she'd be furious at both the perpetrator and anyone closely associated with him," Darcy responded.

Mr. Collins blanched, turning on Wickham, wide-eyed. "What is this?"

Wickham sputtered. "It's not—I wasn't—"

"You weren't trying to fool my sister into believing you loved her so that you could marry her and take on her fortune?" Darcy asked coolly.

"It's not my fault the girl fancied me!" Wickham cried.

Collins stared at him, aghast. Mrs. Bennet tutted. "As I said. *One* ill word, and a visit to Lady Catherine de Bourgh will be in order."

Collins's mouth opened and closed soundlessly. Oliver bit back a laugh—he didn't think it possible for anyone to render the man speechless.

"The both of you should leave immediately," Mr. Bennet said. "Do not attempt to return—neither of you are welcome here at Longbourn ever again."

Perhaps in shock, Collins and Wickham said nothing more as Oliver's father herded them out the door. With a sigh, Mr. Bennet clapped his hands together and turned to Oliver and Darcy. "I'm sorry you had to see that unpleasantness," he said.

Oliver threw his arms around his father again, holding him tight. "Thank you," he said. "Thank you, thank you, thank you."

Mr. Bennet chuckled softly. "Of course, son. Are you ready to reintroduce yourself to the family?"

Oliver pulled back, wiping the tears gathering at his eyes, and took Darcy's hand again. With the other boy's hand in his and the support of his parents, facing the rest of the family, the rest of the world, seemed a little less terrifying. It wouldn't always be easy, Oliver knew, but here in this moment it was clear it would all be worth it. Because *this*—facing the world as his parents' *son*, as *Oliver*—the rightness hummed in his chest like the pure note of a tuning fork.

So, squeezing Darcy's hand tight, Oliver smiled. "Yes," he said. "I do believe I am."

EPILOGUE

OLIVER KNOCKED THREE TIMES, HIS BONES VIBRATING WITH EXCITED energy. The door opened and Oliver faced the reedy young man with the half-moon spectacles again. This time recognition sparkled in his eyes as he smiled.

"Coffee, please," Oliver said confidently.

With a grin, the man pulled the door open all the way. "Welcome back. Your boy is already here, on his usual perch." He jerked his chin toward the back of the room.

Oliver's face warmed at *your boy*, but he laughed and thanked the man as he stepped in nonetheless. He supposed he shouldn't have been surprised that others here had noticed he and Darcy were more than *friends*—after all, they *had* kissed here once before, even if only briefly.

Oliver slipped past the tables of card players and the designated dancing area where people were paired up together as someone played the pianoforte. The music was light and happy, and it buoyed Oliver's mood even higher.

Then he spotted Darcy sitting on the green sofa, his gaze caught intently on the open book in his hand, and something inside Oliver fluttered. The other boy hadn't noticed Oliver yet, and his hair had fallen forward into his face a little as he leaned toward the book; Oliver wanted to reach out and brush it back.

He found himself pausing to take in Darcy's serene intensity. He looked so sharp in his expertly tailored navy tailcoat and perfectly tied matching silk cravat. Not for the first time, Oliver marveled that a stunningly handsome boy like Darcy was interested in a boy like him. That reality made him so giddy that Oliver couldn't help but grin—and it was then that Darcy looked up. Upon seeing Oliver standing in front of him, his face transformed into a grin of his own that left Oliver near breathless.

Darcy closed the book and stood. "I hope you haven't been standing there long," he said with a laugh.

"Not at all."

Darcy nodded and gestured to the sofa. "Would you like to join me? I found the book you were reading the last time we were here and pulled it aside for you."

Oliver supposed it wasn't a shock that Darcy remembered what book he was reading—after all, he *had* recommended the book to him—but the attention to detail was endearing nonetheless.

The two boys sat on the sofa, so close their legs were touching, but neither moved away. Oliver's heart pounded in his throat at the proximity, but when Darcy handed him the book he'd been reading, he took it with a smile that he hoped didn't betray the anxiety buzzing in his chest. The two settled with their books, Darcy diving right back into the text while Oliver stared at the page endlessly, too distracted by the warmth of the boy next to him to process the words. Then Darcy shifted ever so slightly closer, and his shoulder leaned against Oliver's.

Oliver barely breathed. He stared at the open page before him, wondering how on earth Darcy was reading anything at all. Between the two of them, was Oliver the only one so affected by their closeness? He dared peek at Darcy out of the corner of his eye and jumped upon realizing Darcy was looking not at his book, but at Oliver. And he was smiling widely.

"I can't speak for you," Darcy said, "but I'm finding it rather difficult to read with a stunningly handsome boy sitting so close to me."

"Oh thank God," Oliver said before he could stop himself.

Darcy laughed and closed his book again, shifting to face Oliver. "I've often thought about our first encounter here. And while most of the night went better than I'd dared to hope, there is one part I wish I could do differently."

Oliver gulped so hard it was a miracle if Darcy didn't hear it. With his voice a tremble just above the crashing of his pulse, he asked, "And what part is that?"

Darcy smiled. And then his lips were soft on Oliver's mouth, and he went boneless as the other boy's arms wrapped around him.

Darcy's firm chest against his own bound torso triggered a euphoria unlike any Oliver had ever known when he'd pretended to be a girl. This moment, here, kissing a boy *as* a boy, with Darcy's warmth like a furnace against his skin, and Darcy's hands on his back making him feel safe—it was everything Oliver had ever wanted. It was everything he'd dared not to dream.

But it was real, and nothing and no one could take that away from him.

HISTORICAL NOTE

I'D LIKE TO TAKE A MOMENT TO TALK ABOUT QUEER PEOPLE IN HIS-
tory. Specifically in England, during the Regency era.

In the early 1800s, being queer was not, strictly speaking,
illegal—however, sodomy laws very much existed (which, of
course, most frequently endangered queer men). Still, until 1828
the burden of proof was incredibly high, requiring multiple
witnesses. The Regency era was sort of an in-between period;
in the era before it was quite common for people to be openly
queer, but in the era after—the Victorian era—that all ended.
Nevertheless, even in the eras where it was (comparatively) saf-
est to be openly queer, queer men were still expected to marry
women and have children (and queer women were expected to
do the same with men).

As for Molly Houses, they were indeed a part of England's
queer culture in Oliver's time. The name itself, Molly House,
came from the term "molly," which was slang for an effem-
inate man that was sometimes used as a slur and sometimes used as a common noun. While some amount of sex
(and possibly sex work) took place at some Molly Houses,
others were more like clubs (some of which were known to
host early versions of drag balls!) or coffeehouses—like the
one Oliver attends. Unfortunately, Molly Houses were at

times targeted by police raids both in the 1700s and 1800s, leading to arrests and violence, but even with that risk, they provided safe places for queer men in particular to be themselves. (I'll note that though I made the Molly Houses in *Most Ardently* a little more inclusive, historically we don't have much evidence of queer women attending these establishments. We do, however, know that trans people and people in drag were welcome.)

Finally, I'd be remiss if I didn't take some time to address Oliver's inheriting Longbourn. Ultimately, I think it'd be very difficult to say with any certainty whether or not a trans man in Oliver's position had ever successfully inherited property, in large part because if it did happen, it'd be because the law recognized him as a man and wouldn't have taken note of his transness. Interestingly, birth certificates didn't exist in England until July 1, 1837, so there wouldn't have been any record of Oliver being mistaken as a girl at birth. At the end of the day, many of the historical trans people we know about we only know about because their transness was discovered—often, though not always—after death. I like to think there are plenty of trans people we don't know about who lived their lives as themselves, without ever being outed.

So, could a trans man in Oliver's position win a legal challenge to inherit property? I honestly don't know. I like to think if a doctor or midwife along with the entirety of a trans man's family testified that he was indeed a son, that would be enough.

Regardless of whether or not it happened historically, I can say this: in Oliver's case, it's enough.

ACKNOWLEDGMENTS

IF YOU'D TOLD ME JUST FIVE YEARS AGO THAT I WAS GOING TO WRITE and publish a historical book without any magic whatsoever I might not have believed you. As unexpected as it was, I'm so glad this book came to be, and so grateful to everyone who helped make that happen, including:

Emily, I'm so grateful for the way you saw the story I wanted to tell and helped me bring it to the page. For every one of your suggestions and ideas, and for answering each of my anxiety-brain questions, thank you. I'm so happy we had the chance to work on this book together.

Louise, this book wouldn't exist if you hadn't brought me the opportunity to rewrite a Classic. For every strategy call, every excited email and text, every word of encouragement and bit of career advice, thank you.

To the Feiwel and Friends team, including Avia, Kim, and Emily, thank you for your help in bringing this story to life.

To Marlowe and Samira, who have given me one of the most beautiful book covers I've ever seen—holy crap, *thank you*. Marlowe, I cannot get over the gorgeous details of your incredible illustration—I want this cover printed out and framed as an art piece because it is truly stunning. Samira, the design elements truly have brought this book together just perfectly. Thank you both. I truly couldn't be happier.

Alice and Laura, your insights over the years have undoubtedly made me a stronger writer. Thank you, as always, for helping me tell the best versions of my stories over and over again. Melissa and Parrish, your insight was truly invaluable. Thank you for taking the time to help me make the queerness in this story shine.

Jay, I will never stop treasuring all the ways you take care of me. For encouraging me to rest, for checking in on me when I'm buried under deadlines, for being by my side during this roller coaster of a career while celebrating my ups and being there for my downs, thank you. I'm so lucky I get to marry you. I love you. I love you. I love you.

And last but not least, to you, the reader. I treasure every one of your happy and excited messages, particularly as the world has become a more difficult place. Thank you, each one of you, for giving my queer books a chance and helping new readers find them.

AVAILABLE FROM REMIXED CLASSICS

When a dream isn't meant for everyone, sometimes you must create your own.

Two trans boys, Nick and Jay, chase their own versions of the American dream during the Roaring Twenties in this intoxicating tale of glamour and heartache, a remix of *The Great Gatsby*. A National Book Award Longlist Selection.

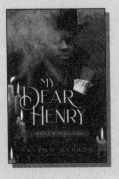

Monsters of all kinds prowl within the London fog, and not all of them are out for blood . . .

A teen boy tries to discover the reason behind his best friend's disappearance—and the arrival of a mysterious and magnetic stranger—in misty Victorian London in this remix of *Jekyll & Hyde*.

Thank you for reading this Feiwel & Friends book.
The friends who made

MOST ARDENTLY

A PRIDE & PREJUDICE REMIX possible are:

Jean Feiwel, Publisher

Liz Szabla, VP, Associate Publisher

Rich Deas, Senior Creative Director

Anna Roberto, Executive Editor

Holly West, Senior Editor

Kat Brzozowski, Senior Editor

Dawn Ryan, Executive Managing Editor

Kim Waymer, Senior Production Manager

Emily Settle, Editor

Rachel Diebel, Editor

Foyinsi Adegbonmire, Editor

Brittany Groves, Assistant Editor

Samira Iravani, Associate Art Director

Avia Perez, Senior Production Editor

Follow us on Facebook or visit us online at mackids.com.
Our books are friends for life.